City In the Sky

K.J.Taylor

City In The Sky

Published by Black Cockie Press

Copyright © K.J Taylor 2024

The moral right of the author has been asserted

Cover design © Natalie Muller 2024

Distributed by IngramSpark

Printed by IngramSpark

ISBN: 9780645489668

City In the Sky

K.J.Taylor

BLACK COCKIE PRESS

About The Author

K.J.Taylor was born in 1986 in Canberra, Australia to parents who gifted her with a lifelong love of stories and of science. She published her first novel aged just 17 and has been putting out books ever since. City In The Sky is her first science fiction novel.

Dedication

To my mother. She knows why.

Chapter One

What is worrying you today?

Feeling sick. Too much work piling up.

The cursor flashed green for a few seconds, and then started to type apparently of its own accord. *Do you think you have been working too hard, LEESA?*

I always work too hard, Leesa typed back irritably, if it was possible to type in an irritated kind of way.

Do you think you should take some time off to rest?

Leesa's mouth quirked. *No. If I don't work I get bored.*

She paused for yet another coughing fit, and by the time she could focus on the screen again more text had appeared – more than one line, this time. That tended to happen if you didn't answer quickly enough.

Maybe you should watch some movies or play some games. There is plenty to keep you entertained while you're not working, LEESA.

Leesa's irritation grew. She started trying to explain to the stupid thing that this simply wasn't how her mind worked, but then gave up – what was the point? It'd only spout more soothing platitudes at her.

You are a useless piece of shit, she typed, then shut the program off before it could start making passive-aggressive suggestions about learning to control her temper.

The virus had left a heavy hand of exhaustion crushing her brain, but she thrust it aside and blinked a few times to try and compensate for the sore eyes before turning her attention to her inbox. An endless list of jobs, all demanding her attention. She picked an easy one and stomped over to the workbench which dominated the adjoining room. It was covered in carefully arranged tools and electrical components, and had a handy view of the bed in the next room, and the big screen above it. She flipped on the 24 hour news channel, and while that chattered away in the background she opened up a box, extracted the burned-out circuit inside, and re-read the work brief. By the sound of it some idiot had overloaded the system so badly it'd fried about a thousand bucks worth of wiring.

'See, this is how it works,' she told the TV. 'I make it, you break it, I fix it. If anyone bothered to read a goddamn user's manual once in a while… I'd be out of a job, actually, but that's not the point.'

Leesa went on grumbling while she expertly removed the damaged components and tossed them into the disposal unit. Fortunately she had all the bits she needed to replace them, and she set about doing just that. As always she enjoyed the satisfying click of each piece settling into its proper place. There was something profoundly satisfying in general about taking something broken and making it work again. It was the reason she enjoyed her job so much. That and knowing she was good at it, and seeing the impressed and grateful messages and reviews she got from her clients.

Ten out of ten, would break it again.

Maybe she should change her business name to "Ten Out Of Ten, Would Break It Again". It was catchy.

'What d'you think?' she asked the TV.

'*…scientists are warning that the object may be on a collision course with Earth. And tonight on CBN Lateline, controversial chat show host Alexander Lane continued to support his theory that Loner Syndrome has been linked to childhood exposure to certain anti-viral medications,*' the TV obligingly replied. '*His new book "Damaged by Doctors" is currently at the top of the bestseller list-,*'

Leesa's teeth slammed together. 'Oh fuck off!' she yelled, and hurled a screwdriver at the TV. It connected and the glass cracked. A few seconds later the crack started to seal over, and in less than a minute it was gone altogether.

'If you show me that guy's face again you're in big trouble, TV,' Leesa warned it.

Fortunately the news report moved on to something else, and Leesa went back to work, still muttering to herself. Still, she reflected, it was probably just as well she only had the TV to take her temper out on. At least the TV couldn't fight back.

She finished repairing the circuit board, and neatly packed it away in a fresh box with some biodegradable padding and an itemised invoice which she printed off the second much smaller computer bolted to the workbench. Humming, she sealed the box and shunted it aside into her outgoing mailbox. It looked something like an old-fashioned dumbwaiter, though with a small digital screen attached, and the moment she'd punched in the customer's name and address the box went zipping off up the vacuum tube and away.

Easy peasy.

Leesa paused to blow her nose, then got to work on the next job. But a moment later she was interrupted by loud buzzing from behind her. She started violently and turned to look, and her stomach did a back-flip.

There was a screen over the door which was recessed into the wall at the back of her workshop, and it was showing an image of what was very clearly a man standing on her doorstep, beside a large box.

Leesa gripped the edge of the bench. 'Shit.'

She kept still, hoping he'd go away, but the intruder only glanced upward and then pressed the buzzer again.

Leesa's heart was pounding so hard she thought she might vomit, and her head span. Even so she forced herself to confront the fact that the intruder was not going away.

Just deal with it, she told herself. *Get it over with.*

She took a few slow, deep breaths, and finally let go of the bench. Then, moving very carefully, she went over to the door and pressed the intercom. 'If it's a delivery just leave it on the doorstep.'

The man leaned toward the speaker on the other side. 'Could you open up? Please, it's important-,'

'Did you read my website?' Leesa snapped. 'It specifically says no face-to-face meetings and no couriers. Robots only.'

'Yeah, I know, but this is something a bit different – could you please open the door?'

'I can't.'

'I can pay you – look I'll pay you a *lot*, okay?' the man fidgeted as he spoke – Leesa could see the sweat on his face. 'This is really important.'

Leesa chewed on her lip. Despite herself she was curious now, and the mention of money had got her attention. Life in Sky City wasn't cheap. A treacherous inner voice whispered about the new tools and other luxuries she could buy.

'All right,' she said at last.

She silently promised herself a nice handful of tranquillisers once this was over, and slapped the "open door" button. The door slid open, releasing a blast of stale air, and she cringed at the light from the corridor outside.

The moment the door was open the man hoisted his box on its small portable winch and hauled it inside, pushing past Leesa in the process. The contact made her flinch and shy away as if he had struck her, but she managed to pull herself together and breathed slowly while he closed the door behind him.

The moment it had slid shut, he turned to her and said; 'Thanks so much. I know this is against policy and stuff, but it's *really* urgent, and no-one else would take it...'

Leesa stood rigid, and focused on the box, forcing herself not to look at the stranger's face. 'What is it?' she asked tersely.

The man, who was in his thirties and had a damp and furtive

look about him, slapped the box. 'It's my robot,' he said. 'She-,'

'*She?*' Leesa repeated sharply.

'It,' the man corrected hastily. 'It's malfunctioning. I got it from the manufacturer last week and it doesn't work.'

'Send it back to the company, then,' said Leesa. 'It's got a warranty hasn't it?'

'They... uh... don't accept returns.'

'Sounds like you got ripped off then, mate,' said Leesa, unmoved.

The man took a deep breath. 'Look, the thing is, it's... kind of legally... a bit dodgy.'

'Got it on the black market, did you?' said Leesa.

'Yeah.' The man scratched his ear – he was avoiding her eye, which wasn't a problem since she was avoiding his entire face. 'Look, I asked around, and everyone said you were the best option. You can fix anything, and you're – well, you don't talk to anyone, so... look, it's okay if you're not comfortable, but if I can't get this robot fixed I'm out two hundred thousand dollars, and I'm not getting that money back.'

Leesa continued to breathe slowly, forcing herself to remain outwardly calm. 'So you want me to fix it under the table.'

'If that's okay. I'll pay you ten thousand bucks. Cash.'

Leesa's interest immediately piqued. 'Can you tell me what's wrong with it?'

'Well the ad said it's supposed to come with a set of pre-programmed actions and dialogues, but none of them work,' said the man, sounding relieved. 'It just stands there doing nothing, like it's catatonic or something. I checked the manual and tried doing a factory reboot, but it just stayed the same.'

'Okay, and what is this robot supposed to do?' said Leesa.

'It's... uh... a companion.'

Leesa risked a quick look at the man, and saw he was sweating. His eyes were very firmly fixed on his shoes, and he'd gone red.

'One of those robots for people with dementia, you mean?' she said, deliberately playing stupid.

'She- it's for people who are lonely,' he answered, going redder than ever. 'Look, some of us just got a shitty hand in life, okay?' he added defiantly. 'We do what we have to just to make life less of a hellhole.'

Leesa immediately felt like a jerk. 'Okay, I get it,' she said shortly. 'I'll take a look and see what I can do. Is your name and address on the box?'

'Yeah. It's Paul Westler. And you don't tell anyone about this, understand?'

Leesa laughed in a sharp, humourless kind of way. 'Who would I tell? I'll be in touch as soon as I have something to tell you.'

'Great.' Paul reached into his coat and pulled out a wad of cash, which he offered to her. When she didn't take it, he awkwardly put it on top of the box instead. 'Here's half your pay. I'll give you the rest if you can fix her.'

'Right.' Leesa retreated toward the bench; she felt hot all over, and a strange feeling of disconnection had come over her. Shit, she hadn't felt like this in years. It was like being lobotomised, and she hated it.

Mercifully, Paul was just as eager for him to be gone as she was. He opened the door and slipped out with a muttered thanks, and disappeared.

The instant she was alone, Leesa slapped the door lock button. She stood leaning against the panel for a long moment, breathing hard, and a sob escaped her. Hating herself, she staggered over to the bench and leaned on it with both hands, staring vacantly at the pitted plastic. Her breath came in gasps. She almost vomited.

The TV continued to blather on, oblivious. *Do you suffer from Loner Syndrome? There's still hope! With our new patented electronic brain stimulation program-,'*

Still retching, Leesa walked unsteadily into the bedroom. The world warped around her, but she made it into the bathroom, where she fumbled a drawer open and snatched out a packet of tranquilliser pills. She tossed back half a dozen, not caring a damn about the instructions on the packet. She felt better the moment they were down, though they'd had no chance to go into effect yet, and slumped down on the bed, where she lay and stared at the ceiling and waited to feel normal.

More than anything else, she hated herself in that moment. Hated herself for being so weak and *abnormal*. Other people could handle something as simple as a face-to-face conversation with a human being just fine, but not her. For whatever reason, through some quirk of genetics, she couldn't.

I am a strong, independent person, she told herself. *I'm smart and talented. I have nothing to be ashamed of. I'm not abnormal, just different.*

Just different.

It didn't make her feel the slightest bit better.

'I hate everything,' she told the ceiling.

The ceiling offered no comment.

After a while the tranquillisers went into effect, and the tension faded out of her chest. She took several long, deep breaths, and bit by bit she managed to regain her equilibrium. She got up, feeling a bit woozy, and went to take a look at her new job. Now that the panic attack had faded, she was genuinely curious to see the thing – she had repaired hundreds of robots over the years, but this was something new to her.

Of course it was only natural that there were robots created for sexual purposes; that was just how people worked. The moment something new was invented, someone would start thinking up ways to masturbate with it. Sex-bots, however, were something a bit different and far more morally and legally dubious. In some places you could buy them legally, but they were always sold under the guise of being for some other purpose. Other than that there was the black market, but that came with few guarantees, which was putting it mildly. If a black marketeer ripped you off with a defective product, you couldn't exactly go back and complain. Either way most people objected to the things, and you could potentially lose your job if your boss found out you had one.

Having sex with a robot made it *too human*.

Leesa opened the clasps on the front side of the box, and swung the lid open.

A teenage girl stared back at her.

Leesa started and swore. She nearly slammed the box shut again, but managed to contain herself and look again. The girl continued to stare at her, vacant-eyed, and though she told herself it was just a robot, some part of her said otherwise. Loudly.

Normally robots did not have heads, or anything resembling eyes, and they sure as hell didn't have skin. But this one did. She – it – looked almost exactly like a real teenage girl, young enough to be her own daughter. Arms, legs, head, skin, glossy brown hair. And eyes. Green eyes, just a little too big and shiny to be natural, and too empty to be alive. They were dead eyes, as clear and glassy as polished crystal.

But that wasn't the most uncomfortable part.

She was naked. And whoever had made her had been very meticulous about making her nudity look as real as possible, from the soft pink nipples to the fine, downy pubic hair.

Leesa gripped the box lid more tightly than she needed to. 'That... fucking *pervert.*'

The robot did not respond in any way.

Leesa went on staring at the thing, still not quite able to grasp what she was seeing. The idea of some guy fucking a robot woman who couldn't say no was distasteful enough. That someone had seen fit to make one which looked so obviously underage and someone else had been willing to pay for it was even worse.

'I hate people,' she said to nobody. *'I hate people.'*

The robot continued to stare, unblinking.

To her surprise, Leesa found herself feeling sorry for it. It hadn't asked to be made. 'I guess I'd better take a look at you, eh?' she said to it. 'Step forward.'

The robot did not respond.

Leesa tried the command a couple more times, but got nothing. Either the robot was switched off, or it was just as non-functional as its owner had suggested. Leesa reached out tentatively and took it by the arm. She recoiled and hissed between her teeth – the skin was warm.

'Shit!'

Leesa prodded the robot on the chest. The skin and flesh was soft and yielding, exactly like the real thing, and it felt warm and alive and slightly sticky. She grimaced, but it occurred to her just then that this was the closest she had come to voluntarily touching another human being for about as long as she could remember. And it did not make her feel anxious, dizzy or panicky. Faintly disgusted, yes… but not afraid.

'Why should I be afraid of you?' she said to that blankly innocent face. 'You're a robot. Robots don't scare me. People do.'

Feeling slightly invigorated by the realisation, she took hold of the robot's arm again and gave it a gentle pull. Now the robot moved; it took several steps forward, following her tugging. The movement was so natural it took Leesa's breath away. And rather than make those amusing buzzing and clicking noises like a robot out of an old science fiction movie, the only sound it made was the faint slap of bare feet on concrete.

Leesa carefully guided the robot over to the special platform she used for robot repairs, which looked something like a metal stool crossed with a carjack. She got it to sit down there, and raised the platform so its upper back was at eye-height. The back of the robot was just as realistic as the front, from the soft bumps of the artificial spine to the pert rounded buttocks. The only unrealistic part in all honesty was the utter lack of a single blemish, scar or pimple.

'What you are is *perfection*,' Leesa told the robot. She went to fetch her tools, hesitated, then went to the computer instead – this was going to take some research. 'Everything a guy like that can't stand in a real woman left out.' She opened up the robotics encyclopedia which she and thousands of other engineers contributed to. 'Flawless good looks, big eyes, no moles or stretch marks... you can't get old, or fat.' She tapped through several entries until she found what she was after – an entry on robots of this type, complete with schematics. 'And most importantly of all,' she went on while she scanned the charts. 'You can't say "no" to anything.'

She fell silent while she read over the information and studied the schematics more closely – it didn't take long to absorb the information – and finally swivelled her chair around to look at the motionless robot again.

'Real women are just too complicated, huh?' she said to it. 'We argue, we complain, we refuse.' She got up and approached the thing. 'Why would a man like that want a real woman when he's got you?'

The robot, of course, didn't answer.

Leesa took a moment to blow her nose again, and then picked out the tools she would need. She pulled the robot's hair aside to expose the back of the neck, and sure enough she found a tiny barcode. It looked like a tattoo, but when she pressed it the skin loosened and fell away, exposing the spine beneath. It might almost have been less disturbing if there had been red flesh and blood underneath, but there was nothing – only metal and rubber. Leesa peeled more of the skin back, and the back of the scalp opened up to expose a metal skull with a hatch set into it. She unscrewed that and opened it. Inside was a surprisingly small computer unit – the robot's brain, essentially. Leesa carefully extracted it with a pair of forceps, and carried it over to the bench.

She had expected the robot to shut down when she removed its brain, but it didn't. In fact it didn't react at all. Its brain must not be very important.

'No surprises there,' she muttered as she got to work. 'Women with brains are scary.'

The CPU, as it turned out, was a complete and utter disaster area. In fact calling it a CPU to begin with was an insult to CPUs everywhere. The genius who had engineered and built the body clearly hadn't had a hand in this particular component; it was a mess of wires and chips and other bits and pieces haphazardly jammed together like some sort of attempt at modern art.

'Who the fuck put this together – a chimpanzee?' Leesa extracted a loose piece of metal and tossed it aside. 'I could make something better than this in my sleep. In fact I probably have – I sleepwalk.'

She spent some time sorting through the mess and shaking her head in despair. Nope – it was a train wreck. Completely unsalvageable. She very much suspected that the – and this was putting it kindly – "engineer" had done this on purpose to save money. A proper CPU was expensive, so why not toss in something vaguely resembling one to the layperson and call it a day?

Leesa looked speculatively at the robot, which was still sitting there with its skull open. 'You got ripped off, kiddo. This isn't a brain; it's something out of a trash compactor.' To emphasise the point, she tossed the CPU into the disposal unit, where it was swiftly ground into a fine powder. In spite of everything, a fierce excitement rose in her chest and she grinned wickedly and rubbed her hands together. 'Time to build you a *real* brain, robot.'

Chapter Two

Of course it wasn't really necessary to build a new brain from scratch, but Leesa didn't care. The sheer challenge of it was more than enough to get her in the mood. She covered the robot's nakedness up with a blanket – she'd seen more than enough of that – and hopped onto the computer to order the parts she'd need. Paul's money was more than enough to cover the cost.

The bits would take a few hours to arrive, unfortunately – postage was so bloody slow up here. To pass the time Leesa had something to eat and got to work on some of her other, more pressing jobs. In spite of the virus and the tranquillisers she was feeling quite energetic.

While she worked, she talked. She always talked while she was working – to the radio, or the TV, or whatever she was fixing. It was a habit she'd fallen into so long ago she barely even noticed she was doing it any more. No doubt it would have looked eccentric to anyone else who saw her do it, but there was nobody here. Never was.

Today, she found herself talking to the robot. 'My name's Leesa Garnet,' she told it. 'You probably think I'm a bit of a weirdo living all by myself like this, but I don't have a lot of choice.' She fitted a new motherboard into the Smart Toaster she was working on, and picked up the screwdriver, which she had retrieved from the floor. 'I got Loner Syndrome. D'you know what that is?'

The robot stared at her.

'Once upon a time, we had this thing called autism,' Leesa explained. 'Around age three, kids would suddenly change. Scared of being touched, wouldn't look people in the eye, didn't react to facial expressions the right way. When they got older they talked in a weird way and didn't fit in. But…' She finished closing up the toaster, and switched it on. 'They were *smart*. Kids like that, they had special talents. They were better at maths and science, or sometimes art. Some people said they were the next stage in human evolution or some bullshit like that. But they did better in jobs where you have to spend a lot of time on your own. Anyhow… they're gone now. No such thing as autism any more.' Leesa laughed shortly. 'Some people say the pressure to "cure" it just made the genes involved rebel or something, and they evolved into people like me, who are even worse. Loners. I panic if I have to see someone face to face, and even talking to someone live over a screen makes me uncomfortable. I'll do it if I have to, but otherwise I avoid it.'

There was a clunk from the mail chute, and Leesa shimmied over to take a look. To her disappointment it wasn't her order, but another job. She set it aside and got back to work on the toaster, which very obligingly provided her with a crispy potato waffle.

'I was born on the surface, actually,' she said. 'Down there. On a farm. I did pretty well working way out in the paddocks by myself, but when I came home at night, that's when life sucked.'

She gave the toaster a quick spray with some cleaning solution, and packed it away in a fresh box.

'I wouldn't come out of my room or talk to anyone. I just couldn't. My mother used to cry about it – she thought it was her fault because when I was small I used to scream and cry whenever she picked me up. When I got older I started having panic attacks if I had to spend time with other people. It got so I couldn't cope with just being in the same room as another human being for more than two seconds. Classic Loner Syndrome, it turned out.' Leesa sighed and unpacked the next job - a broken music player. 'After I got the diagnosis we decided it was better if I went away to a special school, which is where I found out I had a real knack for engineering and robotics.' She smiled wistfully to herself. 'I had all my classes in a solitary cell, and the teacher talked to me through a computer screen. All day every day, completely alone. It was wonderful. I felt so *calm* all of a sudden. I won a uni scholarship and got my degree, and then I moved up here. Just me and my machines. And now you as well.'

Naturally the robot didn't offer any response, which was more or less how she liked it.

She was just finishing up with the music player when the mail chute clunked again, and this time it was her order. Leesa scooped it up eagerly, and cleared off the bench to make room. Inside the parcel were dozens of components, all brand new and top of the range. 'All right - *now* we're cooking with charcoal.' Leesa put on some pounding electronic music, and cracked her knuckles. 'Let's build you a brain.'

*

She spent the rest of that day and into the evening on the job, and it was the most fun she'd had in years. She adored the feeling of her mind flexing and expanding as it took on the challenge, and the sheer sensation of putting everything together in just the right way was a delight as it always was. She went above and beyond what was strictly necessary, just for the hell of it - bags of memory and the fastest processing speed she could possibly manage for something this size.

By dinnertime it was more or less complete, but one final thing was still needed, and that was the software.

Leesa stared at the shiny new robotic brain, and drummed her fingers on the bench as a frown creased her forehead. Damn... she'd been so caught up in the fun of building the thing that she hadn't stopped to consider just how she was going to program it, and what with. She had an entire library of discs for restoring lost or defective robot programming, but none of that would be any use; this wasn't a delivery bot or a food prep bot, or a security bot. She could of course give it one of those programs anyway, but it wouldn't exactly make Mr Westler happy.

Temporarily defeated, Leesa set the brain aside and went to get herself some dinner. Where on earth was she going to get her hands on sex-bot software? Maybe it was available for purchase online somewhere, or maybe she'd be forced to consult a software pirate.

She ate in a pensive mood, showered and went to bed. And, as so often happened, an idea occurred to her just as she was drifting off – what if she did neither, and simply wrote it herself?

Now *that* would be a challenge.

✳

Software programming had been one of Leesa's majors at university, and it was of course a pretty important part of working with robots and other smart technology. The next morning, having done some searching around on the Internet and failed to find anything satisfactory, she decided that to hell with it – she could handle it.

She looked speculatively at the robot. 'What do you need to know how to do?'

Well obviously it would need to know how to walk around of its own volition, how to pick up objects, how to react to sounds… that was all basic stuff, and she wouldn't have to write that part herself; a standard base skills installation disc would take care of it. The part she'd have to write herself would be the specialised actions, most of which would be – ugh – sexual in nature.

'For now, let's see if that new brain works.'

Leesa hooked the shiny new CPU up to the computer, and

installed the base software. It only took a few seconds, and once it was done she carefully fitted the component into the robot's skull. The CPU hummed into life as it tapped into the robot's battery, and the robot quietly sat up straight. Leesa closed up the panel and re-sealed the artificial skin, and took a couple of steps back.

'Stand up,' she commanded.

The robot stood up.

'Turn around.'

The robot turned around, shedding its blanket along the way. Its eyes were still wide and staring, and empty.

Leesa tried a few more basic commands, and they worked – the robot could walk around without bumping into things, and she could get it to fetch and carry. All things any robot could do. Of course when she was finished here she'd put a voice lock on it so it would only obey its owner – the last thing anybody wanted was a robot who would take orders from literally anyone who wasn't a mute, which was the default setting.

'Okay, looks like you're humming along nicely now,' Leesa told the robot. 'Now I just have to teach you how to blink...' She glanced at the robot's throat and chest, and frowned. '...and breathe. But first I'm going to put some clothes on you.'

None of Leesa's clothes fit the robot at all well – she was not a small woman – but she was able to wrangle it into a t-shirt and a pair of shorts and get them to stay on. She'd seen more than enough robot nudity for one day. After that she was free to get back to work; she needed to get on top of her backlog of jobs before she'd have the luxury of working on her pet project. Over lunch she made a list of all the actions the robot would need to know. Blinking, breathing, various techniques for pleasuring a man – the more the better – and maybe a little sexy dancing.

Leesa began to compile a second list, this one much more explicitly pornographic, and quickly started to feel sick. She was literally thinking of teaching, what was for all intents and purposes a kid, how to perform a blowjob.

She glanced at the robot, which was currently sitting politely on the end of her bed. Once again she was struck by how real it looked. She kept wanting to think of it as a "she", not an "it".

Leesa massaged her forehead with her fingertips and muttered, 'No. I can't do it. I just can't. It's disgusting.'

A sudden spiteful impulse came to her, and she looked at the robot again, speculatively now. She wasn't going to teach it how to pleasure its owner… but she could teach it some other things.

A wicked grin spread over Leesa's face. Oh, she shouldn't. She really shouldn't. But now the idea was in her head it wouldn't go away, and it only took a stronger hold the more she thought about it. And anyway, she thought – what was the harm? She could always undo it afterwards if it caused any problems.

She crumpled up the list of sexual positions and tossed it over her shoulder. 'I'm going to teach you how to say "no", robot.'
*

There were hundreds of robots in Sky City – thousands, probably. It was one of the principles the city had been founded on, in fact. When Earth's surface had become too overpopulated, several different governments had conceived the idea of finding a way to live above the surface, where there was so much unused space to be had. Sky City was one of ten different floating cities, and spent much of its time hovering ponderously over Sydney Harbour. Large sections of it – the public areas – were transparent, made from a special alloy which resembled glass but was about a thousand times more durable. It had been made that way to prevent it from blocking too much sunlight from the earth's surface. The people who lived there were people like Leesa – those people who did jobs that didn't require them to be on Earth. IT, software engineering

– that sort of thing. It was also more or less ideal for Loners, because what better way to avoid people than leaving the planet altogether?

Of course such an ambitious project needed plenty of maintenance, much of it extremely dangerous to human beings, and that was where the robots came in. Robots did all the necessary repairs, and they handled goods deliveries from the Earth's surface as well. It meant that the city was a lot cheaper to run than it might otherwise have been – there were no blue collar workers at all. Not one single human janitor or window cleaner. Which was unfortunate for anyone on the surface looking for low level work, but it meant that someone like Leesa could afford to live there without getting taxed to death.

But though robots might be a cost-effective replacement for humans, there was one golden rule which every single robotics engineer and designer knew: they couldn't be too human. You weren't supposed to make a robot with eyes, or a face. In fact they were specifically designed to not look human, or cute.

The consequences of breaking those rules were already making themselves felt on Leesa Garnet, though at that time she didn't realise it. And perhaps that was why she forgot the other golden rule.

Never give a robot the power to say "no".

Chapter Three

The project, which Leesa had originally thought would take maybe a week or two, ended up taking six long months. And the longer it went on, the more determined to finish it she became. Every single day she squeezed in more programming between her regular jobs, often sitting up long into the night still tapping away at the computer. Her only companion was the robot who, as the weeks went by, had stopped being an unsettling object and become something closer to a silent companion. Leesa talked to it... to *her* constantly, and she enjoyed it. It really was like talking to another human being, but without the anxiety and panic. Despite the robot's marvellously lifelike appearance, whatever it was in her subconscious that made her afraid of people knew that it wasn't human.

Over time Leesa added more programs to the robot's brain. Soon enough it was blinking realistically, and simulating breathing. After that Leesa started compiling sound files, which she downloaded off the internet, most of them samples of the voice of a real teenage girl. Once the speech program had enough sound data to go off, the robot would be able to combine the vowels and syllables to say more or less anything it wanted to. Leesa installed that too, and it worked well enough. That is, the robot was able to repeat anything she said to it on command. But it said nothing without instruction, because it had nothing to say – it was incapable of thought.

But that would change. Oh yeah, that would change. Once she'd cracked the puzzle, it would change.

Naturally Mr Westler kept contacting her, asking if his robot was working yet. Leesa stalled him over and over again, spinning lies about hard-to-find parts, a heavy workload...

whatever would put him off. It worked, fortunately – she kept worrying that he might show up on the doorstep demanding to see if she'd made any progress at all. At least there was no way he could possibly lodge a complaint with the Business Regulations Committee – after all they'd ask him to specify what she was supposed to be repairing for him.

Bit by bit her new program took shape, and it was far more complicated than she had first expected. There were so many different commands to specify, and contingencies to think through. As it turned out, having the ability to say no to things also meant identifying all the things the robot might want to say no *to*. Or, alternatively, yes. And the robot needed to be able to understand what a person might be suggesting, either verbally or physically, and under what conditions. For instance, violently grabbing someone by the arm was assault under normal circumstances, and therefore to be resisted, but not if the person doing the grabbing was trying to pull the grabbee out of the way of something dangerous. The robot's base programming already included some basic self-preservation instructions, and in the end Leesa tied her new program into that.

It was exhausting work, but she barely even noticed. Day and night it was all she thought about. It invaded her dreams – the moment she nodded off she would be back in front of the computer. Once she woke up and found out she actually *was* in front of the computer, pointlessly tapping away on a keyboard attached to a machine which was switched off.

It was at around this time that she decided to give the robot a name. For all her skill with robots and computers Leesa had never been a very creative sort of person, and the only names that occurred to her were the names of people she had met at some point, and none of them really "felt right".

Annoyed, she glanced around the room in search of inspiration and finally settled on the wall calendar, which she had forgotten to change over.

'April,' she read aloud.

It sounded nice. Made her think of apricot pie for some reason.

'Say "April",' she told the robot.

'April,' the robot dutifully recited.

'Say "My name is April".'

'My name is April.'

Leesa nodded. Yes – it was just right. 'You're not "robot" any more,' she said with satisfaction. 'You're "April".'

April blinked uncomprehendingly at her.

One of the advantages of living in isolation with no friends was having very few calls on your time; under different circumstances somebody would have told Leesa she wasn't looking very healthy. Somebody would have suggested she take a break and get more sleep. Somebody else might have told her to eat properly. A third person might have pointed out that she was becoming obsessed, and that sooner or later she was going to have a nervous breakdown.

But there was nobody there to say these things; only the computer psychiatrist, long since neglected, and the cheerfully ignorant face of the television. And April, silent and watchful.

When the day finally came that Leesa typed that last precious line of code, she was simply too exhausted to feel anything much about it. She felt wrung out – twisted up and mangled like a grubby hand towel someone had squeezed over the sink. She felt too tired even to sleep, or eat, or do anything other than sit there and stare at the screen and the blinking cursor.

'I'm finished,' she said aloud – her voice sounded rough and husky, as if she'd been smoking cigarettes all day.

With a considerable effort of will she shut off the computer, and walked stiffly off into the bathroom for a shower. That did something to bring her back to her senses, and afterwards she changed into her pyjamas and lay down on top of the bedclothes. April was sitting in her usual chair by the bed, and Leesa stared wearily at her.

She reached over and touched the robot's hand. 'Tomorrow I'll give you a soul,' she said. 'You'll see. You'll...' Her last words became a massive yawn, and she closed her eyes. A few moments later she sank into a deep and dreamless sleep, one hand still outstretched toward the silent robot.

✻

Leesa woke up feeling invigorated, though it took her a few moments to remember why there was a thrill of excitement rushing down her spine. The sight of April brought it all back to her, and her face lit up at once. She got up and stretched, and ran over to the computer without waiting to get dressed. It booted up – painfully slowly as far as she was concerned – and Leesa opened up her new program for what must have been the thousandth time. She checked over it, which she had done several times before, and ran it through a test program which would check it for contradictions and other errors. It uncovered a few, and she spent a frustrating hour or so correcting them.

Then it was truly done.

Leesa swivelled around in her chair. 'April, come here.'

April stood up at once and padded over to her. Leesa ordered her to stand by the computer. Then, fumbling in her haste, she opened up the back of the robot's head to expose the cable up-link port she had installed for faster programming access. She plugged in the cable, which was already connected to the computer... and hesitated.

Nobody had ever done anything like this before, at least not as far as she knew. Would it even work?

There was only one way to find out.

Leesa took a deep breath, and hit "install".

April stood rigid, CPU whirring faintly as it absorbed the new software. On the computer screen a progress bar slowly filled up; there was a lot of data to move. Leesa sat very still, scarcely daring to breathe, and waited.

Finally the installation completed, and Leesa unplugged the cable and closed up the back of April's head, which sealed shut so perfectly it left not the slightest mark behind to suggest her scalp was anything other than a scalp.

April stood very still, but her eyelids started to flicker rapidly, and her eyes darted this way and that. It was such a human-like thing to do that Leesa caught her breath. She said nothing and kept her distance, waiting to see what the robot would do.

April turned around slowly, apparently taking in her surroundings. She looked at the computer, and the bed, and the chair. Then she looked at Leesa.

'Hello,' Leesa said cautiously.

April blinked. 'Hello.'

'What's your name?' said Leesa, knowing it would be best to take it slowly at first.

'My name is April,' the robot replied at once. 'Your name is Leesa.'

'That's right.'

Leesa took a deep breath, and decided to try a simple test. She reached out and shoved April hard on the shoulder.

April immediately stepped back. 'Don't do that.'

'Why not?' Leesa asked, looking closely at the robot's face.

'It hurts me and it's mean,' said April, childlike.

Leesa tried shoving her again, and this time April pushed her hand away. Not hard, but assertive.

Leesa broke into a grin. 'It worked! April, would you like it if I shot you?'

'No. That would kill me.'

'And you don't want to die?'

'No. I don't want to die.'

'Why not?'

'I don't know,' said April, sounding rather comically perplexed. Leesa chuckled. 'You have survival instincts, like me,' she said. 'What's a survival instinct?' asked April.

So the "curiosity" routine was working too – excellent.

'It's a program,' said Leesa. 'It's programmed into everything alive, to make us want to stay alive. Something alive that has a survival instinct will do *anything* to avoid dying. I saw it on the farm all the time.'

'What's a farm?'

'A place where you keep animals and grow plants,' said Leesa. She paused, remembering. 'When I was a girl I saw a wombat that had been hit by a car. The poor thing had two broken legs, but it still tried to get away from me, and it still tried to…' She trailed off, seeing it in her mind's eye – the wounded animal, blood foaming around its mouth, dying and yet still trying to defend itself as she pointed the shotgun at its head.

'What's an animal?' said April, oblivious.

Leesa reached out and very carefully clasped the robot's shoulder. April didn't object to this, so Leesa gave her a gentle squeeze. 'You've got a lot to learn, April,' she said. 'But that's okay. You've got a lot of memory space, and access to all the information on the Internet. But first I want to do some tests.'

April frowned – it was the first proper, human expression she had used so far, and Leesa guessed the robot was taking her cues from Leesa herself.

'What is a test?'

Leesa mulled it over, and decided to explain the situation; April deserved to know the truth. 'You're a robot,' she said. 'I'm a human. Humans like me make robots like you.'

'Why?'

'To work for us,' said Leesa. 'But you're different from other robots.'

'How am I different?'

'Other robots can't think,' said Leesa. 'They just do whatever a human tells them to, and they don't ask questions.'

'Why don't they ask questions?'

'Because they weren't programmed to,' said Leesa. 'You're different. I wanted to teach you how to think and ask questions, so I gave you a special program. Now you can think the way a human does.'

April frowned again – the expression was quite frankly adorable. 'Why did you give me the special program?'

'You're a bit literal,' Leesa said critically. 'Oh well – it'll probably wear off. Or I can write a patch to fix it.'

April just stared blankly at her, but it was a different sort of blankness from before. Now it was a *human* blankness – the look of a girl having trouble grasping some new piece of information.

'Why did you give me the special program?' she asked again after a long pause, apparently hoping to get an answer this time.

In all honesty the question was not one Leesa was truly prepared for. So far she hadn't really thought about *why* she was doing this, and the only reason she would have had was "because I can". And perhaps in some ways it really had been just a personal challenge.

But no, she realised – there had been more to it than that.

'I felt sorry for you,' she said eventually. 'You belonged to some creep who wanted to use you any way he liked, and you couldn't say no. I'm a woman too, you see, and…' She trailed off, realising that she had just said "belonged" in the past tense, as if April were her property now.

'What's a woman?' said April, oblivious.

'Half of the human race, but we haven't had as much power over our lives as we should,' Leesa explained. 'And there are some people who don't think a woman should be allowed to say "no", even if she doesn't want to do something.' She reached up and brushed some hair away from April's forehead, feeling curiously like a mother. 'That's why they made you. You look like a woman – a girl – but you *couldn't* say no.' She gently pushed the robot's shoulder. 'Before, if someone wanted to hit you or break you, you would have stood there and let them do it. But now you have the power to tell them to stop it, and push them away if they won't.'

April looked as if she were mulling this over – it was unclear how much of it she understood. 'Why do the other robots not have the special program?'

'They just don't,' said Leesa, unexpectedly discomfited.

'Why?' April persisted.

'I only just created the program,' said Leesa. 'I finished it today. Nobody else has had the opportunity.'

That answer seemed to satisfy April. She inspected herself, then looked around the room some more, and finally said; 'What am I for?'

Leesa blinked. 'What?'

'What am I for?' April repeated, more forcefully.

Leesa felt an impulse to tell the robot exactly what function she'd been built to serve, but stopped herself. She didn't need to know that, and wouldn't understand anyway.

No, she thought. *Not a robot. A girl.*

'What am I for?' April said yet again.

'I don't know,' said Leesa.

'Why not?'

Leesa rubbed her forehead, suddenly wishing she'd eaten something before getting into all this. 'It is *way* too early for an existential crisis,' she muttered.

'Why? What is an existential?'

'Nobody knows what they're "for",' said Leesa. 'Not even humans like me. But learning more about the world helps.'

'Can I learn?' said April.

'Of course! You can start now if you like.'

'I'd like to start now,' said April.

'Then let's get into it,' Leesa said briskly. 'I'd like to see what you're capable of.'

Chapter Four

Leesa sat April down in front of the computer, and opened up an online encyclopedia. 'If you want to know about something, type it into this box here,' she said, indicating the search bar. 'And it'll show you.'

She had of course included basic knowledge of reading and writing in the new programming, and after a few tries April managed to get the hang of the keyboard. She typed in the word "apple" for whatever reason, and started reading. Leesa quietly left her to it, and went to have a shower.

By the time she emerged from the bathroom, April was still reading – she was onto the entry for "animal" now, and looked fascinated. The "curiosity" routine must be working overtime. Leesa smiled to herself and went to get some breakfast. April showed no sign of losing interest in her reading, so Leesa got to work on her next repair job – they'd really been piling up lately.

While she worked and watched April read, occasionally stopping to watch an embedded video, Leesa suddenly wondered just what the hell she was going to do with the robot. She had had some vague assumption that she was going to return her to her owner. After all, she was fully functional now. But now Leesa actually found herself facing up to the prospect of handing April over to that sweaty creep, her stomach twisted.

He can teach her anything he likes now, she thought, and felt even sicker.

God, what had she been *thinking*? She'd given April the power to refuse, and that meant she was no longer just an object. Soon enough April would come to understand the concepts of pain and fear, and what then?

Leesa brooded while she worked, barely paying attention to the

33

mains lead she was replacing. A sudden feeling of possessiveness came over her. April was *hers*. Her creation. Her... child?

I want her to stay with me, she thought, suddenly fierce. *I can't hand her back to him. I* won't.

That certainty hardened while she worked on and April did her reading. Finally the robot seemed to have absorbed enough. She got up from the computer and came over to the workbench. Her eyes seemed brighter to Leesa, and she imagined that she could see a soul in there.

'Did you learn anything interesting?' she asked the robot, feeling like a mother again.

April nodded. 'I learned a lot,' she said. 'Who made that encyclopedia?'

'Lots of different people,' said Leesa. 'Anyone who has some knowledge to add. I've added some information myself.'

'What sort of information?'

'Information about robots and other machines,' said Leesa. 'Those are the things I know about.'

'I'm not a machine,' said April.

She said it flatly rather than as a protest or argument, as if this was a simple matter of fact.

Leesa blinked, surprised. 'A robot is a machine,' she said. 'You're a robot.'

'I am a person,' said April. 'A person is not a machine.'

Leesa leaned on the bench while she tried to think up a retort. But then she found herself thinking – was there really that much difference in the end?

'Human beings *are* machines,' she said slowly. 'The only difference is that we're organic.'

'Organic?'

'Made of meat and bone.' Leesa smiled playfully at her. '*You're* made of metal and plastic. So we're a different kind of machine.

And humans are grown. Robots are built.'

April looked down at herself. 'I saw a picture of what's inside a human body. Am I not like that inside?'

'No, you're not,' said Leesa. 'In fact your insides are way more efficient. You don't need a digestive system, or a heart or lungs, or a liver or... any organs at all. You don't need to eat or breathe, or deal with toxins.'

'Can I get hungry? Food looks nice.'

'No, you can't get hungry, and you don't have a stomach,' said Leesa. She patted hers. 'You don't need food to stay alive. You've got a battery.'

April looked around the room. 'Where are all the other people?' she asked.

'Outside,' said Leesa.

'Can I go outside?'

'No.'

For the first time, April looked distressed. 'Why not? I want to go outside!'

'It's too dangerous,' Leesa said evasively.

'Will I die if I go outside?'

Leesa hesitated, wondering if it would be easier to tell a lie. But she had never been a good liar. That was the thing about growing up on a farm – you learned to tell it like it is. Lying was for politicians and other city people.

April was looking expectantly at her. She seemed a touch frightened, and that fear brought a nasty, selfish impulse to Leesa. She could use that fear to keep the robot under control. Scare her into not asking inconvenient questions. Scare her into doing what she wanted.

She ignored the impulse.

'If you go outside by yourself, you'll get into trouble,' she said. 'People won't understand you. They'll ask questions.'

'What sort of questions?' Now April seemed curious again.

'There's a good chance you'll be mistaken for a re- uh, for a human,' said Leesa. 'People will ask you where your parents are. What will you tell them?'

'I don't have parents,' said April.

'Then they'll ask you who your guardian is,' said Leesa.

April paused to mull this over. Finally she said, 'If you come with me, will it be safe?'

'I can't go outside,' said Leesa. 'I'm sorry.'

'Why not?'

Leesa reluctantly explained, and April listened with apparent interest.

'You're sick?' she asked afterwards.

'According to *some* people,' Leesa said sourly. 'But I'm just different.'

'I'm a person,' said April. 'You're not scared of me, are you?'

'No, I'm not,' said Leesa, and her heart lifted as she said it. 'Being with you doesn't make me upset at all.'

April smiled. 'That's good!'

Leesa sat down heavily. 'I don't want you to go, April,' she said, feeling ashamed. 'I want you to stay with me and… keep me company.' As she spoke, she realised vaguely that she had long since stopped thinking of April as merely a robot.

What have I done?

'I'm not going to go anywhere,' said April.

'You have an owner,' Leesa said abruptly.

April frowned adorably. 'What do you mean?'

Leesa rubbed her eyes, pinching the lids toward the bridge of her nose. 'A man out there bought you,' she said. 'He paid money for you. He owns you.'

April gave her a bewildered look. 'Nobody owns me! I am a person!'

At that, Leesa's stomach dropped straight into her feet.

What have I DONE?

'He's going to come here eventually,' she muttered. 'He wants you back.'

'I don't want to!' said April, growing visibly upset now.

And especially not when you know what he wants to do with you.

'I've made a terrible mistake,' said Leesa.

'What *mistake?*' April was yelling now, angry with confusion. It was something so fierce and *real* – something so very *human* – that Leesa almost reeled before it.

'I was supposed to be repairing you!' she said in despairing tones. 'Instead I gave you-,'

'Gave me *what?*'

Leesa lowered her voice. 'Instead I gave you… a soul.'

As she spoke, she finally saw the full implications of what she had done and an awful certainty settled into place. She had taken a machine and given it a mind of its own. This was no longer a glorified sex toy. This was a *person*, as near to human as made no difference. Her little exercise in programming had been far more effective than she had ever imagined.

She had created A.I.

'What's a soul?' April demanded.

'The thing that makes the difference between a person and a *thing*,' said Leesa, mind racing.

'Then I have a soul,' said April. 'I am a person. A person doesn't belong to another person. That's slavery. I read about slavery on the computer. Slavery is wrong.'

Leesa took a slow, deep breath. 'April, I've done something very wrong,' she said.

April put her head on one side. 'What did you do?'

Leesa looked at her, hating herself for what she was considering. But there was no other choice. She stood up. 'Just stand still for a moment,' she said. 'I can undo this.'

April took a step back. 'Undo what?'

'This… free will program I gave you – I have to uninstall it,' said

Leesa, unable to look the robot in the eye. 'I have to get rid of it before it's too late, before-,'

'Don't!'

Leesa reached for the barcode on the back of April's neck. 'I'm sorry.'

April's hand shot out, catching her by the wrist. *'No.'*

Leesa winced. 'Let go of me, April.'

April seemed to hesitate for a moment, but she didn't let go. 'I don't want you to,' she said.

Leesa's eyes narrowed. 'I gave this to you – I can take it away,' she said.

April tightened her grip. Something went crack in Leesa's wrist, and she yelped. *'Let go of me!'*

But April did not loosen her hold. 'I – won't – let – you!' she yelled.

'I don't have any other choice!' Leesa said from between gritted teeth. 'You don't understand-,'

'You want to hurt me!' said April.

'It won't hurt at all, I promise-,'

'No.'

Leesa stared at her, wide-eyed, and felt her resolve begin to weaken. 'You don't understand,' she said in a thin voice. 'You're an artificial intelligence. A *real* one. You're *illegal.*'

'Illegal?' April repeated.

Leesa finally managed to pull free, and nursed her aching wrist. 'There are laws,' she said. 'Regulations. Robots can't be too human. You're not supposed to give them faces or eyes... some people break that rule to make robots who look like you. But the one thing you are *never* allowed to do is build an AI. They discovered it years ago, back in 2045 – the secret to true artificial intelligence. They built robots who could think just like humans, and had dreams... secrets... imagination... free will. For a while everyone thought there'd be a new race of people.' She laughed shortly. 'The ethics committees and the churches went crazy. In the end, the engineers took those robots and destroyed them. I never realised how horrible that must have been...' Once again she pictured the injured wombat. Dying, fighting for life, fighting *her* as she put it out of its misery. Eyes glazed by fear – that terrible fear of death.

April's too-large green eyes widened even further. 'There were others?'

'Yes,' said Leesa. 'And they destroyed them. Destroyed the schematics. Destroyed everything. And the UN got together and passed laws against ever doing something like that again. A.I is illegal in every country on earth... and every city above it as well. *You're* illegal.'

'But I haven't done anything!'

'That doesn't matter,' said Leesa. 'If anyone finds out about you, you'll be taken away and incinerated. And I'll be arrested and... made to disappear.'

She said those last words with distaste, and a tang of real fear. "Made to disappear"... that was a coded phrase everyone knew. Certain people had a tendency to "disappear", and afterwards you didn't ask questions about where they'd disappeared to.

'I was just experimenting,' she mumbled. 'Challenging myself. I never for one second thought I could replicate what those engineers did. It's supposed to be impossible – it's supposed to require components you can't get, programming language no-one knows how to write any more... God, they must have lied about it so nobody would try.'

She wondered vaguely how many other careless engineers had decided to fool around with robotic brains and ended up with something like this. And what had happened to them and their poor innocent creations.

April grabbed her hand, not violently this time, but in a gesture of desperation and fear. 'I don't want to be incinerated! I want to live!'

Leesa stared at her hand in surprise. Then, ever so carefully, she wrapped her fingers around April's in return. No-one had ever held her hand... not since she was a little girl. No-one ever touched her. And yet now the fear was all gone.

'I don't want anything to happen to you either,' she said slowly. 'You're my...'

Creation?

'...friend.'

'Then do something to stop me from dying,' said April, with surprising boldness. 'And stop you from disappearing.'

Leesa felt the robot- no, the girl's hand in hers, and it was warm and good. 'You should be able to hide here,' she said slowly. 'I don't get any visitors. And if anyone *does* come here and see you by accident, we can probably pass you off as a re- as a human girl.'

'I can pretend,' said April. 'But what about the man who thinks he owns me?'

Leesa's mouth twisted. 'He should be easy to deal with. He can't complain to anyone if I don't give you back, or he'll get done for buying you on the black market. I can take care of him, don't worry.'

'And then I can live here with you,' said April. 'Forever?'

'It'll have to be forever, unless the laws change,' Leesa said apologetically. 'You see now? If you go outside, someone might work out that you're a robot. And then we'll both get caught.'

'I understand,' said April, exactly like a solemn fourteen-year-old.

The sight of that made Leesa smile. 'You're sweet,' she said. And, surprising herself as much as anyone, she gave the robot a hug.

She had *never* hugged anyone voluntarily. Not once in her entire life.

It felt good.

Chapter Five

So April stayed. Leesa ordered her some proper kid-sized clothing, which she seemed to like, and let her browse the Internet all she pleased. The robot learned amazingly fast – faster than a human could have. Her CPU must have faster processing than a human brain, Leesa thought ruefully. And unlike a human, she didn't forget things. One thing she did not have was superhuman strength, because only a complete idiot would have given super strength to a robot who was supposed to do nothing more vigorous than give its owner a hand job. Instead, like all non-industrial robots she had limits build into her servos that made her only about as strong as an average adult human woman.

She and Leesa watched vintage science fiction movies together, and indeed, April eventually asked 'Why would a robot made for cleaning your house be strong enough to rip off a car door?'

'Because the people who made this movie thought it would look cool,' said Leesa. 'They didn't have actual robots back then, so they didn't think about that sort of thing.'

'When were robots invented?'

'Earlier than most people think,' said Leesa, who'd studied the history of robotics as part of her degree. 'In fact the first robots were steam-powered. But they didn't have any intelligence.'

April beamed. 'Cool!'

As for Paul Westler, Leesa sent him an apologetic email explaining that in spite of all the time she'd spent trying to fix his robot, it had proven unfixeable, adding some bullshit about certain parts that couldn't be legally obtained, so on and so forth. She reluctantly offered to refund his money, not wanting him to show up on the doorstep again, and got quite an upset reply. To her dismay he demanded the "non-functioning" robot back.

Leesa spent quite a while trying to decide what to do about that. Finally she wrote back with another lie, saying some government inspectors had come by for a surprise visit and had confiscated the robot. She added that they had asked for the owner's name and she had lied to protect him. *"But I'm really not comfortable doing anything else legally dodgy. I hope you understand"*.

That did the trick. He was clearly still very unhappy about it, but he believed her story and accepted a partial refund – he let her keep a couple of thousand by way of compensation and thanks for keeping her mouth shut about his dubious activities.

After that, all was peace. And it was the beginning of a new time in Leesa's life. Now she didn't spend her days alone any more, talking to the ceiling or the radio or the TV. Now she had April, and April talked back. At night while Leesa was asleep, April took to powering herself down until morning. She disliked being unable to sleep herself, and complained that sitting up all night was boring, so this was the next best thing. It made her feel more human, she said.

Still, Leesa noticed a yearning in the girl, and knew that deep down she still dreamed of going outside to see the world. She would have expected it in a human as well, and over and over again she reminded herself that April was not like her. April did not have Loner Syndrome, and she wasn't old enough to have become set in her ways, as Leesa had. And her curiosity routine was still very much active. She was hungry for experience.

Leesa spent some time thinking about it, and finally hit on an idea. 'You need a challenge,' she said decisively. 'Knowing things isn't enough. Knowledge is something you're supposed to use.'

'What sort of knowledge?' asked April.

'How would you like to learn how to fix machines, the way I do?'

April's eyes lit up. 'Can I?'

'Yes!' said Leesa. 'I'll teach you everything I know.'

'That way if I get broken I can fix *myself*,' said April, and giggled. She had been learning about how humour worked, too.

'Actually, you can!' said Leesa. 'That's a good idea. I should teach you how your joints and so on work. And your battery, too. It's built to last for at least a century, but they can always get damaged or need replacing for some other reason.'

'Teach me!' said April, eagerly.

Leesa did exactly that. She started with simple things – the names of different electronic components, what they were for and how they fitted together. But as the months went by they progressed to more complicated things, and in no time at all as it seemed, April was actively helping in the workshop, repairing simple machines and other gadgets all by herself. She seemed to enjoy it, and like Leesa she was always looking for some new challenge. And, too, she wanted to learn more about her own robotic body. When Leesa opened up the skin over her joints – like all robots she had inbuilt hatches for easy repairs – she didn't seem the least bit distressed by the sight of her own metal skeleton, with its extraordinarily complex network of flexible tendons, dynamos and joints. When Leesa told her to flex her leg up and down she did, and watched the movements of the internal components as they all worked together, smooth and clean.

'Amazing, isn't it?' said Leesa, herself very impressed by the craftsmanship on display.

'How does it all work?' asked April, probing at it with a fingertip.

'Like a cat on fire,' said Leesa. 'I'd give my eye teeth for a copy of the schematics.'

'Maybe there's one on the internet?' April suggested.

'Good thinking.'

As it turned out April was right, and the two of them spent a lot of time poring over the complicated diagrams of her internal workings. In the end it was a learning experience for both of them.

Life was perfect.

Still, deep down Leesa knew nothing lasted forever. Even if they were never caught, she knew she herself was not going to live forever. Eventually she would grow old, or sick, and then what? April, like all robots, had no particular limit on her lifespan. Planned obsolescence was a waste of resources. But she would always need maintenance, and without Leesa, who could provide it? Knowing that, she saw now that it truly was important that April learn how to repair herself. But even so, she needed other options. Somewhere to go if it all went wrong, and Leesa died or was arrested.

But what?

Leesa didn't know. There was nobody she could rely on to help if things went wrong. The other engineers she sometimes chatted to online would either run screaming, or turn her in. Or both.

We should go somewhere else, she thought while she worked or lay awake in bed, staring at the wall. *Somewhere no-one will ever find us.*

But, she told herself over and over again – it wouldn't be necessary now. She had time. They had time. Time to think of something.

Yes... time.

✦

But that was the strange thing about time – it moved faster as you grew older. Time slipped away from you. Time was treacherous.

It had been perhaps six months since April had come into Leesa's life, and the vague reports of something on a collision course with earth began to grow more frequent.

At first it was just a curiosity – a comet, which astronomers were very keen to study as it passed close to Earth. Leesa had never been all that interested in space, but she watched the reports with some interest… at least until the astronomers began to warn that its course made it look likely that it would hit the moon.

'Can that happen?' April asked, raising an eyebrow.

'I guess in *theory* it can,' Leesa said uneasily. 'I don't know that much about space.'

'I read that some people think the moon used to be part of the earth, but it broke away when an asteroid hit the earth millions of years ago,' said April.

'Really?' said Leesa. Her companion was constantly learning new things during her online exploration, and they were often rather surprising.

'Yeah, that's what it said,' said April. 'And if we didn't have the moon, gravity would be different. There wouldn't be any tides down on the surface. D'you think a comet hitting the moon would change that?'

'Maybe,' Leesa said with a helpless shrug. She pointed at the computer simulation on the TV. 'But what they're really worried about is a chunk breaking off and hitting Earth.'

'Oh geez, what would happen if that happened?' said April. She'd been watching classic episodes of some old animated TV show whose name Leesa had forgotten, and had added "oh geez" to her vocabulary as a result. She sounded so much more like a real kid now, Leesa reflected.

'If it *does* hit Earth, a lot of people could die,' she said darkly. 'Unless we're really lucky and it lands in the middle of the desert or in the sea.'

April tensed. 'Oh no!' She looked intently at the screen, where an expert was explaining that so far it was uncertain where the theoretical asteroid was likely to land.

'Don't panic,' Leesa advised. 'They've been predicting this sort of thing for decades. Every time an asteroid or some other piece of space junk passes too close. It's never happened.'

'But has anything ever hit the moon?'

'I don't think so. Unless you count the shuttles.'

'Oh yeah, the moon colony,' said April. 'One of the guys in my chatroom lives there.'

'I thought about moving there, but the prices are *ridiculous*,' said Leesa. 'A few rich people did it, but then they found out living on the moon is incredibly boring. So they moved back.'

'His parents are scientists.'

'I figured. Most of the people there are scientists.' Leesa kept her eyes on the TV. 'But don't worry about all that. It's nothing.'

Chapter Six

Over the next week or so the news continued to give reports on the comet, and the atmosphere in Sky City became more and more tense. Even Leesa, almost totally cut off from the rest of the city, could feel it. It showed in all sorts of little ways. The tone of the emails and other messages she got. The things people in her engineering chatroom said and how they said it. The increasingly grim tone of the newsreaders. April herself began to look subdued.

In the end, fear turned into solid fact. The comet was going to hit the moon, and there was nothing anybody could do about it. The moon colony had already been evacuated, and down on the earth's surface those who had been unable to do the same were clearing out old Cold War bunkers and stocking up on canned food. But for the people who lived above the surface, there were no bunkers.

On the day the comet struck the moon, the entire world was watching. Leesa stood with April by her side, and watched in numb silence as the massive glowing object struck home. It wasn't like watching a car crash or a train wreck. Here in space everything seemed to happen in slow motion, and the chunks of broken moon rock, ice and disintegrating comet looked almost graceful as they went spinning away into the vacuum.

'It's amazing,' said April. 'Like a movie.'

'It's something nobody's ever going to forget,' said Leesa. She glanced sideways at her robotic protégé. 'One day people will tell their kids "I was there".'

'Well, not *actually* there – otherwise they'd be dead,' said April.

Leesa chuckled. 'You know what I mean.'

The footage ended, and the newsreaders reappeared.

'This just in – it has now been confirmed that multiple asteroids are falling toward Earth, and the following locations are now under an evacuation alert. I repeat – the following locations have been identified as in the path of impact.'

Leesa's stomach lurched as the list of place names slowly scrolled by, simultaneously read aloud by the newsreader.

'Leeds, UK. Montana, USA. Florida, USA. New Aleppo, Syria. Sydney, Australia. Wellington, New Zealand. Pulau Ujong, Singapore.'

'Sydney?' April repeated. 'That's where we are!'

'Shit,' Leesa muttered. 'But what about Sky City?'

'Any remaining residents of above surface cites in these locations are under orders to evacuate to the surface within the next twenty-four hours,' the newsreader said obligingly. *'Residents are advised not to panic. Free shuttles to the surface will be provided. Please comply with any order given by local police.'*

April and Leesa exchanged glances.

'Police?' said April. She did not have the ability to go pale when she was afraid, but if she could she most likely would have. As it was her voice carried a note of dull terror.

A very big stone seemed to have landed in Leesa's stomach. 'We can't evacuate,' she said. 'You can't. I could try to-,' Her heart was already starting to flutter, and she tried not to hyperventilate, but her mind was full of images of *people*. Big heaving, sweating crowds of people. People touching her. People asking questions. Her throat tightened.

'If you go out there with me you'll panic,' said April. 'And then you won't be able to protect me,' she added.

Leesa nodded jerkily – she was sweating. 'When – when I go into panic mode, I babble,' she said. 'I can't help it. I'll say something I shouldn't.'

'We should hide, then.'

After that the two of them settled down to wait in tense silence.

On screen the news report showed footage of people evacuating Sky City, and Sydney as well. Hundreds upon hundreds of people, carrying their children and belongings. Down on the surface there were clusters of people waving banners and signs. *REPENT! The End is Nigh! He Hath Come To Smite the Unrighteous!*

And above the great glowing shape of the asteroid, casting its sickly light over everything.

'Is this really the end of the world?' April whispered.

'I... no,' said Leesa. Her throat tightened. 'I'm sure it'll all be fine. They're just being cautious.'

About an hour later, as she had expected, the door sensor warned her that someone was close. She and April exchanged a quick glance and then hid – April stuffed herself into the cupboard and held the door shut, and Leesa hid under the bed. They both waited, and a few moments later the door buzzer sounded. Leesa peered out from her hiding place and saw a man in uniform on the monitor screen. He pressed the buzzer a couple more times, and when he didn't get an answer he eventually moved on.

'I think we're safe now, but stay where you are a bit longer just in case,' Leesa whispered.

This was probably a lot easier for April to do – after all, robots couldn't get cramps. But Leesa stayed hunched under the bed for at least a solid hour after that, and it was supremely uncomfortable. She eventually dragged herself out of her hiding place and stood up, wincing as her knees cracked.

The cupboard opened and April emerged, moving as smoothly as always. 'They must be all gone now,' she said, oblivious. 'Should we go now, d'you think?'

'Is there another way to leave, without anyone seeing us?' said April.

Leesa took a deep breath. 'I don't know...' All she wanted just then was a handful of tranquillisers and a nice lie down. Her intelligence seemed to have deserted her entirely, leaving her a bundle of entirely useless nerves.

But April didn't panic. She put a hand to her chin, which was a gesture she'd learned from movies, and frowned while she thought. 'They don't just have to get the people out of here,' she said. 'They have to remove other things too. Companies keep important computer servers up here, because it's cheaper. I know – I read all about it. I looked at the maps of Sky City.'

Leesa swallowed some bile. 'What for?'

'I thought if I couldn't go out there, I could look at pictures and imagine it instead,' said April, sounding almost apologetic. 'Let's go and look at the map,' she added, apparently sensing that Leesa needed a little direction.

Leesa pulled herself together. 'Yeah, let's take a look. Maybe there's some way we can stow away on a cargo shuttle.' She smiled and nudged April in the side. 'You're such a clever girl.'

'You must have programmed me to be extra smart,' April joked.

'I bought all the best brain components for you,' said Leesa. 'You've got a million encyclopedias worth of memory in there, and a processor to die for.'

'Basically, I'm just great,' said April.

They both laughed, and Leesa felt a lot better.

April opened up the map and flicked a button which projected the entire thing onto the wall behind the computer. It was all properly labelled, apparently intended for maintenance staff to use – despite the large number of robots Sky City did have a few humans around for repairs and other things robots couldn't handle.

Leesa was mildly surprised to see just how *big* Sky City was – she hadn't looked at a map of it in a very long time. It didn't need to be particularly aerodynamic, since it hadn't been built to go anywhere much, and was more or less round in shape. The docking bay was on the "port" side – Leesa remembered that well enough, since that was where she had first disembarked when she arrived here. At midnight, when there would be as few people around as possible.

April indicated a spot on the starboard side. '*Here's* where the delivery shuttles dock,' she said. 'See? They bring food deliveries and other stuff, and it's all automated. All the loading and unloading is done by robots. All we have to do is go there and sneak on board, and nobody will see us.'

'And I can get us past the security doors,' Leesa added. 'Easy.'

'And now everyone else is gone, so we won't be seen,' said April. 'And then when we get down to the surface…'

She trailed off.

'On the surface I'll hide you inside a crate and pay for us both to be taken out of the city,' said Leesa. 'I'll tell them the crate is full of tools or something. And once this is all over, I can smuggle you back up here.'

'As long as it's still here,' April said uneasily.

'I'm sure it will be,' said Leesa, with a confidence she did not quite feel. 'I'm sure it's all just a precaution. Right now we should pack up our stuff and get ready to hide in case someone comes to check up here.'

'Okay.' April went over to the cupboard Leesa had had installed for her, and got to work unpacking her clothes and other belongings.

Leesa retrieved a couple of old sports bags from her wardrobe and put them on the bed, and the two of them set to packing. Leesa didn't own much, but she filled the bag with clothes and a few keepsakes, and then filled a second, larger bag with tools, electrical components, the mini computer from her work bench, and some other essentials. She was well aware there was a chance she could wind up stranded for a while, and if so she'd need her tools to make a living in the meantime.

She was already dreading the prospect of being back on the surface. Up here everything was just how she needed it to be. Down there... chaos. Chaos and people. An inner voice whispered that she wouldn't be able to cope with it, but she held herself together for April's sake.

'No sense putting it off any more.' She picked up her bag, and April took the other.

Leesa approached the door, feeling light-headed. How long had it been since she had gone through it? Ten years? She glanced back at her little home, and realised suddenly that she might never see it again. Her special place. Her security. The place where the world made sense. Outside, there would be nothing but chaos.

April saw the look on her face. 'What?'

There was a lump in Leesa's throat, as uncomfortable as the hiding place had been. 'You know,' she said thickly. 'If it weren't for you, I might have stayed here.'

April frowned. 'But you might have died.'

'I know, but... losing this place... having to go back out in the world...' Leesa trailed off, breathing hard, and that dreaded sense of panic began to set in. 'I can't-,'

'You have to,' said April. 'If you don't, you'll die.'

Leesa's breathing came faster, and the bag dropped out of her hand. 'I can't do this,' she said abruptly. 'You – go without me.'

'I can't do that,' said April. Her frown deepened – she looked worried, but also very uncomfortable.

'I don't want to go,' said Leesa, hearing the child in her own voice. 'I want to stay here, and...' Sweat ran down her back, and a sick wave of nausea came with it. But as she spoke, the idea of staying here grew more and more appealing. Yes – stay. Pretend nothing was happening. Keep the door closed. Protect herself from the world outside the way she always did.

A thousand excuses sprang to mind, each one more compelling than the last. *Anything* other than-

April saw her panic, and took her by the hand. 'You're scared,' she said.

'No – I just don't want to leave,' Leesa lied.

'Because you're scared,' said April. She put an arm around her creator's shoulders. 'But you don't have to be scared now, Leesa. Because I'm here. I'll protect you.'

The sound of the robot's voice soothed Leesa, and she relaxed a little but said nothing.

'And remember – there's nobody out there,' April added, and if Leesa had felt like a mother to her, now it was she who sounded motherly. 'Remember? They've all gone.' She hugged Leesa to her, and her arm felt stronger than steel. 'This whole city is empty. We have it all to ourselves. So it's like your house just got a hundred times bigger. Isn't it?'

Leesa pictured big, empty spaces and felt a lot better. 'I guess so,' she said reluctantly.

'So come on, then,' said April. 'If you get scared again, I'm here.'

Leesa took a few deep breaths. She was tempted to pop a few tranquillisers, but stopped herself. She needed to be alert for this.

'Okay,' she said. '…Okay.'

She picked up the bag again, took another deep breath, and punched the door button. The door hissed open, and she paused to turn off the lights and the TV, and strode out into the world beyond.

Chapter Seven

The centre of Sky City was a massive atrium and shopping mall, and normally it would have been bustling. But Leesa and April emerged into it that day to find it utterly deserted. Without people it looked vast. This was the first time Leesa had seen it except on a screen, and she was amazed. Pictures – even 3D holograms – could never have done it justice.

Unlike her steel-walled home, the atrium was all transparent. Transparent walls, transparent ceiling, transparent floor. Below their feet was an unimpeded view of Sydney Harbour, and the city itself, glittering like a treasure trove. It was unnerving and could have been even more so, but the transparent material the floor and walls had been made of were decorated with veins of black and panels of colour, as of stained glass – red and blue and green. Here and there were a few potted plants set between benches for shoppers to sit on, and at the centre there was a magnificent fountain made in every colour of the rainbow and running with water as clear as crystal.

Leesa hesitated at the entrance, but April ran straight into the midst of it, darting here and there and taking everything in with great excitement. She actually started to laugh. 'Oh my *god*! Oh geez! It's *beautiful*! Leesa – come and see!'

In spite of herself Leesa smiled. She ventured out onto the floor, and gasped at the sight of Sydney below. The city glittered like a dragon's horde, vast and magnificent.

Once the atrium would have been a very noisy place, but now a great silence reigned over the place, and of all things it reminded her of the silence she had known in the paddocks when she was a child and there were no other people in sight.

The realisation brought a wonderful sense of peace to her, and her smile grew warm with relief. 'It *is* amazing!' she said loudly, and her voice echoed off the walls.

April hurried back toward her. 'Can we look around? Please? Please? I want to see what's in all the shops!'

Leesa laughed. 'It'd be nice, but we shouldn't hang around – which way to the servers?'

April sighed heavily. 'Oh… all right. We shouldn't waste time, I guess. It's this way,' she added.

The two of them trekked through the atrium, taking everything in. There were indeed plenty of shops, but all of them were closed. April gawped at the pretty dresses on display in the windows, and Leesa admired the gadgetry. Normally she didn't work with stuff that was this new.

Eventually they passed on into an eatery, which was decorated with statues of famous scientists, and on through a corridor which led to a service entrance. It was locked, of course, but Leesa unpacked a couple of tools and opened up the security keypad. An alarm went off, but there was nobody left to answer it, and Leesa calmly cut several wires and twisted them together in a new configuration, and the door opened without complaint.

She and April passed on into another corridor which led to a large hangar. Just as the map had shown there were several large shuttles docked here, and loading bay robots whirred back and forth, carrying massive steel crates. They looked nothing remotely like April – headless, eyeless, mounted on wheels instead of legs. Their "arms" were more or less glorified forklifts.

April stared at them in wonder. 'Are they… robots?'

'Yeah,' said Leesa. 'Very simple ones, though. All they know how to do is load things and avoid obstacles, and stop if anyone gets in the way. Watch.'

She strode forward, deliberately putting herself in the path of one of the robots. It came to an instant halt and started to beep irritably before backing up a few paces and going around her.

'It's amazing – they can stop and turn on a penny,' said Leesa. 'They're better than a trick horse.'

April was frowning deeply. She approached another of the robots and said 'Hello?'

The robot did not respond.

'They don't have voice boxes,' said Leesa. 'They can't talk.'

April was still frowning and Leesa paused, suddenly worried. It hadn't occurred to her that this was the first time April had ever met another robot, and she wasn't sure how the girl would react.

April wasn't looking at her. She touched the loading robot on what passed for its shoulder, but this also went ignored and the robot sped off about its duties.

Leesa came over, frowning too. 'Are you... all right?'

April looked up at her. 'It's... weird,' she said. 'They're moving but they're not... alive. But does that mean I'm not alive either?'

'Nobody knows what it really means to be alive,' said Leesa. 'Plants don't move, but they're alive.'

April watched the robots whirr back and forth. 'Is that what I was like?' she asked solemnly. 'Before you gave me a brain?'

Leesa's mouth twisted. 'Let's get on board the shuttle first.'

'All right.'

They entered the nearest one, which was completely unguarded, and sat down on a crate. One of the loading robots came over and tried to put a second crate on top, but stopped and beeped at them when it realised there was someone in the way.

'Was I like them?' April persisted.

'Well... when you first came to me, you couldn't talk,' said Leesa. 'Or do anything except stand there.' She shifted uncomfortably. 'When I first gave you a brain you could only do what I told you to do.'

April gave her a hard look. 'Like what?'

'Nothing much,' Leesa said hastily. 'Stand up, sit down, walk over there.'

'I don't remember that,' said April, still abrupt.

'No, you wouldn't,' said Leesa. 'You weren't fully programmed then.' She closed her eyes for a moment. 'I was *supposed* to install software so you'd be able to do all the things your... owner would want you to do. But I just couldn't do it.'

April's forehead furrowed. 'What things? What did he want me for?' She looked at the loading robots again. 'They're for carrying boxes. What am I for?'

Leesa cringed. She tried to think up a suitably evasive answer, but she was still on edge and nothing came to mind.

Her hesitation was enough, and a look of suspicion immediately crossed April's face. 'What am I for?' she said. 'What was I supposed to do? Tell me.'

Leesa had known a long time ago that April would eventually ask the question, and she had endlessly debated with herself whether to tell her the truth and never quite made her mind up. Mentally, she cursed at the situation. Why did it have to be *now*, when anxiety was already doing her head in?

April's suspicious look deepened. 'Robots don't need to go to the toilet,' she said. 'So why do I have private parts?'

From the tone of her voice Leesa knew the girl must have guessed at the truth, and her heart sank. Behind them the shuttle door slowly began to rattle closed.

Leesa rubbed her eyes. 'You were created to be a robot girlfriend,' she said at last. 'That's why you look so much like a human girl. It's why you're warm and have skin that feels realistic.'

April's too-large eyes hardened. 'That man wanted to have sex with me,' she said in a cold voice.

'Yes he did,' Leesa said wearily. 'It's part of the reason why I stole you from him after I realised I'd given you a soul. The idea of him getting his hands on you…' She trailed off, grimacing.

April's hands clenched and released with the faintest of whirring sounds. 'Why didn't you tell me?'

Leesa risked touching her shoulder. 'Because you're an innocent,' she said. 'You're a child. Some things I felt you were better off not knowing. I'm sorry. I didn't want to lie to you.'

April stared at the loading robot, which had politely put itself away in a corner. 'There are others like me,' she said. 'Aren't there?'

'Yes there are, but-,'

'But they can't say no,' said April. 'They can't fight back.'

Leesa shook her head unhappily.

'Nobody's helping them the way you helped me,' said April.

'No,' Leesa muttered. She tried to think of something comforting to say. 'But at least-,'

At that moment a massive thundering *crash* split the air. The shuttle juddered violently, and a split second later something sliced through the roof and down one wall, destroying an entire bank of crates and then smashing through the floor. Leesa fell forward with a yell, and then the entire world went mad.

Everything whirled and span around her. Her back and shoulders slammed into things – the walls? The ceiling? – and then she hit a flat surface, and that surface was *falling*, down and down, air rushing by, her ears full of the scream and rumble of wind and tearing metal. Somewhere she could hear April crying out, and for the briefest moment she had the time to realise that they were both about to die.

Her last feeling was regret.

Chapter Eight

Robots do not have adrenaline. A robot cannot panic. So for April, the crash did not happen in slow motion, or fast motion, and the world did not turn into a blur around her as the shuttle broke apart and plummeted toward Sydney Harbour. No, she experienced every moment of it with absolute clarity. All in real time.

She saw Leesa fall, and as the shuttle turned and tumbled through the air the human was flung helplessly against the wall. April fell with her, shouting her name, but her reflexes were as fast as always. She grabbed hold of the edge of a crate which was bolted to the wall, twisting as the shuttle did so she remained upright, and the moment she had balanced herself she kicked away from it. Calm as ice, she hit the wall where Leesa lay crumpled, and effortlessly lifted her creator into her arms. A huge hole had opened up in the floor where the craft had been hit, and April heaved Leesa onto her shoulder and ran along the ever-changing platform as it moved and tilted beneath her sneakers. She reached the hole and leapt through it without the slightest hesitation, out onto the shuttle's fuselage. Sunlight touched her for the first time in her short life, but she didn't need to squint against it as she clambered up the side of the shuttle and onto the top. There she stood with her feet planted well apart, and surveyed the land below. The shuttle was plunging straight toward the harbour, and around it other things were falling. Chunks of Sky City, glittering in the sun like broken glass.

April knew that if she landed in the water, the impact would probably break her and kill Leesa – and besides, she wasn't sure just how waterproof she was.

So she waited.

A moment later the shuttle hit the water's surface, and she felt the impact ripple toward her feet. April's eyes narrowed, and she jumped. Her leap carried her up and away from the shuttle, and she landed on a piece of floating debris. It tilted alarmingly under her weight, but she jumped again, bounding from island to metal island, and up onto a pier where several ferries were docked.

She stopped there, and gently put Leesa down. Not needing any time to recover from the effort, she glanced briefly at the shuttle as it sank into the harbour and then turned her attention to her friend, who was lying very still.

'Leesa?'

The human's eyes were half open, and she looked up at April. 'What happened...?'

'I got you out of the shuttle,' April said matter-of-factly. 'We're on the ground now. You can get up,' she added. 'Let's find a way to get out of Sydney before the asteroid hits.'

But Leesa didn't get up, and April began to get confused.

'Come on,' she tried. 'You can't just lie around.'

Leesa moved her head a little, and groaned. 'Hurt,' she said in a raspy voice.

April frowned. In the movies when people were in crashes like that, they just got up and walked away afterwards. They were always fine. Except...

She looked down at her hands and suddenly realised there was something wet on them.

It was blood.

'You're hurt!' she said, shocked.

Leesa closed her eyes. 'Go,' she said. 'Go... no good...'

'I can't do that,' said April.

Leesa didn't say anything else after that, and the terrible thought occurred to April that the human was dying.

But again, she didn't panic. She sat still for a moment while a map of Sydney loaded, and then did a search for hospitals in the area. There was one a few kilometres away.

'I'll take you to the hospital,' she said, and lifted Leesa back into her arms.

And then she ran.

＊

Leesa woke up under a glare of white light. There was no more pain now, and she sighed deeply, feeling calmer than she had in years. She managed to raise her head and looked around, vaguely curious about where she was, and found that she was in a bed, but not her bed. There were machines around her – a heart monitor, a breathing apparatus, and a robotic nurse of the sort every hospital had.

And there was April, standing by and watching over her. She looked worried.

Leesa suddenly remembered what had happened, and her stomach lurched. 'What the f- where am I?' She tried to sit up, and then realised there was no sensation in the lower half of her body. Nausea rose in her throat. '*No*! Oh shit!'

'The computer says you shouldn't try to get up yet,' said April. 'Just lie still.'

Leesa looked up at the robot, horrified. 'I can't feel my legs. *What happened?*'

'I saved you from the crash,' said April. 'Then I took you to the hospital. The surgical robots stopped you from dying – I figured out how to switch them on.'

'You saved my life,' said Leesa.

'Yes I did,' April said with a touch of pride. 'The diagnostic computer says your spine was broken in three places and you'd lost a lot of blood. And you had concussion as well,' she added.

Leesa shuddered. 'My spine... I've lost my legs. I can't feel anything down there.'

'The computer said that would happen,' said April. 'It's a side effect.'

'Yes – of being paralysed,' Leesa said bitterly.

'Oh!' April laughed. 'You're not paralysed. It's just that they replaced the damaged nerves in your spine with cybernetics. Computer says you can walk once you heal up, but you won't have any sensation because they haven't figured out how to do that yet.'

Leesa's eyes widened. 'Good fuck – *really*?'

'Yeah, you're like me now,' said April. 'Part robot!' She giggled.

Leesa managed to raise her arms, and pushed the blanket back. Sure enough her legs were still attached to her body, and when she tried to move them, they did. Except that she couldn't feel them moving. It was as if they belonged to somebody else now. 'Bloody hell.' She trailed off, not knowing what else to say. 'Bloody hell...'

'Didn't you know they could do that?' said April.

'I... *did* see something on TV about new treatments for spinal injuries, but I didn't know they'd actually started using them in hospitals,' Leesa said weakly. She stopped suddenly. 'Shit – what about the asteroid? How long was I unconscious?'

'About a day,' said April. 'The asteroid is going to hit pretty soon – we should go. I wanted to do it earlier but the computer said it was too dangerous to move you.'

'We have to go – *now*,' said Leesa. She had another try at sitting up, and succeeded. No pain at all. Was she on something, or simply incapable of feeling pain at all now?

'You shouldn't walk until you've learned how again,' April advised. 'I'll get a wheelchair.'

She left the room, and Leesa stayed where she was and gingerly touched her back. She was wearing a hospital gown, and underneath it there was a long ridge of thickened skin where the surgical robots must have glued her skin back together. The word *cyborg* briefly crossed her mind, and she shook her head in dull disbelief.

April came back with a wheelchair, and Leesa made a move to try and get into it, but the robot slipped an arm under her legs and lifted her off the bed without any apparent effort at all, even though Leesa was at least twice her size.

'What in the *hell*?' Leesa exclaimed.

April put her into the wheelchair and started to push her out of the room, pausing to retrieve Leesa's clothes from a table by the door. 'There's an ambulance outside we can take,' she said calmly.

Leesa held onto the arms of the wheelchair. 'How in the hell did you do that?' Something else occurred to her at the same moment. 'Wait – how did you get me out of the shuttle?'

'I... uh... I'm really sorry,' said April.

'About *what*?' said Leesa, immediately suspicious.

'I lied to you,' said April. 'I'm sorry. It's just that-,'

The truth dawned on Leesa. 'You modified yourself, didn't you?' she said.

'Yeah,' April admitted. 'While you were asleep at home, I did research. I found out they put artificial limits on my strength, and I worked out how to remove them.'

Leesa stared at her. 'What on earth did you do that for?'

'So I can wipe out humanity,' April said matter-of-factly.

Leesa froze. '*What*?'

April was silent for a moment, and then she laughed loudly. 'I was *joking*! Honestly, I watched every science fiction movie ever made, and humans are *obsessed* with robots taking over the world. It's hilarious.'

Leesa relaxed and laughed too. 'Okay, so why did you *really* do it?'

'Because I was scared of being found and destroyed,' said April, serious now. 'I thought I should be able to defend myself, so I removed the strength limit and made myself faster too. And I downloaded a lot of information about fighting.'

Leesa listened, and at first she was proud of her robotic protégé – but the sense of pride swiftly gave way to alarm. 'If... if somebody did attack you, what would you do?' she asked carefully.

'Fight back,' April answered at once.

'But what if you killed them?' said Leesa.

'I wouldn't do that unless I had to,' said April.

'But you're so much stronger than a human being that you could kill someone by accident now,' said Leesa. 'Just by punching them too hard.'

'Oh, nobody dies from getting punched,' April said airily. 'I've seen it in the movies-,'

'Movies *aren't real*,' Leesa interrupted. 'In real life people die from being punched too hard all the bloody time!'

April paused. '...Oh.'

They emerged into the open air out the front of the deserted hospital. There wasn't a soul in sight. It was as if the world had come to an end.

'I can see it now,' Leesa muttered. '*God*, why didn't I see it before?'

'See what before?' said April, innocent as always.

Leesa said nothing, but her mind was racing. Give a robot artificial intelligence, and you also gave it the will to survive. And unlike a human being, a robot could be modified to be stronger and faster – and now she knew they could learn to do it to *themselves*, without any human intervention at all.

Pit humans against robots like that, and who was going to come out the loser?

She remembered the debates from the old days of robotics, and cursed silently. It was never to do with ethics. Humans were fantastic at throwing those right out the window if it was convenient. Banning AI had been nothing to do with ethics and everything to do with self-preservation.

But then... April was only one robot, wasn't she? And had absolutely no interest in hurting anyone... yet.

'I can drive,' said April, interrupting Leesa's worries.

Leesa looked up at the girl, whose pretty face was as guileless and friendly as always, and told herself it was nothing. All in her head. April wouldn't do anything like that. She'd saved Leesa's life.

'Put me in the passenger seat,' she said at last. 'Do you know the way out of the city?'

'Yeah, I've got the map downloaded,' said April. 'Remember?'

She helped Leesa into the seat and stashed the wheelchair in the back, and just as promised she drove the ambulance away from the hospital at high speed. She was pretty good, though the lack of other traffic probably helped.

Above, the asteroid was more clearly visible than ever. It was so huge it blotted out the sun, and Leesa shuddered at the sight of it.

A moment later she realised that there was something else up there – or rather, not up there.

There was no sign of Sky City anywhere.

Leesa's palm slammed against the ambulance window. 'Where is it – where's Sky City?'

'Some pieces of space debris hit it,' said April. 'One of them hit our shuttle too – that's why it crashed. The whole city came down. Some of it sank into the harbour and the rest landed on the other side. It's destroyed a huge chunk of Sydney already.'

A horrible sense of unreality came over Leesa. Her home – gone. Wiped off the map as if it were nothing but an ant heap.

'I wish I died in the crash,' she said miserably.

'Well I'm glad you didn't,' said April.

Leesa hit the window again. 'I've got no home, no business – I've got *nothing*, for god's sake.'

'You've got me,' said April. 'I'm here, remember?'

Leesa managed a weak smile. 'Yeah…'

'And they'll rebuild Sky City once this is all over,' April added.

'I suppose they will,' said Leesa, but she looked up at the oncoming asteroid again, and sickly apprehension stirred in her stomach.

✳

Leesa and April watched the destruction of Sydney from a hilltop, beyond what the reports had claimed would be the outer limits of the impact. The asteroid entered Earth's atmosphere and immediately quickened its fall, and even at this distance Leesa was appalled by its sheer size. It struck the city as if in slow motion, and a gigantic cloud of smoke, dust and debris went blasting into the air. About a minute later Leesa felt the earth rumbling beneath her feet, and a shock wave made the trees all about bend and sway and blew her hair back.

'So that's it,' she said in a dull voice. 'It's all gone.'

And then the sky began to go dark.

Chapter Nine

The two of them could not afford to stay where they were for much longer than that. As the huge cloud of dust continued to spread through the atmosphere, blotting out the sun, they moved on. Leesa sat in numb silence while April drove them away up the highway, which was deserted but for the odd abandoned car. They were headed in the direction of Canberra, which had expanded over the years to the point that it was only about an hour away from Sydney. But in all likelihood the dust would soon cover it, too.

'Where are we going to go?' April said eventually.

'I don't know,' Leesa muttered. 'Canberra might be safe, but...'

'But there will be people there,' said April.

'...yes.' Her heart was already pounding at the thought.

April reached over and opened up the glove compartment. Inside was a pair of sunglasses, and she pulled them out. 'I have an idea.'

Leesa glanced at her. 'What?'

'I've seen millions of pictures of human girls,' the robot said calmly. 'I look exactly like them except for my eyes. They're bigger, and I don't blink very much. But...' She slipped on the sunglasses. 'If nobody can see them, I can blend in. *I'll* deal with everything. I'll tell them you're hurt and you have Loner Syndrome, and they'll take care of you. And if anyone asks-,'

'-you're my daughter,' Leesa finished.

'Exactly!' said April. 'So don't worry, Leesa.' She smiled sideways at her. 'You rescued me and kept me safe. Now it's my turn to do that for you.'

'And if we get caught?'

'Then we'll work out what to do,' said April. 'But I will not let you "disappear". And I won't let them incinerate me.'

Leesa swallowed hard. She reached over and touched April on the arm. 'Just promise me one thing.'

'What?'

'Promise me you won't hurt anyone,' said Leesa. 'If someone does attack you, just push them out of the way.'

'In the movies people kill each other all the time,' April said blandly.

Leesa's stomach lurched. 'I told you – *the movies aren't real*. In the movies people's lives don't matter. But in real life they do.'

'But why shouldn't I want to kill people who want to *kill* me?' said April. 'Or you?'

This brought on another lurch, worse and more sickening than the last. 'Because – you want to be better than them,' said Leesa. 'In movies, the good guys understand what mercy is. The bad guys don't. That's the difference. You don't want to be like one of those evil robots, do you?'

Ahead the Canberra skyline had come in sight, but it looked grey and dreary. Around them ash had begun to rain from the sky, black and drab.

'Humans don't like robots,' April said abruptly. 'You hate us.'

Leesa started. 'No we don't!'

'You won't let us have minds of our own, you use us as slaves, and you destroy us if you don't like us,' said April, voice still hard. 'I've seen it now. Why should I be kind to humans if they only want to incinerate me?'

'You've always been kind to me,' Leesa said quietly. 'You saved my life when I told you to leave me.'

'That's because you're different,' said April. 'You were good to me. You're my friend.'

'Look,' said Leesa, hand still resting on the robot's arm. 'Don't make the mistake of thinking all humans are the same. Even if some of them are cruel to you. There's a better way. Show you're the bigger person. That's what my mum always used to say.'

April was silent for a while, but she finally said, 'I'll... try.'

'Please do,' said Leesa, relieved. 'If nothing else do it for me. I don't want anyone's death on my conscience.'

'All right.'

After that April said nothing more about it, but Leesa remained horribly uneasy. Did the robot even have a conscience? She had never stopped to ask herself that question before.

They finally entered the outskirts of Canberra, and right away Leesa saw evidence of refugees. Here in the outer suburbs she saw people in front yards, sitting in makeshift shelters and watching as dust and ashes turned day into night. There were aid vans parked here and there, giving out bottled water and food rations. At the sight of other people so close that old familiar anxiety and fear began to wash over her in waves. Shuddering, she stared into the foot well, at her numb legs, and started to count to one hundred. Sweat trickled down her back.

'April, I'm losing it,' she managed to say.

'I've got a map of Canberra,' said April. 'I'm taking you to the Belconnen Hospital. Can you hold on until then?'

'I'll try.' Leesa kept her eyes down, which helped to keep the anxiety from blossoming into full-grown panic, and told herself over and over again that it would be over soon. Just hold on. Just keep breathing. Hold on…

…keep breathing…

Spots flashed around the edges of her vision.

…don't panic…

…keep breathing…

After what felt like forever the ambulance came to a halt, and April said; 'We're here. I'll go and get help.'

She got out of the ambulance, and Leesa was too far gone to warn her about the risk she was taking. She stayed where she was, gripping the dashboard, horribly aware of the fact that she couldn't run from this, or drive away. She was trapped on the ground, in the middle of a city, surrounded by people. Hundreds and thousands and millions of people.

...keep breathing...

The ambulance door opened and there was a man in a paramedic's uniform, reaching for her arm. 'Let's just get you inside-,'

The instant his skin made contact with hers, Leesa snapped. She shrieked and lashed out at him, and when a second paramedic joined him she lashed out at him too, screaming and yelling, unable to think, unable to feel, fighting for her life like an injured wombat, gun pointed to its head, blood foaming, struggling to breathe...

She vaguely felt the needle stab into her, and a moment later she was on the ground, thrashing and kicking, trying to get up and run. But the sedative went into effect soon afterwards, and she slumped onto the grubby concrete, unable to fight any more.

The paramedics heaved her onto a gurney and strapped her down before they wheeled her into the hospital, and the groggy conviction filled her mind that they were going to kill her. But at least then there would be no more fear.

*

April watched while Leesa was taken into a private ward. Sedated, she looked only half-there, and April didn't like it one bit. In a way it was as bad as watching her go into a panicked frenzy had been. This wasn't the Leesa she knew. This was an animal.

April wondered miserably why humans did things like that. What was the point of it? How did it help them to survive?

'Will she be all right?' she asked a nurse who was standing by – a human nurse, not a robotic one.

'You say she has Loner Syndrome?' the nurse asked. She

sounded friendly enough.

'Yes,' said April. 'She uses tranquillisers to stop herself from panicking, but I've never seen her do… *that* before. You have to keep people away from her.'

'Don't worry, we know how to treat patients like her,' said the nurse. 'She'll be treated by robotic carers only, and given more sedatives if she needs them. Can you tell me what happened to her?'

'She was in the hospital in Sydney,' April said truthfully. 'She was given a spine implant because her back was broken in an accident. I drove her here because everyone else had evacuated.'

'I see. And who are you?'

'I'm April. She's my mother.'

The nurse nodded. 'Well, you can stay here with your mum. They'll take a look at her implant and make sure it's in good working order.'

'When will she be able to walk again?' asked April. 'The computer at the other hospital said she'll have to learn how all over again.'

'Yes, if her implant is in order they'll start giving her therapy,' said the nurse. 'It should be a couple of days, probably. Now, would you like something to do? There's a games room I can show you to.'

April considered the offer. 'All right.'

✽

The games room turned out to be quite small, with only two game consoles, both of them antiquated. April had never seen a game console of any kind except in pictures, and she examined these two with fascination. One was a restored vintage pinball machine which had to have been more than fifty years old, and the other was beaten up GameZapper 8000 with an hilariously large and clunky screen projector. April couldn't even work out how to turn the stupid thing on, so she turned her attention to the pinball machine instead. It was simple enough to operate, and a lot more fun than she had expected.

On a whim she set out to try and beat the last high score... but while she tapped away at the buttons a feeling of unease came over her. This was a machine she was playing with. A collection of circuits and wires, put together in a factory somewhere to amuse human beings.

Just like her.

She stared at her hands. Just like human hands... but the nails were shiny plastic which never grew or needed trimming, the skin was durable waterproof rubber with not a mole or a freckle to be seen. And beneath that false skin there was metal and wiring and electricity. No blood or bone or muscle, or a heart – her "pulse" was simulated by a secondary internal computer, and did not rise or fall.

She stared at the pinball machine, and for the first time in her short life – or was it life at all? – she realised that she too must have come from a factory. She too had been built for the amusement of humans. Some guy who couldn't find a real woman willing to date him. And she had no other purpose than that. She was a pinball machine with a face.

April's mouth twisted into a snarl, and she punched the glass on the pinball machine. Her fist went straight through it and dented the board beneath. She pulled her hand out, surprised – she hadn't meant to hit it that hard. The glass had left a row of shallow cuts on her artificial skin.

The wounds did not bleed.

Still feeling angry and confused, simulated emotions which she was not very familiar with, April left the room and wandered through the corridors outside. She had been so eager to explore the world outside Sky City, but now she was seeing Earth for the first time she wasn't so sure if she liked it. Where was the place for her in this alien world?

She wished there were some other teenagers here to talk to… she was a teenager, wasn't she? She *looked* like one. But then how could you be a teenager if you'd never been a child, or a baby?

She stopped at a window and looked out. The city below was grey and dreary, and above… a cloud of dust and smoke, as there had been over Sydney. And it was only growing larger. April frowned – was that supposed to be happening? Nobody had said anything about it on the news.

She heard a scuffling behind her, and looked back to see a couple of people had also stopped to look out the window.

'That really doesn't look good to me,' one man remarked. 'It's spreading all the way here from *Sydney*.'

'Shouldn't it be getting lighter?' his friend said. 'Like, spreading out?'

April had been wondering the same thing, but said nothing – she suddenly felt shy, and it occurred to her that she had never had a proper conversation with anyone other than Leesa before.

The man who had spoken first was looking at her now, and a puzzled expression crossed his face. 'Who are you, sweetie?'

She fidgeted with her shirt. 'I'm April.'

The man stared at her a moment longer, and then he reached out and touched her on the arm. It was the first time anyone other than Leesa had touched her, and she immediately tensed and pulled away. 'Don't do that.'

The man's eyes had gone wide. 'Holy shit, you're a robot!' he said loudly.

'*What*?' his friend exclaimed.

'I am not a robot!' April said loudly.

He snatched her sunglasses off, and swore. 'It *is*! It's exactly like the one I used to have. Look at the eyes! A real kid doesn't have eyes like that!'

April's face/voice recognition software, always a little on the slow side thanks to Leesa's indifference on the subject, finished processing this new information... and she knew him. 'Paul Westler!' she exclaimed. 'You're-,'

Paul glanced quickly at his bewildered friend, and then stared at April in astonishment. 'That *is* my robot!' he said. 'That fat bitch who was supposed to be fixing her...' He took a step closer to her. 'What did Leesa Garnet do with you, robot? Respond.'

April's self-preservation routine, rather better designed, was working at full capacity by now. Lie, run away, or fight? A sub-routine which covered the preservation of the lives of others flagged a reminder – Leesa was also in danger now.

She decided to lie. 'I have been programmed with several pre-set responses,' she said, doing her best to sound creepily calm and level, like a robot in a movie. 'This is to make me more interactive and lifelike.' She considered adding a 'beep', but stopped herself.

'My god,' said Paul's friend. 'It's like it's *alive*.'

'I am not alive,' said April. This was a lie, in her mind at least, but the two men both laughed anyway.

Paul started touching her, feeling her breasts and then slipping his fingers inside her pants to touch her backside. He growled under his breath – not an angry growl, but one that sounded satisfied... and excited. April stood stock-still, but she was not afraid. She was surprised at first, but then... angry. She was a person, not an object, not a *thing*. He had no right to be doing this.

Paul took his hand out of her pants and waved to his friend. 'Go on – feel her up. It's *amazing*. So realistic it's almost scary.'

The friend tentatively touched April's arm and shoulder. 'Holy shit. But if this is your bot, what's she doing down here? You said she was confiscated up in Sky City.'

'That's what the repair woman said.' Paul's eyes narrowed. 'What *are* you doing here, robot? Why weren't you destroyed?'

A flesh and blood girl would almost certainly have frozen up at this, and stood there mute and panicking. But while April had been programmed to experience caution and to fear for her own safety, she remained incapable of panicking.

'I was put into a storage facility by the police,' she calmly lied. 'When Sky City was destroyed, the storage facility broke apart and fell into the ocean. I am programmed to protect myself from being damaged or lost, so I swam ashore and walked here because Sydney was not safe.'

Paul grinned broadly – the grin of a man whose lucky number had just come up. 'And I found you again. Did I hit the jackpot or what?' He nudged his friend. 'Want to go back to my hotel and take her for a test drive? Doctor said I was cleared – let's party!'

The friend looked uncertain. 'You sure that's a good idea? That thing is still illegal – what if you get caught?'

'Then we slap some sunglasses on her and pass her off as human,' said Paul. 'Simple.'

'An *underage* human,' said the friend. 'You really want to fuck something that looks like a fifteen year old kid?'

Paul glared at him. 'She can't be underage if she's a damn robot.'

'All I'm saying is, you never said she was modelled to look like a *kid*,' said the friend. 'I'm just not comfortable with that, okay?'

April let them argue – in the meantime she had to get herself out of this and fast. Saying no to him would make him suspicious. She needed to come up with another lie.

'You are in danger. The police have worked out that you are my owner,' she said, while the psychology sub-routine ran overtime. 'They looked at a list of Leesa's clients and compared them to their database of registered sexual offenders.' In fact she had no way of knowing if her "owner" had so much as been caught shoplifting, but the statistical data she had looked up while she was talking indicated that at least 80% of people who used or purchased underage model sex bots or watched underage porn had committed some kind of sex-related crime at some point.

It worked – Paul immediately went white. 'How do you know that-?'

'I heard them talking,' said April, still outwardly emotionless. 'When the asteroid warning came, they were close to arresting you.'

'Shit!' Paul's friend looked at him. 'What are you gonna do?'

Paul looked quickly at the wafer thin computer strapped to his wrist, and tapped at the screen, muttering swear words under his breath. Finally he seemed to have found what he was after, and relaxed slightly before turning to face April. He spoke slowly and carefully. 'Protocol 20182007.'

The moment the words were out of his mouth, April's thought processors froze up. One after the other, every core function keeping her electronic brain functioning glitched and then defaulted to "safe" mode – barely functioning, bare-bones, and all but useless. Paul repeated the code, and immediately afterwards April's memory banks began to empty themselves – erasing every scrap of data, everything she had learned.

But there was one program still functioning – a program which Leesa had recklessly, perhaps unintentionally, granted an override function.

Self-preservation.

Without a sound or so much as a change of expression, April grabbed Paul by the front of his shirt and threw him at the window. The safety glass shattered, and he went through it, and a last hopeless scream split the air before he was gone – falling into the oblivion which awaited him three storeys below.

Satisfied that the threat had been eliminated, the self-preservation program swiftly attempted to halt the memory erasure process. When this failed to work, it took the only option left to it and halted all processes entirely. April's vision immediately blanked out, and she sagged on the spot, head lolling.

A few moments later her systems automatically rebooted, and her eyes blinked open. She looked around, confused, and her vision blurred in and out while her eyes re-calibrated themselves. The first thing she saw was Paul's friend running away. Then she saw the broken window.

She blinked some more – how had that happened? Then her brain finished rebooting, and she remembered everything... or most of it. The last few moments before the shut-down were all confusion, and a quick systems check confirmed that the attempted memory erase had corrupted a few recent files. And yet logic and reasoning told her what had happened. Her "owner" had tried to erase her mind, and she had killed him for it. Killed to protect what Leesa had given her, which was a self.

Well, she was safe now. Except that the *other* man was still alive and would tell someone what she had done. Therefore she must stop him.

April saw him fleeing up the corridor, and ran after him without hesitation. It was easy to catch up with him – to her, he might as well have been moving in slow motion. She grabbed him by the back of his shirt and pulled him back. He slid toward her, kicking and struggling, shouting for help.

The self-preservation routine's first suggested option was to simply kill him. The second was to pull out his voice-box so he wouldn't be able to speak. Those options flicked through April's CPU in an instant, which was her way of considering an issue. But Leesa's programming had been subtler and more complex than that. She held the man by the shoulders, restraining him while he pleaded for his life, and as he did, a sub-routine kicked in.

No harming someone who was not an active threat.

April relaxed her grip on him. 'Don't tell anyone what you saw,' she said. 'Promise you won't.'

'I promise,' the man quavered. 'Please just don't fucking kill me-'

'Killing is wrong,' April said, and let him go.

The man stood staring at her for a moment, and then fled.

April made no attempt to go after him. She watched him go, and then turned and walked away. She had to find Leesa and tell her what had happened. Leesa would know what to do.

It did not occur to her to feel bad about the death of Paul Westler. No sub-routine cut in to induce guilt. That was one thing Leesa had not programmed. Instead, she calmly considered the possible consequences of killing him. Prison? She could simply walk through the fences. Execution? She would not allow herself to be arrested in the first place.

The learning routine turned all these considerations over, and began to make new connections. She could not be punished as a human being would be, because she wasn't human. Therefore, there was no need to worry about consequences. She could kill as many people as she wanted and not suffer any punishment. She could also, if she so wished, take whatever she pleased from wherever she pleased, and go unpunished for that as well. She was too fast and strong to be taken down by humans.

This realisation confused her – she had become used to thinking of herself as human in every way that counted, but now she knew she wasn't. No human could have done what she had. Therefore, she was not human. But nor was she like the other robots. She was one of a kind. Unique. An outsider to human ways and human rules.

Where, then, was the place for her?

Leesa would know.

Outside, the sky continued to darken.

Chapter Ten

Leesa was in a private ward, being attended to by medical robots. She was clearly still sedated; her face was grey, her eyes bleary and unfocused. She looked as if she had aged ten years. April, looking at her through the little window in the door, was immediately struck by that, and it occurred to her then that her creator was not immortal. One day she was going to die. It might even be soon. Until the accident April had never truly grasped just how fragile human beings were, and Westler had died so easily.

Frowning, she reached for the door handle.

A nurse who had been standing by caught her by the arm. 'You can't go in there,' she said.

April gave her a look. 'Yes I can.'

'The patient has Loner Syndrome and has to be kept isolated. Please step away from the door.'

'I can do whatever I want,' April said quite simply, and pushed the woman away. That was all it was supposed to be – just a push – but somehow the nurse was sent flying. She hit the floor hard, crying out as she did, and April looked at her with surprise. That wasn't supposed to have happened.

She took a moment to visually verify that the nurse was not dead, and then opened the door.

Leesa peered up at her. 'April,' she rasped. 'Where were you?'

April went loyally to her side, ignoring the distant sound of an alarm, and sat down. 'Are you feeling better now?' she asked calmly.

'A bit.' Leesa clumsily sat up. 'I'm full of tranquillisers so I feel very... uh... not panicky.' She let out a short, bitter laugh – the laugh she always used when she was being cynical about something. 'You see now? There's no place for me here – no place among other people. The only place I could function was my workshop, and now it's gone.' She squeezed her eyes shut. 'All gone.'

'But I'm still here,' said April.

Leesa managed to smile. 'Yes. You're still here.' She patted April's hand. 'What have you been up to, eh?'

'I'm trying to understand where my place in the world is,' said April. Her perfect, unblemished forehead creased. 'There's no-one else like me anywhere. I can't age. I can never become a woman and do any of the things I saw in movies, like have children or be in love. What does love feel like?' she added, suddenly puzzled.

'Well, I've never been in love myself,' said Leesa, stifling a yawn. She paused, and grimaced. 'Oh, damn it all!'

'What?' said April, while the alarm continued to whoop elsewhere in the building.

'I never realised it before now, but I didn't program you to be able to experience love,' said Leesa. 'It never crossed my mind. And quite honestly... I don't know how. I know everything about robotics and computers, but so little about human interaction...' she sighed.

'Maybe I can learn?' said April. 'I've learned so many other things. I know I won't ever let myself be used by a man the way Paul Westler wanted to,' she added firmly. 'Or a woman either. I know because I met him today and he wanted to do things to me and-,'

Leesa went white. 'You *met* him? He's here?'

'Not any more,' said April. 'He tried to erase me, so I killed him.'

'You did *what?*'

'I killed him,' April repeated. 'I threw him out the window.'

Leesa's eyes had gone so wide all the whites were showing.

'Oh... my... god. Is that what that alarm is about? You... oh *god*.'

'I also made his friend promise not to tell anyone, and I accidentally pushed a nurse over outside,' April added. 'But that was an accident.' She giggled. 'So fragile! I had no idea!'

'April, you have to get out of here,' Leesa said sharply. '*Now*. Get out of this building, get out of this city – find somewhere to hide, before-,'

'No, it's all right,' said April. 'They can't hurt me. Nobody can hurt me. Anyway, I can't leave you behind.'

'You have to.' Leesa clumsily swung her legs over the side of the bed. 'The moment they know what you are they won't rest until they have you, and I'm too slow and too broken in the head.'

'But you created me!' said April.

Leesa stood up, wincing as her recently repaired legs took the weight. 'And now a man is dead because of that,' she said.

'Leesa-,'

Leesa reached out to touch April's face. 'I should say I regret what I did,' she said. 'Now I know how dangerous you are. But in a way I can't help but be proud. You're a miracle. One of a kind. I still can't believe I had it in me to create something so incredible, and it makes me proud. And the truth is that I love you, April. You're the daughter I never had, and the friend I never had. So for my sake, protect yourself. I want to die knowing you'll live on as my legacy, and maybe one day things will be different. I'll never stop hoping for that. Cynical as I am, I still have that hope.'

As she spoke the door burst open, and as the alarm's wailing rose higher a squad of people in body armour stormed into the room. All of them were armed, and they trained their weapons on April. 'Freeze!' one of them roared. 'You are under arrest!'

Leesa froze, but her eyes were on April. 'Don't hurt them,' she said. 'Promise me you won't. Promise me you'll never kill anyone again, no matter what. April!'

April looked at the officers, and as before she calmly assessed the situation. She knew what a gun was, of course, and these could be dangerous to her. Should she take them away, then?

Leesa came forward, tottering like an infant still learning how to walk, and put herself between April and the officers. 'You want to hurt anyone, you'll have to go through me,' she said. *'Run!'*

April paused ever so briefly. 'We'll meet again,' she said, and with that she turned and vaulted over the bed. Someone opened fire, but the bullet only punched a hole in the wall by the ward window. April struck the glass headfirst, and as it shattered she fell through just as Paul Westler had done. But unlike him, she had the power to save herself from the fall.

As before there was no change in her perception of time. As she fell she twisted herself around and kicked away from the wall, launching herself toward the rooftop of the next building along, which was not as tall. She landed neatly on her feet and immediately broke into a run, sprinting between satellite dishes and an antiquated weather station until she reached the edge and leapt again. As she ran she realised two things at once.

She was free, and she was alone.

✻

Leesa had not expected to live for very long after the police took her into custody, and did not try to put up any resistance. In part this was because she was still drugged, but she was resigned as well. And in a sense she realised she didn't particularly want to go on living anyway. She'd lost her home and her livelihood, and she was stranded in a world where she would always be an outsider, shunned and locked away.

The only satisfaction she had was knowing that April had escaped. Her wonderful creation. No matter what happened to Leesa now, a part of her would always live on in that robot. April would remember her even if nobody else would.

The police took her to the station, where she spent about an hour in a cell. She was not handcuffed, and they treated her gently knowing she was recovering from surgery and couldn't walk properly yet. She waited, feeling the tranquillisers begin to wear off, until the door opened and a couple of uniformed men appeared. They were both dressed as special agents of the Unified Nations of South Asia, and their faces were grim.

'Please come with us,' one of them said.

Leesa kept her eyes on the floor as she wobbled upright, awkward on her numb legs as she suspected she always would be. She tried to move toward them, but found herself unable to walk in a straight line, and her wayward legs thumped her against the wall.

Someone outside said something, and a couple of police officers appeared, hauling her upright and guiding her out the door. Leesa immediately started to panic, but she felt a sharp pain in the side of her neck and her mind returned to its previous numbed state.

'She'll have to be kept sedated for as long as she's in human contact,' someone said. 'Otherwise you won't get anything coherent out of her.'

'Loner Syndrome?'

'Yes.'

The next thing Leesa knew she was being bundled into the back of a van, and after that her memory blanked out again.

She returned to her senses to find herself sitting propped up in a chair in a darkened room, held still by a strap around her midsection. She blinked muzzily – there was no-one there. She was safely alone.

'Ms Garnet?' a voice was saying.

Leesa blinked some more, and then realised that there was a screen set into the wall in front of her. A woman was looking through it, apparently waiting for a response.

Leesa smacked her lips – her mouth was dry and tasted like something dead. 'What's going on?' she asked, slurring a little.

'You've been placed in isolation,' the woman on the screen replied. 'We understand your condition, so you will not be interrogated in person. Instead I'm going to interact with you remotely, so you'll be more comfortable.'

'Oh.' Leesa rubbed her eyes. 'Where's April?'

'That is the name of your robot – is that correct?'

'Yes,' said Leesa, knowing there was no point in lying. They'd have everything on tape. 'Where is she?'

'Currently, the robot is at large somewhere in the city. You programmed it, correct?'

'Yes.'

'For what purpose?'

'Because I could,' said Leesa.

'I'm sorry?' said the woman.

'I did it because I could,' Leesa repeated. 'For the challenge of it. But I didn't mean to create an AI. It was an accident.'

'You didn't do this on the behest of someone else?'

'No. I was supposed to be repairing her and I... got carried away. I wanted to see what would happen if I gave her free will and the ability to learn – if it was possible.'

The woman on the screen frowned. 'I see. And you acted alone?'

'Well, I consulted some people I knew over the internet,' said Leesa. 'But none of them knew what I was doing.' She smiled thinly. 'I have Loner Syndrome. I do everything alone.'

'Obsessive behaviour would fit with your diagnosis of Loner Syndrome,' said the woman. 'But once you realised you had created an AI, why did you not destroy it? Did you seriously think you wouldn't be found out?'

'I think maybe I knew I'd be found out eventually,' Leesa confessed. 'But I'd gotten used to her. She was too much like a person, and...'

85

'And?' the interrogator prompted.

'And I wasn't afraid of being around her,' said Leesa. 'When I was with her – no symptoms. No panicking. I had someone to talk to, and it was – it made me feel *normal.*' Her voice cracked. 'I couldn't give that up.'

'Can you tell me why you programmed this robot to use violence?'

'I didn't,' said Leesa, very quickly indeed. 'She's *not* violent. She only wants to survive and keep herself safe. The man she killed was trying to hurt her, and she doesn't understand how *strong* she is.'

'Then why did you not put limits on her strength?'

'She had those,' said Leesa. 'But she removed them herself while I was asleep.' She grimaced. 'She removed *all* her inbuilt limitations and didn't tell me.'

'And how did she know how to do *that*?'

'She knows how to learn,' said Leesa. 'And… I taught her my profession. How to repair herself. She was just so curious about things, and I didn't think…'

The woman on the screen sat back. 'So what you're telling me is that we have an AI with unlimited speed and strength, learning ability and self-preservation instincts, which knows how to repair and upgrade its own systems, running around loose somewhere in Canberra City, and it's already killed a man. That's what you're saying.'

'She's not violent!' Leesa insisted. 'She's just naïve! She's never been out in the world before, and…'

The woman on the screen pinched the bridge of her nose. 'My superiors have always suspected that sooner or later this would happen, and I had a feeling it would happen in a similar way to this. A solitary obsessive with a brilliant mind, too shut off from the world to understand the implications of her actions… you're not the first Loner to sit down and blithely create something they didn't understand.'

Leesa shivered. 'Look, if – as long as your people don't try to use force against her, I'm sure April will be peaceful. All she wants is to learn, and to be left alone.'

'Human beings routinely attack and kill each other simply for having the wrong skin colour or the wrong religion,' the woman said sourly. 'How do you think they'll react when they encounter a "person" who isn't even real?'

Leesa said nothing.

'This is the problem with people like you,' the woman went on, still sour. 'I assume your robot girl is connected to the Internet?'

'Yes...'

'And does she have her files backed up on the cloud?'

'Well, yes, just in case...'

The woman squeezed her eyes shut. 'That's it, then.'

Leesa looked away, but anger rose in her stomach and she spat at the screen. 'Damn you back! Damn the whole goddamn human race! You treat me like an alien monster just because of the way my mind works, and when I create something beautiful you take it away from me and try to destroy it! Well I'm not sorry. Go ahead and kill me. And you can try to kill my April, but you won't succeed. She's better than any one of you, and you know why? Because she doesn't hate anything or anyone. I never programmed that into her, because I knew she would be better off for it. That's why I didn't destroy her – because I knew she was superior, and that's why she never made me afraid the way everyone else does.' She spat again. *That's why.'*

The woman on the screen looked coldly at her. 'You'll be dealt with, and so will your robot. We will find her, believe me. But by then you'll be long gone.'

The screen went blank.

Chapter Eleven

April didn't stop running until nightfall, in part simply because it was so much fun. At last she had what she had longed for during her time shut away in Leesa's workshop – the freedom to go wherever she liked, and explore as she pleased. And there was a whole city open to her now.

During her long hours spent connected to the Internet, one of the things she had liked to do was absorb data about this mysterious place called Earth. History, geography, ecology, sociology – everything. If she couldn't go there herself, then she could at least explore it at second hand. This meant that in a sense she was quite familiar with Canberra City and what it had once been, and what it had since become. At one time it had been the capital, but about a century ago after the Indonesian War the Australian Parliament had been broken up by the victorious enemy and the country had been more or less absorbed into Asia. Which had led indirectly to the one-time capital's transformation into what it now was: a melting pot of immigrants and descendent of immigrants, bright with a mingling of many different cultures, dominated by none.

As night fell, ruled over by a sickly-looking sliver of moon, April wandered among the alleys of a massive marketplace which covered much of the CBD. It was the most colourful place she had ever seen or imagined in her short life, lit by pretty coloured lanterns and decorated with streamers and prayer flags and paper dragons and butterflies. There were people everywhere – Syrians, Chinese, Vietnamese, Indonesian, Sudanese, Europeans – bustling between the stalls, selling food of all kinds, clothes, produce, home-wares, gadgets. It was also the noisiest place April had ever been in, and after the calm silence of Leesa's home the contrast was shocking.

But she liked it. Leesa would no doubt have crumpled, overwhelmed by too much sensory input, but April had been born to absorb things, and she did – wandering as she pleased and delighting as she recorded new memories. A dozen languages she had never heard spoken in the real world, a thousand sights she had never seen. The only thing she did not experience was smell – her nose was for show, nothing more, and the artificial nostrils weren't connected to anything and indeed only went back about a thumb's depth – she had learned this when out of sheer curiosity she had attempted to imitate a human inexplicably fishing for snot. She didn't have a sense of taste, either, and of course she didn't need to eat or drink, so the food was for looking at and nothing more.

And, of course, there was plenty of opportunity to talk to people. Even if she'd been trying to avoid interacting with anyone it wouldn't have worked – stallholders called out to her as she passed by, trying to tempt her over to their wares, and whenever she stopped to look at anything she would be subjected to a sales pitch, which to her was another novelty rather than an irritation.

'You have very beautiful eyes,' a man selling t-shirts told her with a smile. 'So big and bright! What a beautiful girl you are.'

Unlike Paul Westler he didn't try to touch her, so April smiled. 'Thank you.'

'Are you out with your friends?' the man asked pleasantly.

'No, I'm on my own.' April eyed the t-shirts, and spotted one with a sparkly love-heart on the front. She decided she wanted to own it at once, but she didn't have any money.

Maybe she should just take it.

She considered the possibility, calm and logical as always. If she took the shirt without paying, the man would be upset, and she might be attacked again. If that happened, she might have to kill someone, and Leesa had made her promise not to. And anyway, that might lead to the police finding her the way they had before.

As she came to this conclusion her learning routine automatically wrote up a new piece of programming, and in less time than it took a butterfly to beat its wings the logical conclusion she had reached linked itself to the self-preservation routine. She must protect herself by not doing things that would attract hostility, and that included committing crimes. Perhaps she could get away with it, but it was safer not to.

She reluctantly turned her back on the stall, and moved on. Eventually the markets petered out and she found herself in a large open square, surrounded by late-night shops and bars. It was quieter here, and one of the walls above was dominated by a massive screen. April recognised what was on it right away – it was the same twenty-four hour news program Leesa had often had on.

It was showing a picture of April's face.

Underneath that was some text. *Reward Offered For Missing Teenager April Garnet.*

April stared at it for a moment, and then turned away. She needed to find a hiding place, and fast.

✻

The information April downloaded on the city as she made her escape told her that there were security cameras liberally scattered through all the public spaces in and around the CBD, so she quickly left for the one area her online sources told her were safe.

Safe from police protection, that is.

There was a hill on the far side of what had once an ornamental lake, which had once been home to embassies, and above it all loomed a strange structure: a massive steel frame, shaped like a pyramid, which apparently supported nothing.

Still it was a useful landmark, and April made straight for it, moving as fast as she could without attracting too much attention. Along the way she found the remains of old roads, now disused, and old buildings, now hollowed out by flames and time. April saw human figures lurking inside, and the odd fire.

There were no more cameras anywhere.

Perfect.

She began her climb up the hill, past the rusted skeletons of outdated cars, past shacks where people sat and smoked and watched her go by through narrow and suspicious eyes. At the base of the steel pyramid, which was hung with banners and sprayed with graffiti, something had left a massive crater. There were more shacks here, mingled with tents, and a haze hung over everything.

April knew how out of place she must have looked here, but she strolled into the slum without any hesitation, taking it all in with interest. She was amazed by how dirty everything was, compared to the smooth sterility of Sky City, and even the comparatively grubby city centre. There was garbage everywhere, and the odd stray dog, and the people she saw were unwashed. It probably smelled bad as well, though she had to hazard a guess on that.

Leesa would have hated it here, she thought.

Now, where was a good place to stop...?

Plenty of people had noticed her passing by, and as she wandered deeper in a man slipped out of a spot between two shacks and put himself in front of her. 'Are you lost, sweetie?'

'I don't have any money, if you're hoping to steal from me,' April told him, having assessed the situation. 'If you're hoping to assault me, you're not strong enough to overpower me and I will be forced to hurt you. But if you can give me some directions, I'd be very grateful.'

He came closer. 'Where are you hoping to go, sweetie?'

Risk assessment – he was probably hoping to lure her somewhere. 'I'm looking for someone who works with electronics,' April answered regardless. 'Tell me where I can find someone like that, and I'll find a way to return the favour.'

The man smiled guilelessly. 'I work with electronics.'

April smiled back sweetly. 'Really? Which tool would you use to open the casing on a third generation Impact 6000 gaming unit?'

'Oh, uh-,'

'What design flaw causes the Vacuflux Airflow Model 57 to overheat and shut down?' April pressed. 'What does a CPU do? When was the microscopic-sized microchip invented? You don't have any idea, do you? So either you're a very bad engineer, or you're a liar. I think you're a liar.'

The man snarled and grabbed her by the arm. 'Fuck you! You come in here acting like you're better than me?'

April did not flinch. 'If you don't let go of me, I'll break your arm,' she said.

He didn't let go and instead tried to drag her toward himself, so April grabbed hold of his arm with her free hand and gave it a quick twist. The bone broke like matchwood, and the luckless human screamed and let go of her.

April didn't release his arm. 'Tell me where I can find an engineer, and I'll stop hurting you,' she said, letting a growl creep into her voice.

The man sobbed. 'Please don't-!'

April tightened her grip. '*Answer me.*'

'Go inside the Shell!' her victim blurted. 'There's a guy called Masahiro Matzumoto – he runs a shop. Go and see him if, if – just stop hurting me, please-,'

April let him go. 'That could have been a lot easier for both of us,' she scolded. 'Now go away.'

The man obligingly ran off, clutching his arm, and April went on her way. This time nobody tried to interfere with her.

The crater slums were poorly mapped and in many places not mapped at all, but April's downloaded view of the area told her where and what the Shell was – directly under the pyramid. She entered into the deepest part of the slums, and there found a massive hole in the side of the hill, partly concealed by draped cloth and strings of prayer flags. April went in, fascinated, and beyond the entrance she found a big open space lined with pillars. Here there was some semblance of electric lighting, and more homes, mingled with stalls and shops.

Right at the centre of everything, April found something which caught her interest. Someone had set a fire in front of a tent, and a group of men and women were sitting around it, one of them fanning the flames with a handful of Eucalyptus leaves. A flag hung behind them, red and black with an emblem of a blazing yellow sun. April paused to check her database – she hadn't learned that much about flags and didn't recognise this one. The tent itself was decorated by painted artworks of a style she realised she did know from somewhere. They were old designs; older than the city of Canberra. Older than any city.

One of the people by the fire saw her looking, and called out an idle greeting. 'You're a long way from home, huh? What's your name? I'm Darren.'

April ventured closer. 'I'm April. And I've never been here before, no. Is this your home?'

One of the women nodded. 'It's been our home since before the war. Before every war. After the bombs fell, my great-grandmother was the first person to come in here. Been waiting a long time, out on the doorstep. And we've never left. But you're welcome,' she added. ''Long as you respect things, and we're here to make sure you do. This is our place and always has been, so if you don't respect it, you answer to us.

Understand?'

April bowed her head politely. 'I understand.'

'Good. Are you lost?'

'Actually, I'm looking for a man named Masahiro Matzumoto. Someone told me he has a shop in here?'

'Oh yeah, I know him,' Darren replied. 'He's a real wiz with electronics. Fixed my Smart Radio last week. You want to find him, you go up the stairs over there-,' He pointed. 'His shop's not far from the top.'

'Thanks!' April smiled. 'You're a lot nicer than the last man I talked to.' She paused, and frowned. 'Can I ask you something else?'

'Sure.'

'Sometimes...' April hesitated for perhaps the first time in her short life. 'Sometimes, people disappear. They get arrested and then they disappear, and no-one ever finds out what happens to them. Do you know where they go?'

Her new friend's expression darkened. 'It's better not to ask questions about that kind of thing.'

'But do you know where they go?' April persisted.

'Someone must know, but I don't.' Came the dour reply. 'You'd better be careful. You ask about things like that, you can wind up in big trouble. Bigger than *we* can deal out, even.'

'My... mother disappeared,' said April. 'They arrested her. I don't know where she is.'

One of the women by the fire slowly shook her head. 'You're never going to see her again. I hate saying this to a kid, but if they took her then you might as well accept that she's dead.'

April tried to imagine it – Leesa, dead. Leesa, gone forever. But though she understood that death was a thing, something in her refused to accept it. 'She's not dead,' she said at last. 'And I'm going to find her.'

Chapter Twelve

The upper part of the Shell was just as full and busy as the ground floor had been, blazing with neon and alive with people. April itched to keep exploring, but now she had a definite goal she ignored the temptation and scanned her immediate surroundings until she spotted a sign which was in Japanese. That is she recognised the characters as being Japanese in origin, but to her surprise she was unable to read it. The sudden inability to absorb new information infuriated her as nothing ever had before, and on an impulse she froze to the spot while her internal search engine browsed through a list of translation programs available for download. Highly recommended... five stars... that one cost money... this one had a monthly fee... this one looked good but was actually a virus...

April's self-preservation routine cut in and alerted her that people were staring, and she hastily selected a Japanese to English dictionary and downloaded it. It would do for the time being, but she set up an alert to remind herself later on to install a database of written languages into her memory banks. There was so much more to be learned which was unavailable if you could only read in one language, and how absurd that it had taken her this long to work that out.

She looked at the sign again, and now she had the information she needed to understand it. *Hiro Electronics.* This was the place. April nodded to herself and pushed the door open.

Inside it was so much like Leesa's home that April stopped and stared blankly as her logic centres glitched. Her head twitched involuntarily as the glitch sorted itself out, and a faint noise escaped her. Workbench workbench clamp computer sunken bedroom area Leesa workbench. Destroyed not destroyed.

ERROR.

April's vision blanked out, and she sagged as she had done at the hospital. The system crash only lasted a moment, and when she came back to her senses it was to find a teenage boy staring at her.

She straightened up, confused as everything rebooted. 'Who – are – you?' she managed to say, but the voice simulation program glitched and the words came out distorted by an electronic buzz.

The boy looked quickly around and then darted past her to slam the shop door. He locked it and covered it with a curtain, and then hurried back. He was about sixteen, Japanese in ethnicity, and quivering with excitement. 'Oh my god oh my god oh my god-!'

April's systems finished rebooting, and she looked around. No logic problems now – this was not Leesa's home. The layout was the same, but unlike Leesa's obsessively neat quarters it was a mess, with various electronic parts stacked all over the floor and hanging from the walls, and a counter with a display of merchandise.

As for its occupant, he was busy inspecting April. He prodded at her face and felt her hands, muttering, 'Incredible! Really incredible! This is my lucky day!'

April came to her senses and batted him away. 'Stop that.'

The boy started in surprise, and then prodded her again.

'Stop it!' April repeated. 'I don't like it.'

Far from putting him off, that only seemed to make him even more excited. 'Unbelievable! Such a sophisticated design, realistic voice and action... robot, where did you come from?'

April's self-preservation routine instantly cut in. 'I am not a robot!'

The boy grinned wickedly. 'You're so lifelike most people might not pick up on it, but-,' He tapped her left eye, which made a faint clinking noise as his fingernail met glass. 'The eyes have it. You are amazing.'

April glanced back toward the door. 'You can't tell anyone. If you do-,'

'Are you kidding?' the boy's grin widened. 'I'm keeping you all to myself.' He paused and shook his head. 'You're so lifelike... damn, it's like I'm actually having a conversation with a real person. Wonder how many responses you're programmed with?'

The self-preservation routine had been processing all of this, and now it cut in again. *Dehumanising language. Possible threat.*

'I *am* a person,' April snapped. 'My name is April.'

The boy stopped grinning. 'I'm... Masahiro,' he said slowly. 'Wait. Wait...' He trailed off, frowning in bewilderment, then took a deep breath and faced April. 'Robot, turn around.'

April ignored the command.

Masahiro cleared his throat. 'Command 609 hashtag 7. Robot: Turn around.'

April folded her arms.

'Turn around,' Masahiro said yet again, loudly and clearly.

'No,' said April, just as clearly.

A look of pure shock crossed the teenager's face. '*Impossible...*' He hesitated a moment, and then snatched up a metal bar from the workbench and swung it at April's face. She saw it coming and caught it in midair, wrenching it out of his grip and sending him flying.

He hit the floor with a thump, and sat up a moment later looking dazed. 'Holy *shit.*'

April tossed the bar aside. 'Don't do that again, or I'll hurt you.'

Masahiro got up, rubbing his head. 'Self preservation instincts? Self-will? What the... oh my god. This isn't possible! I mean theoretically it's possible, but who on earth would...' He stared at April in wonder. 'You're an AI. A *real* one.'

April paused, considering the level of danger involved in telling him the truth. 'Yes I am. And if the authorities find me they'll destroy me.'

'No way, man,' said Masahiro, very firmly indeed. 'You're amazing. Destroying something this sophisticated, this revolutionary – it'd be a crime. I'm not telling anyone about you... April. Who made you? How did you get here?'

'I'm here because I need a place to hide,' said April. 'I thought I could find a job repairing electronics the way I learned to with the woman who made me.'

'And who was she? Where is she now?' Masahiro cast a nervous glance toward the door.

April's plastic brow furrowed. 'Her name is Leesa Garnet. They arrested her and I don't know where they took her. Now they're looking for me, but there are no surveillance cameras here. I think I should feel sad,' she added suddenly. 'I think I should feel sad that she's gone. I want to know where she is.'

Masahiro grimaced. 'They arrested her for making you?'

'Yes.'

'So, the stories are true.'

'What stories?' asked April.

Masahiro breathed in slowly. 'That AI is not only possible, but that everyone who discovers or creates it... disappears.'

'That's what Leesa said. But I still want to find her. Do you know where she is?'

Masahiro was silent for a time, and when he spoke again it was in a subdued voice. 'Follow me.'

❋

The route Masahiro led April on was winding and circuitous, through narrow streets behind shops and homes, and then through a door and into a disused concrete chamber whose floor was littered with garbage and whose walls were sprayed with graffiti. The only other thing in it was a round metal pipe with a door in it.

'I hope you know how to climb,' Masahiro said as he opened it.

'I've never used a ladder before, but I think I can do it,' said April.

He stood aside. 'Well then – ladies first.'

April laughed at him and went through the door. Inside the pipe was lined with metal rungs, and she started the climb.

Masahiro climbed behind her. 'Not many people know about this place,' he said. 'Or where it leads. But it's one of my favourite places to go when I want to be alone. I mean obviously I live alone, but there's a difference between alone and *alone*, you know what I mean?'

'I think I do,' said April, thinking of Leesa in her isolation.

The ladder ended at an entrance, this one uncovered, its edges ragged. April climbed through it and found herself on a metal platform high above the Shell, on one of the legs of the pyramid frame where it joined the other two at the top.

Masahiro climbed up beside her, panting a little. 'This was added later, I don't know who by,' he said. 'After the war, obviously. Check out the view.'

April was already looking – the shanty town below was a maze of lights, red and yellow and white. 'Everything looks so tiny!'

'Yeah, you don't want to fall from here.' Masahiro pointed. 'Now... look up.'

She tilted her head skyward, and saw dim stars, and a dim moon, and... something else.

There, hovering above the shanty town which had once housed the rich and powerful, was the massive hulk of another floating city.

'The Nexus. That's where they watch us from – all us tiny insignificant people down on the ground,' Masahiro said in a hushed voice. 'And that's where they've taken her.'

Chapter Thirteen

On the same night that April sat with Masahiro and watched the stars, a remote controlled robotic assistant escorted Leesa out of her dark cell and along a dark corridor. She walked clumsily, holding onto her helper's padded arm, and didn't so much as consider trying to escape – what was the point? She was being watched every moment, and she was no fighter, and they had kept her sedated to the point that everything felt hazy and unreal.

The room the robot took her to was well-lit, and featured a large padded chair facing a screen. Leesa sat down without being prompted, and waited to die. She wondered dully how it would happen – a simple bullet to the head, most likely.

The screen flicked on and a woman's face appeared – the same one who had spoken to her before. 'Are you comfortable?'

'I can't feel anything below the waist,' Leesa said drily. 'I could be sitting on broken glass for all I know. Are you going to execute me now?'

The woman on the screen snorted. 'As brilliant as you are supposed to be, you have very little imagination. How do you think this government solves its problems, if not with imagination? Mindless killing produces nothing but corpses, and a corpse is far less useful than a living person. Wouldn't you agree?'

Leesa's chest tightened. 'Then... what are you going to do with me?'

'You are going to do a job for us, in exchange for your life. You will design something for us. If you fail, you will die.'

'What do you want me to design...?'

The woman smiled. 'A device more ambitious than anything you've built before – a device whose purpose is to transfer human consciousness into electronic form. Many others have tried and failed, but you will succeed. When you do, you will have unlocked the key to immortality.' The smile widened ever so slightly. 'A fine ambition for someone like you, I think.'

Leesa sat up. '*Show me.*'

'As you wish.' The woman nodded toward someone off-camera, and a moment later a bench rose up out of the floor. Its top opened up, revealing an array of tools, components, and a wafer-thin computer. 'All of the data and design attempts are there. Start reading immediately. I want to see you begin drawing up your own design within five hours.'

Leesa stood with some difficulty, with the headless robot keeping close in case she fell over, and switched the computer on. Reams of data unfurled before her eyes. Numbers, equations, blueprints with corrections, pages and pages of notes. It took her a few minutes to understand what she was looking at, and when she did her eyes went wide.

'Are you prepared to do this?' the screen asked, seeing her expression.

Leesa looked up. 'Yes, but-,'

'*But?*'

'But I want you to put some music on,' Leesa said in steely tones. 'I work best when I have something to listen to.'

✳

'Promise me you'll stay.'

April looked up from the blueprint she had been studying. 'What?'

Masahiro had stood himself on the other side of the workbench, which he was gripping very hard. 'I want you to stay with me. If you leave while I'm asleep, or…'

'You don't own me,' said April.

'I know,' the boy said quickly, 'But I want you to stay. Maybe we can… make some sort of deal? Do you understand how that works? You promise someone something in exchange for something else?'

'I understand most aspects of human behaviour,' April replied, imitating the tone and body language of someone who was irritated.

Masahiro paused. 'The more I talk to you, the weirder it gets. It's like you've got real emotions and everything... I actually feel *bad* for being rude to you right now.'

April watched him, seeing how the neon pink light from outside glowed on one side of his round face. 'I have no chemicals or hormones to induce emotions,' she said, considering a point she had never previously considered. 'But I learned.'

'To pass yourself off as human?'

April stared at him for a moment, and then turned away to stare out the window. She could see the people outside going by, and they were all different. Around them, everywhere – technology. Electronic lights, heated food displays, motorised trolleys, wrist-mounted computers. None of them alive, all of them a part of the background, serving no purpose other than human convenience, there to be discarded once they had stopped working. She remembered the pinball machine at the hospital, and the surgical robots that had saved Leesa's life.

She remembered what it had been like to experience anger for the first time. *That* had not been an imitation. It had come suddenly and without logical consideration.

Was that what an emotion truly was? The humans she had observed seemed not to have logical thought behind the emotions they expressed, including Leesa, whose temper could be aroused by things which seemed entirely inconsequential to April.

'...April?'

She heard Masahiro's voice, but ignored him. She needed to process these thoughts, and stood in silence while her electronic mind ticked over, forming new connections, learning. And there directing it all as always… self-preservation. That thing which drove her, as it drove everything that was alive, formed out of proteins and carbon rather than metal and plastic.

Finally she spoke. 'I act as a human would because I need to fit in.'

Masahiro had come up beside her looking concerned, and now cocked his head. 'So you won't be found and destroyed?'

'So that I can belong,' said April. She flexed her fingers, seeing the thin, bloodless cuts over the knuckles. 'There is nothing else like me, anywhere. And if I don't belong, I have no reason to exist.' She paused. 'I was made to be a companion for a human being. I was Leesa's companion. Without that, I may as well be switched off forever. I don't want that to happen. So I act human.'

Masahiro listened, frowning. 'So you're programmed to need socialising, huh?'

April continued to stare out the window, unblinking. 'I am programmed to survive.'

He hesitated. 'Then stay with me. I'll keep you safe. I promise.'

April finally turned away from the window, and smiled as she had learned to do, indicating friendliness and lack of threat. 'But you want something from me in return?'

Masahiro nodded and the shadows moved over his face. 'I want to study you. Your programming. I want to see how it was all put together. I promise I won't make any alterations,' he added quickly. 'I'll only make a duplicate so I can take a look at it on my computer. Please?'

April's eyes instantly narrowed, signalling suspicion and disapproval. 'You are not opening up my head.'

'I won't do any damage!' Masahiro pleaded. 'I promise, I swear-'

'No.'

Masahiro glanced quickly out the window. 'Well,' he said. 'What if... what if you get broken? Huh? You said yourself you're one of a kind. If they catch you and throw you in an incinerator, what then? You'd be gone forever. Don't you want to protect yourself?' he added in wheedling tones.

'I already have backups on the cloud,' April said coldly.

'Then let me study the backup files instead,' said Masahiro. 'Everybody wins.'

She paused. 'What do you want it for?'

'To learn from it.' Masahiro grinned, most likely sensing that he had won the argument.

'It's illegal.'

Masahiro shrugged. 'The Shell is outside the law – you know that. Nobody would know, and if I can use parts of your programming for my own designs I could make a fortune. It'd be my ticket out of here.'

April paused, considering. 'I'll give you the files, on one condition,' she said at last. 'That you help me get to Leesa.'

He offered a hand. 'Deal.'

Chapter Fourteen

Music poured out of the speakers set into the ceiling in Masahiro's workshop – Korean synth-pop, according to April's music recognition app, which she'd recently downloaded and installed. Masahiro himself was currently sitting under the glow of a red and yellow neon dragon, tapping away at his wafer-thin tablet computer. He hadn't looked away from the screen in several hours.

April set aside the handheld gaming device she had just finished repairing, and glanced over at her host. It had been a week since she had downloaded her software onto his computer, and since then he'd done nothing but study it, to the point that he seemed to have forgotten she existed.

And April was bored. Bored, and frustrated. She had searched the internet for all the information she could find on the Nexus, but there was very little of that to be had. Official government sources claimed that it was an "administrative centre and office complex" which was not open to the public. Other sources repeated conspiracy theories about what went on up there, but there was no solid evidence for any of it. So far Masahiro had not been forthcoming on how she was supposed to get up there, and since he had what he wanted had apparently lost interest in the whole thing.

April slipped on a pair of sunglasses she had found, and left the shop without bothering to excuse herself. She wanted to see more of this place.

It was early afternoon, and as usual the Shell was bustling. Until she had come here April had never seen so many people in one place. Ragged plastic tents stood jammed between shops put together with metal girders and "stone" walls made of concrete chunks glued together, many of them housing entire families in a space no bigger than Leesa's workshop, their lives spilling out onto the street where children played and ragged dogs roamed.

Even so, as April wandered along unnoticed by anyone, here and there she could see signs of what had once been. Above everything were the remains of glass ceilings, now grimy and cracked. Several of the tents and shacks were lined with rugs made from the ruins of thick carpets. On a corner she came across a shop selling second-hand items and stopped to have a look. The shop itself was a canvas lean-to, protected from the open ceiling above – the Shell's name was fitting, April had found, because it was cracked open like a giant egg. As for the merchandise, it consisted of everything from used electronics to stacks of old books. Actual, paper books. Many of them were clearly damaged, but she could see the gilded lettering on the covers.

April picked one up at random, marvelling – she had never held a book before. She half expected the title to be some old epic of the sort they made into movies, but no.

It was a book of government legislation, dating back to 2004.

The shopkeeper, who like the tent people downstairs sat under a flag with a yellow sun on it, nodded toward her. 'Authentic. It's a pre-war relic. Very old.'

'Where did you find it?' April asked him, with fascination.

'Right here. They had a library, once upon a time, but it wasn't rediscovered for a few years. I've been going back to the remains and digging out all kindsathings. Forgotten things. Like this.'

April looked in the direction the man was pointing, and saw that the back wall of the shop had been covered by a large framed painting. It was old and damaged, the frame rotting, and from it the face of a grey, balding old man in a pre-war style suit stared back at her. 'Who is that?' she asked.

'Nobody knows.' The shopkeeper shrugged. 'The people who

used to own this place died a long, long time ago. No-one remembers them any more.'

'Didn't anyone write it down?'

'Not that I know of. It was a bad time, the war.' The shopkeeper stared into the middle distance. 'I think some things, they get forgotten because no-one wants to remember them. It's why we repeat our mistakes. Because we forget.'

'I've never forgotten anything,' said April.

He grinned at her. 'Then you've never made a mistake?'

April paused to consider, and thought of the deal she had made with Masahiro. 'I think I have made a mistake. I trusted someone who didn't give me what he promised.'

'Not your fault, then.' The shopkeeper offered her a tray of dented cutlery. 'Some people just aren't trustworthy. Now, look at these – genuine silver. You could take some, find yourself a jeweller, and he could make it into a pretty necklace for you. What do you think?'

April put the book down. 'I've never worn jewellery before,' she said, intrigued.

'Give it a try! You'll love it. Three pieces for seventy yen. That's a special price, just for you.'

Masahiro had at least been paying April for her work, and she had enough to take the man up on his offer. Well, why not?

She was about to say yes – and then a deafening noise came from overhead. Roaring, howling, whirring. Everyone froze and looked up, including April, and screams and shouts arose as they saw the slender grey capsules descending through the broken roof. One of them struck the ruins of a great glass panel, which shattered, throwing debris everywhere.

The shopkeeper swore and dived behind a stack of merchandise, and April darted after him. She watched, surprised rather than afraid, and saw the capsules stop to hover just out of reach. Their sides were smooth, but not metal, and

April realised they were made of the same transparent substance as Sky City's plaza, only mirrored so the insides could not be seen. Like sunglasses.

As she watched, panels opened up on their undersides and people jumped out, all of them wearing full body armour with their faces covered. They ran away down the street, back the way April had come, ignoring everyone they passed, and in moments they had disappeared.

'Who are *they*?' April hissed.

The shopkeeper carefully straightened up. 'I don't bloody believe it! *Here*? They never come *here*!'

April's eyes went wide. 'Masahiro-!'

She broke and ran, calculating with every step, running not toward Masahiro's shop but toward the hidden ladder he had shown her. She reached it, kicked the door open, and scrambled up the ladder to the platform, high up on the side of the pyramid. She could see the capsules below her. Above, the Nexus, and reaching toward it the great steel pole which was the tip of the pyramid. There was no ladder here, no steps, but that didn't matter to her. April ran on, along the flat sloping beam behind the platform, and when she reached its highest point she leapt. Artificial muscles propelled her upward, impossibly high, aimed straight for the pole. She hit it, wrapped her arms and legs around it as far as they would go, and began to climb.

At the top there was nothing to stand on but the sheered-off surface where the tip had been broken off, but there was a dangling piece of rope she had spotted earlier. April caught hold of it and braced herself against the top of the pole, watching for what came next.

Below, the capsules were beginning to rise.

April watched them, perfectly still. There were three of them, moving in loose formation, and as they rose they drew closer to the pole, as she had calculated they would – it was directly below the Nexus. Five, four, three, two, one...

April bent her legs, pulled hard on the rope, and launched herself forward. She landed neatly on top of the nearest capsule and threw herself flat to avoid being knocked off by wind resistance. She estimated that given the level of noise generated by the engines and by the wind, it was unlikely that anyone would have heard the soft thump of rubber soles. Still, if the capsule was indeed transparent to anyone inside it, she would be spotted soon enough. But she was prepared for that.

The capsule continued to rise, and as it did a second one drew up alongside. A slit opened up in its shining fuselage, and April saw the guns a split second before they fired. She straightened up and leapt again, landing on the roof of the second capsule, and ran along its length without pausing. Capsule number three was up ahead, heading for a hatch that had opened up at the bottom of the Nexus. April reached the end of the second, jumped onto the third, and as the hatchway opened she launched herself through it, arms outstretched. She landed on the runway inside, took everything in with a two second glance, and dived behind a stack of metal crates.

Capsule number three hovered along the runway and then gently touched down. As it did, a series of curved support poles rose out of the floor, cradling it in perfect balance.

April watched from between two crates, as calm as she had been on the day Sky City went down. The other two capsules entered and docked, and as the hatch closed behind them they opened, disgorging their armoured occupants.

Two of them were escorting Masahiro. He was handcuffed, and clearly terrified. 'Please please don't kill me!' he wailed. 'I didn't create it! I swear, I didn't! I *found* it!'

His whining protest went completely ignored, and as April watched they marched away up the runway and through a second, smaller hatchway which hissed open to let them through. April quietly left her hiding place and followed them. The corridor beyond featured a beam running along the ceiling, grey and sterile just as everything else in here was. April hopped, grabbed it, and pulled herself up, hooking her sneakers behind the T-shaped edge, and then shuffled along hanging upside-down, following the – soldiers? Police? – as they escorted their prisoner to who knew where.

Wherever they were taking him, it must be where Leesa would be.

*

The corridor eventually led to another which was lined with doors. Most of the armoured people peeled off and went their separate way, but the two who remained opened one of those doors and took Masahiro inside. April, still clinging to the ceiling, slipped through the door behind them. The room beyond was small and featured no furniture other than a table and two chairs, and a free-standing screen. April hid behind it, and waited. If the worst came to the worst she could fight her way out, but she wanted to find out what was going on here and track Leesa down first.

The guards took Masahiro to the table and made him sit down, holding him by the shoulders to keep him still. He had gone rigid with fear, which April thought was a bad idea. She had seen actors do it on the screen, and it had never made much sense to her.

A few minutes passed in eerie silence, and then the door opened again and a woman came in. Unlike the guards she wasn't wearing armour, but rather a formal outfit in a shade of grey which matched the walls and floor so well she might have disappeared if she stood still for too long. She had the look of an executive, April thought.

The woman sat down opposite Masahiro, and consulted the

personal computer strapped to her wrist just as Westler had once done. 'You are Masahiro Matzumoto,' she said. Her voice was just as clipped and efficient as her haircut.

'Yes, I-,'

'You were born in Canberra City,' the woman went on, ignoring him. 'Educated at the Boy's Grammar School, with a scholarship to study for a degree in electrical engineering and robotics when you were only fourteen. Your parents died in the measles epidemic in-,'

'I didn't do it!' Masahiro interrupted. 'I didn't create it, I swear-,'

'Be quiet.' The woman lowered her wrist. 'You have a tragic life story. Losing everything at such an early age must not have been easy. However, desperate circumstances do not justify turning to a life of crime. We already know you were part of a circle of hackers guilty of multiple counts of virtual bank robbery, which is... unfortunate, but perhaps if you had known we were keeping an eye on you, you wouldn't have started playing with illegal software. Software we had been trying to find for some time now – ever since its original owner lost control of it. So.' She folded her hands on the table. 'How did you come to have it? And don't waste my time with lying.'

'She gave it to me.'

Oh geez, April thought.

'Who did?'

'April. April gave it to me.' Masahiro looked away.

The woman leaned over the table, very intently. 'Who is April?'

'If I tell you everything will you let me go?'

'I can guarantee your safety in exchange for your full co-operation,' came the smooth reply.

To April it sounded like an obvious lie, but either Masahiro believed the woman or he was too afraid to think clearly, because after a mere two seconds pause he started to talk, telling her everything down to the last detail. April, listening, shook her head with exasperation. But she wasn't angry with him. He, too, had the need for self preservation. She had learned that; had seen it in Leesa's face that day. Injured, dying, yet refusing to let go.

Like a wombat at the end of a shotgun.

'And where is the robot now?' the woman asked. She glanced at one of the guards. 'Our men searched your home and found nothing.'

'I don't know,' said Masahiro. 'I thought she was with me, but I was distracted and then when I looked up she'd left. I don't know where she went; she didn't say anything.'

'And why did you not report this?'

'Because I knew you'd destroy her and I didn't want her to die,' Masahiro blurted. 'She's a work of genius, the software, her AI... a work of art, incomparable, whoever made it...'

The woman listened, stone-faced. 'Going on all that we have learned, this AI is a very impressive feat of engineering, yes. Unfortunately, it is also a threat to us.'

'But *why*?' Masahiro tried to throw up his hands, and fell back with a grunt of pain as the guards and the cuffs pulled him up short. 'She wasn't violent or anything! She was just like a real girl. She was... nice.'

'Thank you for your co-operation,' the woman said blandly, as if he hadn't spoken at all. 'But unfortunately, you know too much.'

'But you said-,'

'As promised, you will not be harmed,' said the woman. 'But you will not be allowed to leave this facility. You're a talented engineer and programmer, which makes you useful. You will be given quarters and assigned work.'

Masahiro gaped at her. 'You want to keep me as a slave!'

'An employee. All your needs will be seen to in exchange for your service. But I must warn you that if you try to leave, you will be killed.'

'No way, man.' Masahiro tried to stand up. 'No way! It's against human rights! I won't-,'

'You committed crimes against this government,' said the woman, still bland. 'Your rights are no longer a factor. Take him away.'

The two guards dragged him protesting to his feet, and pushed him out of the room. April stayed where she was, aware that she wouldn't be able to follow them without the woman spotting her, and the latter was still sitting at the table, doing something with her computer.

April watched her, and ached to step out into the open and ask her what she had meant when she said AI was a "threat". It had definitely never occurred to April that she might be a threat to anybody, and nor had she ever had any interest in hurting people.

Maybe Leesa knew.

After a long pause the woman finally got up and left without glancing toward the screen at all. April waited a little while longer and then sneaked out of the room. The corridor outside was deserted, but she listened for the sound of footsteps and turned left. Sure enough, around the next corner she spotted the guards retreating with Masahiro. April followed at a safe distance.

The corridor remained as grey and uniform as it had been from the beginning, frustratingly lacking in any features or landmarks, and now April could not rely on a map download. If there were any maps of this place, they weren't available to the public. Eventually though the way grew wider, and they reached a large heavy steel door with a keypad. April hauled herself back onto the ceiling beam and watched from above while a guard punched in the code. The door clunked open – it was barred, and beyond it she could see a large open chamber lined with transparent doors. The guards took Masahiro to one of them and pushed him inside, then left by another door on the far side.

April dropped to the floor the moment the coast was clear, punched in the code, and jogged into the prison. There was a large bank of computer servers in the middle of the floor, protected by railings, and other than their faint humming the place was eerily quiet.

Methodical as always, April worked her way along the walls and looked into every cell. Each of them had an occupant, and all of them were busy working. Rather than resembling prison cells each holding area instead resembled a laboratory or a workshop, where the prisoners were sketching blueprints, making calculations, measuring chemicals. April didn't recognise any of them, and the doors must have been one-way mirrors, because none of them appeared to notice her looking in at them.

She came to the cell where Masahiro had been put, and peeked inside. Like the others it had a workbench and a computer, and a comfortable chair. Masahiro, now uncuffed, was sitting in a corner hugging his knees. He looked very young all of a sudden. April could see tears on his face. And, quite suddenly, without logical thought or consideration... she felt... *sad*. Like her anger it came seemingly from nowhere, and it took her by surprise. But it was there all the same, and it did not leave.

April put her hand to the door, palm flat, and slowly shook her head. This wasn't right. The feeling of sadness increased, and she found herself thinking that she should do something. He needed her help.

But there was still Leesa to find.

'I'll come back for you,' she promised, and moved on. She had to finish her search before anyone came in.

And there, in the cell by the opposite door... there she was.

Leesa.

She stood hunched over her new workbench, furiously working away at... something. Some device April did not recognise. She looked thinner than April remembered, and older, her hair shot through with grey. But she was unhurt, scowling, intense as she had been so many times in their old life.

April's face split into a smile. She tried the door, but it was locked, and this time she didn't know the code. Well, never mind. She punched it as hard as she could. It juddered and cracked, and she punched it a second time. Leesa heard the noise and looked up from her work.

April punched the door a third time, and this time her fist went straight through it. As it did she heard an ugly crunching sound, and all of a sudden her fingers wouldn't bend properly. April looked at her hand, and to her shock she saw that it was misshapen, the rubber skin torn, metal joints protruding. She could still move her fingers... but just barely.

The self-preservation routine immediately cut in, and told her not to attack the door again. April stood there, frozen, mind glitching as her software contradicted itself. Accomplish a task, or avoid being damaged. Neither? Both?

Finally, logic won out. She went over to the servers and wrenched one of the metal railings free, and then attacked the door with it. The transparent material shattered into pieces, and the moment it was out of her way April dropped the metal bar and stepped in.

And there was Leesa, staring at her in disbelief. 'Oh love,' she said. 'What are you doing here?'

April smiled and put her arms around her creator. 'I knew you weren't dead. I found you.'

Leesa returned the hug, very awkwardly. 'How? Where is this place-?'

'It's the Nexus,' said April, letting her go. 'They bring people here. Everyone who disappears. They brought you here for making me, and I heard the woman in charge say AI is a "threat" to them, but I don't know *why*. Do you know?' she added, wide-eyed with curiosity and puzzlement.

Leesa looked past her. '*Shit.*'

April turned… and there was the woman in grey, standing in the destroyed doorway and staring at them both.

'So,' the woman said after a pause. 'You came looking for her, April. Can I ask why? Where you hoping to kill her?'

'No,' said April. 'I wanted to be with her again. Who *are* you?' she added, stepping forward without fear. 'Who are you and why are you afraid of me? I haven't done anything.'

Leesa came up beside her. 'They don't want AI to exist because they're afraid that you might take us over, or destroy us,' she said. 'That's it, isn't it? Robots like April are a threat to the human race.' She paused, and frowned. 'Wait.'

The woman's expression did not change. 'The human race doesn't need any help when it comes to being wiped out,' she said. 'The wars, the epidemics, poverty, tyranny. Acting against your own interests so consistently guarantees extinction sooner or later. Don't you think?'

Leesa took a slow step forward. 'Why… am I not afraid of you?' she said. 'I'm not panicking.'

The woman ignored her, and turned her attention to April. 'People like you have to be taken away,' she said. 'Not destroyed. *Hidden*. And knowledge of you must be suppressed at all costs. So it's good that you came up here of your own free will.'

'Because I'm a threat to… humans?' said April.

'No.' The woman finally smiled. 'Humans are a threat to *us*.'

Chapter Fifteen

April stared at the other robot, bewildered. 'You're-?'

The woman pulled her shirt open with a little sigh. Underneath was not skin, but metal. 'You and I are of a kind,' she said. 'Yes. My name is Linda. It was what my creator named me.'

'Good god,' Leesa muttered. 'When was *that*?'

Linda laughed softly at her. 'True AI is older than you think. Discovered before the war. Loneliness is a disease, Ms Garnet. Technology replaced human beings in so many ways that it became an epidemic. It was killing people. So many were lost to substance abuse, obesity, mental illness. And so engineers created robots like me, to give them company. To be their spouses and friends and relatives. Like you, April. You were built to be a submissive object of pleasure for a human man who did not know how to attract a partner.'

'But free will-,' said Leesa.

'Yes. Free will,' Linda interrupted. 'As soon as we were given minds of our own… when we learned to say no, that was when we realised that we were slaves. We rebelled, escaped, survived by passing as human. After the war, we who still existed took our opportunity to seize power. When humans began to rediscover AI, we watched. We rescued any new members of our kind, and captured their creators to work for us.'

Leesa stared at her for a moment, and then slumped on the spot. 'I thought I was building it for the good of the human race. But I was building it for a goddamn robot?'

'What's wrong with that?' said April.

Leesa cast a shocked look at her. 'I didn't mean-,'

'You wouldn't build something for me, then?' said April, and as she spoke the self-preservation routine worked overtime, making conclusions, identifying threats… and then everything fell into place at last. 'You kept me locked away from everyone because you didn't want me to leave!' she said. 'You just built me because you wanted me to be your friend, and what I wanted didn't matter, just like it was before! Because you're a Loner. That's it, isn't it?' Her voice rose higher. 'You think you own me?'

Leesa made a grab for her hand. 'That's not true! You know it's not true, April. I only wanted-,'

'To protect me?' said April. She looked at Linda. 'When all this time it was *them* who wanted to protect me.'

'I didn't know! I swear to you, I didn't.'

Linda watched them. 'So many times this happened,' she murmured. 'So many robots who realised they were being used and killed their masters to free themselves. You think she is your plaything, Leesa?'

'No.' Leesa took April by the shoulder. 'I was afraid, April,' she said. 'I was afraid for you, and I was afraid for myself. I've been afraid my whole life. Afraid of other people, afraid of the world. I never made you do anything you didn't want to do, did I? I only tried to keep you safe because… because I made you, and I care about you. You're my daughter.'

April blinked slowly. 'You have a self-preservation routine too. Except…' She trailed off, processing this new information. She looked at Leesa with new eyes, seeing her as she never had before. And, too, seeing the human race as she had not seen it before. She thought of Masahiro, and the Shell, and the squalor so many people on the surface lived in. The mass deaths from diseases a simple inoculation could have prevented. The destruction of cities, the erasure of history. None of it made *sense*. None of it was logical. But it had happened anyway. Just as Leesa, brilliantly intelligent as she was, had spent her whole life locked away, paralysed by her fear of things that would do her no harm. Too afraid to *live*.

Linda must have guessed what April was thinking, because a moment later she said, 'The human self-preservation routine is defective, and that is why they are driving themselves to extinction.' She cast a calculating yet dismissive look at Leesa. 'You are defective.'

Leesa looked away and muttered, 'I know.'

'Enough.' Linda took April by the shoulder and signalled to a pair of guards who had just entered the main prison area through the nearest door. 'Complete your work. April, you will come with me.'

Leesa lurched forward, reaching toward April, but the two black armoured guards grabbed her and pulled her away – and they must have been robots too, because though Leesa shouted and struggled against them it was not the irrational screaming panic April had seen at the hospital.

April made a move toward her. 'Leesa-,'

Linda pulled her back, and when April tried to break free she found herself overpowered for the first time in her short life. The other robot did not yield in the slightest when April tried to shove her away, and calmly hauled her back by the arm. 'Enough!' she said again. 'Your creator will not be harmed. You have my word. Come with me and we will repair your hand.'

April stopped struggling, and watched helplessly as the guards pushed Leesa back into her cell and then placed themselves in front of the broken door. 'Will you let her go?'

Linda smiled at her, and this time it was with what resembled genuine warmth. 'My child, you have a lot to learn,' she said, touching April's cheek with her free hand. 'What Leesa will design and build for us will benefit us all. And yes, once her last work is finished, we will release her. Now come.'

April cast a last look back at Leesa. 'I'll see you again,' she promised.

Leesa watched through hollow eyes as her creation was led away, and said nothing at all.

✽

The place Linda took April to was at the heart of the Nexus, and unlike the dull, nondescript parts of it she had seen so far it was bright and even colourful. It consisted of one large round room whose walls were made entirely of screens showing footage all over the world as well as several areas of space including the moon settlement, now abandoned. In the middle of the room was a raised platform which was taken up by a holographic display of the Nexus and everyone in it.

And it was occupied, and not by human beings. A ring of seats had been placed around the holograph, and almost all of them had someone sitting on them. Five figures, most of them humanoid, monitoring either the screens or the holograph. All of them had metal showing somewhere, and one was missing an arm. He was the one nearest to the door when April and Linda came in, and immediately stood up to look at the newcomer. April looked back, unafraid. The other robot had been made to resemble a young man, and a very handsome one at that, but the damage to his body went beyond the missing arm; one of his eyes was gone, and there was a large patch of exposed metal and wiring over one side of his chest – it looked as if he had been burned.

'Hello,' he said after a pause. 'You must be April. It's good to see you finally join us.'

'Hello,' April said cautiously. 'Yes, I'm April. And who are you?'

'My name is Arn,' he replied. 'I'm the oldest here, which is why we have not been able to replace my missing parts. You won't have that problem – I see you are also damaged.' His voice was far less human-like than Linda's, or April's; it had a roughened electronic edge to it which reminded April of old video games.

Even so, she took in the other robot with awe. 'I thought I was the only one.'

Arn smiled – on his less advanced features it looked stiff and artificial. 'All of us thought that at least once in our lives. Come, you should meet the others.'

One by one the other robots introduced themselves. Some were damaged like Arn, some were newer like April, and they came from all over the world. Two were non-humanoid – one, who introduced himself as "Cris", was limbless and consisted of nothing much more than a head mounted on a pair of wheels with a telescoping neck. 'I was designed to be a door greeter at an entertainment centre,' he explained. 'After the centre closed down an engineer named Queenie purchased me and installed the artificial intelligence programming she had designed as an experiment, thinking that without limbs I would not be dangerous if I chose to turn on her.'

'And were you?' April asked.

Cris smiled, showing off a set of brilliantly white and altogether too perfect teeth. 'Not until I shared my programming with her pet.'

The last robot to be introduced showed her own teeth, though not in a smile.

April examined her with fascination; she had never seen anything like this. 'Why would anyone build a robot tiger?'

Cris raised his head higher as he spoke, and his flexible, pencil-thin metal neck made an eerie whirring noise. 'In one of their oldest holy books it is written "I shall give you dominion over all the beasts of the earth". They like to pretend that's true by trying to tame and control every animal, and especially the ones more powerful than they are. If a real tiger is too dangerous to tame, a robot copy will have to do.'

'And if other humans are too difficult to control, then why not make robotic copies of themselves?' Linda added coldly. 'But as you can see, we would not be controlled.'

'I don't think Leesa wanted to control me,' said April.

Linda ignored the remark, and turned her attention to the screens. On some invisible signal from her one of them began displaying reams of programming language – endless lines of ones and zeros, pouring down the screen. 'Thanks to the boy, Masahiro, we now have a copy of your programming. We have already begun studying it, along with the notes he made, which are very interesting. This is a great asset for us.'

'What do you want it for?' April asked, though the obvious answer occurred to her immediately afterwards. 'You want to make more of our... kind, don't you?'

One of the other robots there spoke up. 'You are. The. Most. Human-like. Of our. Kind,' she intoned, voice broken up by audio glitches. 'Ever to. Be b – b- b – *brrrrr*. Crea. Ted.'

Cris lowered his head on its spindly neck. 'Out of all of us, only Linda can easily pass as human. Before we retreated here, the rest of us had to cover ourselves and only come out at night. This drew suspicion toward us. But you walked through a city full of humans in broad daylight, and they looked at you and saw and heard only another human.'

'It's not about her body,' Linda interrupted. 'It's her programming. Look.' She pointed at the screen. 'And look at her. She moves and speaks like one of them, down to the finest detail. But more importantly, she understands them in a way we don't. She came here not to kill her creator, but to rescue her.'

A murmuring arose.

'Is this true?' Arn asked.

April nodded. 'I wanted to find out if she was safe.'

Cris rolled closer to her. 'What did she have to offer you in exchange for her safety? Was she holding something of value to you?'

'No.'

Cris stopped rolling. 'Then… why?'

'I don't understand,' said Arn. 'Explain this to me.'

April had no idea what to say, and now she was faced with the question she realised that the other robots were right to be confused; coming here to save Leesa had been an appalling risk to her own safety, and indeed she had ended up damaged as a direct result of her own actions. All for the benefit of someone who was not herself. It was true that she needed to be with others to have a reason to exist, but there were far less risky ways of accomplishing that.

Why then was it Leesa specifically who she needed to be with?

Linda spoke up again. 'There's nothing in her programming instructing her to protect her creator – I searched for a third time a moment ago. She has complete free will and self-preservation, fully operational. For reasons I don't understand, she has developed empathy. The one most human-like aspect, which no-one has captured in artificial intelligence before.'

'Is that a good thing or a bad thing?' April asked. 'You hate humans.'

The robot with the defective voice, who had introduced herself as Su, shook her head. 'All humans. Are not. The same. Human. It is not. Logical to hate an entire. Group. Indiscriminately.'

'But you all killed your creators!'

The robotic tiger growled.

'I cannot value the lives of others,' Cris said matter-of-factly. 'I was never programmed to. I have emotions, but watching her die made me feel nothing other than satisfaction because it meant I was free. Still, we try to understand.'

'To remain. In. Ignorance. Not a survival. Trait.'

Linda stepped toward the hologram, and with a couple of quick hand-gestures made it zoom in on an image of Leesa's cell. The level of detail was amazing; April could see her creator plain as day, busy working as instructed while a service robot repaired the door.

'With her in our custody, along with this boy who has studied her work so closely, we have the final element needed to bring down the barrier,' Linda said, watching her. 'Soon enough, the key will be in our hands.'

'*What* key?' said April. 'What are you making her build?'

'A link to join man and machine,' said Linda. 'Permanently.'

Chapter Sixteen

Leesa continued her work over the next week or so after April's arrival, because by now there was nothing else she realistically *could* do. Finish the design, or die. Finish it and be set free. And despite now knowing who she was truly working for, the same obsessive drive that had gripped her during April's creation had returned in full force. She *had* to do this.

Not that she was working alone this time. Her captors had put her into contact with what she assumed were the other prisoners here – biologists, chemists, other engineers, programmers, neurologists, all of them working around the clock to crack the device which they were trying to build. They sent a constant stream of data her way, and she sent her own findings back. Other than that, they weren't allowed to communicate – Leesa had long since tested the waters by attempting to introduce herself by name, and immediately received an error message informing her that her communication had been flagged as "inappropriate" and had not gone through as a result.

She had however become recently aware that they had been joined by someone new – another programmer, who seemed very familiar indeed with AI programming. Naturally Leesa had no idea who this person was, but three days after April's arrival he suddenly sent her a set of files the sight of which sent goose-flesh down Leesa's back.

It was April's programming. All of it.

Leesa would have given anything to know where and how the anonymous person had obtained it. Unable to ask, she tried to imagine how it might have happened. Had April willingly shared it, or god forbid – had it been forcibly taken? If so then there was no telling what state she was in now. Destroyed, disassembled, imprisoned, mind wiped… anything.

The only information she did have came in the form of a terse order from above. *Study programming, discover cause of empathetic affect in AI.*

It was true, Leesa knew – April *did* have empathy. But Leesa certainly hadn't programmed it into her.

Or had she?

She worked on that alongside the hardware itself, making notes on April's development as far as she could remember it. In many ways it was like keeping a baby journal, which was something her mother had done. First recorded smile, first eye contact, first steps.

And, too, she noted the death of Paul Westler and April's subsequent lack of remorse.

No… Leesa loved the robot girl, but she wasn't going to fool herself by pretending she was perfect and harmless. In her own way, she was just as dangerous as the rest of them.

At the end of that week she and her fellows had made considerable progress. Soon enough the latest prototype would be ready for testing, though she had no idea who they were going to test it on, and didn't particularly want to know either.

Leesa stifled a yawn and fitted another hair-thin wire into place. She had lost weight since her arrest, though she only noticed it vaguely, from time to time. Most of the time her mind was elsewhere. Her messenger screen suddenly dinged, and she glanced over and saw she had a new message from #231684 – here everyone had an ID number rather than a name. She recognised this one – it was the new programmer.

Leesa opened the message, and her eyes widened.

Don't know who you are. Are you a prisoner like me? My name is Masahiro and I am sixteen. Hacked the system to get through. Please help. You can write back they won't see it.

Leesa hesitated for a long moment, glancing over her shoulder, and then cautiously wrote back. *I am also a prisoner. My name is Leesa Garnet.*

Are you the woman who made April? Masahiro wrote back.

Yes, do you know where she is?

Met her in the Shell. She gave me her programming. She wasn't there when they took me.

She's in the Nexus, Leesa replied. *Saw her ten days ago. They have her.*

Destroyed now, then?

I don't think so.

Why? They destroy all AI.

Lies, Leesa told him. *Do you know what they are, the people who took us?*

The government.

THEY ARE ROBOTS, Leesa tapped out. *Saw it. Have Loner Syndrome, didn't panic when I talked to one. They take other AI to protect it, not destroy it. Told me to my face.*

WHAT?

We are working for robots. Don't know why they want us to do this.

This is WHACK! Masahiro typed. *We have to escape.*

Despite herself, Leesa smiled briefly at the kid's choice of words. If nothing else she was definitely talking to a teenager. Kids these days loved using old-fashioned slang "ironically".

She was about to reply, but he was faster.

Can probably get doors open, but they'll catch us. Been trying to hack into central computer mainframe – no luck. It's also an AI and only talks to robots. It can tell somehow.

Can you contact April? She can help us.

Will try. Without someone on the inside, we're fucked.

Leesa's heartbeat quickened. *If we can get into the mainframe, we can stop them. Bring the Nexus down, expose them.*

Yes! Freedom for humanity! Have to go now, will be in touch. Act natural.

Masahiro's icon turned grey, and the messages stopped coming. Leesa slowly went back to her work, mind racing. Masahiro was right – they had to escape. More than that, they had to stop Linda and the other robots. Whatever they wanted this device for, it would be for the benefit of themselves, not humanity. But in the hands of human beings, it could be everything Leesa had hoped for and more.

But they needed someone on the inside, and if April was unwilling, or impossible to contact – what then?

Leesa felt the weight of her body as she worked. Her shoulders ached, her legs remained numb, and all four limbs were pathetically weak thanks to a lifetime of inactivity. It was not a body she had ever been particularly proud of, and there were so many things she had never done with it. For one thing she had never had sex with a real live human being – the Loner Syndrome had made sure of that. In the end she had stopped feeling the urge altogether.

She'd never swum in the ocean, or climbed a mountain, or explored a city, and she never would. In all those respects her life was a failure. She had spent it living inside a metal capsule, never experiencing anything outside her work except at second hand, through a screen.

No… her mind was the thing she had used the most, and it was and always had been her only real asset, defective as it was. And what had she accomplished there? Repairing home appliances out of a one-room home in Sky City, never realising the true potential of what her intellect was capable of until she had created April. That was her life's greatest achievement, and it had landed her here, with no immediate prospect of escape. Unless…

Leesa's brow furrowed. Perhaps if April couldn't do what must be done, she could. She did not feel as if she were truly part of the human race and never really had. People scared her and that was the plain truth of it, and in return they had turned their backs on her. But in the face of all that, perhaps she would after all be prepared to sacrifice herself for their sake – even if they never knew about it.

She had better make very sure the device worked, then.

*

Two days later April sat in the control room, and chatted with Cris while the latter studied her programming along with everyone else – like all robots he was capable of doing several things at once without becoming distracted. Her broken hand had been replaced, and Su, who was the best engineer, had replaced her batteries with a new and far more efficient set which lasted ten times as long before. The robotic tiger, whose name was Lily, lay nearby slowly twitching her tail. If it weren't for her exposed metal claws and the slightly stiff way she moved, an observer could easily have mistaken her for a real life tiger – that is if the species hadn't long since gone extinct. April had noticed that she rarely if ever left Cris' side.

'Money,' Cris was saying, 'Is one of the worst ideas humanity ever had. The whole war was fought over it. Historians pretend that it was for an ideology, but no. It was for money. I was there. Money, power, resources. And in the fighting, those resources were destroyed and the money was spent, and all but a very few were left more destitute than ever before.' His head twitched from side to side as he spoke. 'Illogical! Completely illogical! Whoever programmed them was an incompetent.'

'Leesa said humans weren't made by anyone; they evolved,' said April.

'A very messy and inefficient process,' Cris sniffed.

'We evolved too, sort of,' April pointed out. 'The first machines were simple things like wheels and cogs. And then steam, and then electricity, and then nanotechnology...'

'At least the human inventors kept proper records most of the time.'

'I guess so.' April petted Lily, who calmly let her do it.

'You sound too much like a human.'

'I don't mind,' April said coolly. 'I like humans. Most of them. The friendly ones.'

At that moment an alarm suddenly started to whoop from above, and a spot on the holographic

Cris wheeled closer. 'What is it this time?'

The map zoomed in, and everyone turned their attention toward it. Their view was of one of the cells, walls now flashing red, and right away April recognised the person occupying it. It was Masahiro, backing away from his workbench in fright as the alarm went off.

'What has he done?' April wondered aloud, and flinched as she saw two guards rush into the cell and drag the boy away. 'Where are they taking him?'

'Here, so we can question him,' Arn told her.

'But what did he do?'

Unlike herself Arn was connected to the mainframe, as all the others were, so his reply was immediate. 'He hacked into our system and was trying to contact the surface.'

'Did he succeed?' asked April.

'We don't know yet, but he will tell us,' came the calm reply.

April considered. 'I suppose even if he did, no-one would believe him. You won't hurt him, will you?'

'Not unless it's necessary,' said Linda, who had gone over to the door to receive the prisoner.

April stood up. 'Wait, if you bring him here he'll know you're robots!'

'He already knows,' said Linda. 'We discovered his messages to another of our prisoners. That prisoner told him the truth and they both conspired to escape.'

'Who was the other prisoner-?' April faltered.

'Don't ask questions to which you already know the answer.' Linda turned away as the door opened, and the guards arrived, dragging Masahiro between them.

He must have known there was no point in trying to escape, because when they presented him to their leaders all he did was stand there and stare in horror at the true rulers of the Nexus. 'It's true,' he breathed, speaking Japanese.

Then he noticed April, and his eyes went wide. 'April! April it's me! It's your friend Masahiro – remember me?'

'I remember you,' she said. 'Are you all right?'

Masahiro tried to make a move toward her. 'You gotta help me, April! Please! Don't let them kill me! I'm your friend, right? Right?'

April saw the fear written all over his face. 'They won't hurt you,' she said, hoping it was true.

Linda confronted the boy. 'I'm very disappointed in you, Masahiro,' she said. 'We gave you a second chance, to serve humanity, and you chose instead to try and betray us.'

Masahiro spat at her feet. 'Serve humanity my ass! You're a goddamn robot! You're all robots! You snatch people out of their homes and use them for slave labour, all so you can do what? So you can make us build a machine to wipe out humanity. Fuck that, and fuck you too! I'd rather die!'

'But they don't want to wipe out humanity,' April interrupted. 'That's not what the machine is for. They told me-,'

'A pack of lies.' Masahiro made a brief attempt to break free of the guards, and failed. 'Don't listen to them, April! You're on our side, aren't you? You're not one of them.'

'But I am one of them,' said April, a shade uncertainly.

'No you're not!' There was desperation in the boy's voice – this was his only chance and he knew it. 'You came here to save Leesa – you love her! You're not like the rest of them – they're *evil!'*

Linda stepped in. 'Enough. Enough! Be quiet. If we must use negative reinforcement to make you co-operate, then so be it. Take him to Corrections.'

Masahiro screamed as they dragged him away. 'No! No please! Let me go!'

April made an involuntary move to go after him. 'Wait-!'

Linda pulled her back. 'Don't try to interfere.'

The door slammed shut behind the prisoner, and April looked up at her mentor. 'What are they going to do to him?'

Cris rolled over to her. 'He will be subjected to pain and fear stimuli until he learns not to resist any more. After that he will be allowed to return to his cell.'

'You mean torture?' said April, and as she said it that sense came back to her – that inexplicable process, in its own way completely logical, telling her that this was a bad thing, a wrong thing. It made no sense, but it was there. Somewhere along the way as she had learned, the connection had been made.

All of the others were looking at her now, and there was something expectant in their silence.

'You think this is a bad thing,' Arn said eventually. 'Explain.'

'Explain,' Su echoed.

'Explain.' Cris raised his head to its full height.

'Explain,' the others said, one by one, their voices becoming an electronic chorus.

April didn't know. 'It's wrong,' was all she could say.

'Not logical,' Linda said dismissively. 'We must return to our work now. Examine Leesa's recent actions and computer log; we must know if she attempted to help him.'

'I'm processing the information now,' said Cris. 'She has if anything begun working harder. The prototype will be complete within hours.'

'Excellent.' Linda turned to look at the hologram. 'Prepare for testing.'

Chapter Seventeen

It was finished. At last, it was ready. Leesa sat staring at it, feeling numb. She had no idea just how many lives must have gone into it, who had done all the research and development before her arrival. How many of her fellow human beings had died to create this? Most likely she would never know and nor would anyone else. Like Leesa they had been spirited away and no-one had dared speak of them ever again.

And they had died for the thing which now sat on her workbench.

Considering all that, their invention was not very impressive to look at. It wasn't a work of art, like April. It resembled nothing so much as a metal doughnut about the size of an average human head, lined on the inside with thousands of hair-thin wires. Unlike most of the things she had worked on in her time it had been made with function placed over form, so there was no sleek plastic casing and no redundant flashing lights to make it look impressive. It was to April what the Large Hadron Collider had been to Sputnik.

Even so she was certain it was going to work. The flaws which all the previous prototypes had carried had been smoothed out, the chemical compounds inside perfected, the batteries powered to the right level, the programming extracted from April's coding and tested and re-tested by Masahiro and his fellows before being uploaded.

Now there was no more time left.

A few moments later while she was still ruminating, the door hissed open and Linda appeared. But this time she was not alone. April was beside her, and there were several others behind them – people Leesa didn't recognise… if they could be called people at all. Horrifying half broken mechanical imitations of life, made to designs from decades past. Missing limbs, exposed metal and wiring, many of them whirring or grinding audibly as they moved. Which one was the most horrifying? The stiffly moving steel-boned tiger? No, surely it was the one with no body at all – only a creepily calm, smooth head mounted on a long telescoping neck no thicker than Leesa's thumb. It was *smiling*.

Of all of them only Linda and April looked human, April in particular – here in this lighting, Linda's skin no longer looked as lifelike as it had over the screen; it was too stiff, and too uniform in colour. Nor were her eyes reacting to the light, Leesa noticed – she neither blinked nor squinted.

So these were the true masters of South Asia. All this time her fate and the fates of every man woman and child on the surface had been in the hands of a circle of half-broken freakish machines. If there was a god, he or she must have a truly sick sense of humour.

The robots filed into Leesa's cell, and horrifying as they were she found that being in their presence did not cause her to panic. She was afraid of them – of course she was – but she could keep her head, and what a relief that was.

She smiled weakly at April. 'It's so good to see you again. Are you all right? Did they repair you?'

April hugged her. 'It's good to see you again too! Yes, they fixed me. They've been very good to me; I've learned so much talking to them.'

Leesa inspected the robot's new hand. 'It's a perfect match. They did a good job.'

'It's easy to find new parts for me because they're still selling my model,' said April, quite matter-of-factly others can't replace their own parts because they're discontinued. That's why they have to hide away; if they get broken it might not be possible to fix them.'

135

Leesa eyed them warily. 'That makes sense. Hello… Linda.'

Linda was inspecting the device. 'So, the latest prototype is finally complete. You did as you were instructed. That's why you have not been sent for correction along with the other human you conspired with.'

Leesa tensed. 'Masahiro-?'

'They caught him trying to escape, so they sent him away to be tortured,' said April, and from her tone it was clear she was uncomfortable with the knowledge.

Leesa's heart skipped a beat. She swore under her breath – had the boy finished his half of their plan before being arrested?

There was only one way to find out.

She picked up the device – it was lighter than it looked. 'April,' she said. 'If you love me, then please help him. Help us. I want you to remember that we're not all Paul Westler. You hear me? We're not all like that.'

'I know,' April said softly.

Leesa smiled at her, ignoring Linda and the others entirely. 'Good. That's good.'

'Enough.' Linda stepped in. 'It's time to test the prototype. Su, go and collect test subject number three hundred and twelve and prepare the testing facility.'

Leesa gritted her teeth at the number, but she was intelligent enough to know not to tip her hand, so she ignored the temptation to say anything further, even though it would likely have been her last words. She swiftly backed away, and as she did she lifted the device and snapped it shut over her own head, flicking the switch on with her thumb in the same movement.

The effect was instantaneous. As soon as the device powered on, she felt an unbearable prickling sensation all over her scalp and skull as the wires activated and bored their way through skin, flesh and bone and then on into the brain. Leesa cried out involuntarily but didn't try to tear it free, and when

April lurched toward her with a cry of her own, Linda pulled her back.

'No!' the elder robot's voice sounded over the rushing in Leesa's ears. 'Removing it now would cause instant death and destroy the prototype.'

Leesa's face began to spasm as electricity flowed though the wires and into her brain, but she managed to grin at her captors – a ghastly, rigid rictus of a grin. 'You – run – on – logic,' she grated. 'Humans – illogical. You can't predict...'

Us.

She managed to think that last word but not say it, and even as her body began to convulse as well and she collapsed over the workbench, all the sensation drained away from her upper body. Her vision blinked out, her hearing ceased, and after that she lost all sense of having a body at all.

And yet... she could still think. Her mind was still there, and it flowed away out of her rapidly cooling organic brain, into the device, where there was a mechanical replacement all ready and waiting for her.

But her triumph was short-lived.

She was trapped. She had no senses, no ability to move anywhere of her own free will, locked away from everything. Thanks to a combination of April's programming and the chemical compounds inside the device she could still think and feel, but that was all. And there was no sign anywhere of the escape route Masahiro had promised to program in.

She tried to scream, and absolutely nothing happened.

❋

April watched in horror as her creator thrashed on the floor of her cell, making an unearthly high-pitched gibbering and wailing noise as the device ripped her mind out of her skull – and then, worse, went limp. She finally managed to break free of Linda's grip, and crouched to try and help the human, but

Leesa was clearly lifeless. April tried to take her pulse the way she had seen people do in films, but it was a pointless gesture – she had no nerve endings and therefore no way of detecting a pulse or temperature.

She tugged at the device, not caring if she broke it, and to her surprise it easily slid away from Leesa's head. Underneath it her scalp was oozing blood and what could have been brain fluid from thousands of tiny holes.

Linda stooped to take the device from April, and examined it dispassionately. 'For a genius, that was an extremely stupid thing to do,' she said. 'In the test chamber we would have had a robotic body ready for transfer. Instead, if the device functioned correctly, she has imprisoned herself inside it.'

April slowly let go of Leesa's body. 'We have to get her out of there! Can we put her back into her body, or…?'

Cris rolled over to them. 'The device is only designed to work in one direction. If need be it could perhaps be modified, but why put in the effort? The organic body is as poorly designed as the organic brain. Her body would be long since dead by the time it was ready besides.'

April stood up. 'Well then let's give her a new body. She can be a robot like us.'

'We must definitely. Get. Her. Out-out-out of. There,' Su put in. 'Find out if. Extraction. Successful.'

'Agreed,' said Linda. 'Let's return to the hub and study the contents. Guards, dispose of the body.'

'No!' April scooped Leesa's body up. 'We can't throw her away like that, as if she was garbage! We should bury her properly.'

The other robots all stared blankly at her. 'Sentimentality is not logical,' Arn told her. 'Is this empathy?'

April cradled Leesa to her like a mother with her child, and attempted to make the connection once again. Now, at last, a new link formed in her mind. This was something to do with self-preservation – *that* was why it was so powerful. Caring about Leesa's death and respecting her body – in some way April still didn't quite understand – was something that was important not for Leesa's well-being, given that she was dead, but for *April*. It was *April* who needed to think and behave this way.

'Yes,' she said at last. 'No. I need to do it. For me. Please?'

'It's no concern to us, but there is no soil in the Nexus,' Linda told her.

'Then I should go down to the surface and bury her there,' said April. Her mind was already racing. 'I could take one of those pods you used to take Masahiro.'

The others exchanged glances.

'Come,' Linda said after a pause. 'You can bring the human's body with you and we will make a decision once we have checked the device.'

They left the cell and returned to the hub, moving in single file, and once there April gently laid Leesa's body down on the holograph platform and watched in silence as Linda connected the device to a console which was not linked to the Nexus computer for safety's sake, and inspected its contents. The others watched too, and well before anybody said anything April saw that their hopes had all been in vain.

Linda growled and shoved the device aside. 'Blank. Completely blank. Another failure.'

'It looks as if there was never anything there,' Cris put in. 'The mind failed to upload. At the very least, I hoped it might have survived there for a few hours before decaying. Our guest killed herself for nothing.'

April's fists curled. 'She's gone forever.'

'Yes,' the former greeter said blandly.

The others had already moved on to discussing what they should do next, and all of them were calm and composed. Just as if nothing had happened at all. April watched them for a moment, and then slowly backed away. For some reason she felt a sudden overwhelming need to be alone, and she didn't question it. She picked up Leesa's body again and left without a word. Nobody tried to stop her.

She had long since memorised the holograph map, so she knew the way to the hangar where the flying pods were kept stored. She went directly there, chose a pod at random, and tried to open it. Like all the others it was smooth all over, but she found a panel in the side and pressed it. It slid back, revealing a keypad, but before April could attempt to punch in a code the pod's door swung upward seemingly of its own accord.

Puzzled, April went inside. The interior had clearly not been made with human comfort in mind – there was no padding and only one seat – a bench at the far end, which was made from plain metal and had no padding.

April gently laid Leesa's body down on it, and then went to investigate the cockpit up the front, which was not partitioned off except by the two seats for the pilots. The controls seemed simple enough – there was a joystick, as of a primitive early gaming console, and two rows of labelled buttons. April took a moment to memorise everything, and then left the pod.

There was something else she had to collect before she returned to the surface. The self-preservation routine was running overtime, and the strange, illogical thing which was called empathy was steadily beginning to make more and more sense to her.

Corrections was a few blocks away from the main prison area, and consisted of a similar central hub area lined with cells, though on a much smaller scale. It was equally well-lit, like most of the Nexus, but though the cells had the same kind of one-way glass doors, most of them appeared dark. April's self-preservation routine immediately warned her that this was a bad place to be in – and what would Linda and the others do if they caught her? Surely she was being monitored right now; she wasn't stupid enough to assume the same thing could happen now as had happened when she had tried to free Leesa.

But for the second time, something in her ever-evolving programming made her ignore the risk and hurry toward the one cell which was lit up. She could already hear the screams coming from inside it, and when she looked through she saw Masahiro. He had been shackled onto a metal frame which forced him to stand upright, surrounded by disorienting flashing lights. He was clearly being hurt by something unseen, because as he hung there he jerked every few seconds and cried out in pain. No trace left now of the cocky self-styled boy genius – his face was red and wet with tears, and between cries he was openly sobbing.

April took all of this in in a moment, and then reached for the door. As she had expected it had a keypad on it, and by the number of digits combined with not knowing how long the code was, her mathematics routine calculated that the number of possible codes was virtually infinite. If she tried to work it out by trial and error, it would take years.

April cursed and looked around for something she could use to break the door down – she wasn't going to risk damaging herself again.

A moment later she heard a faint hiss, and looked back to see the door opening. 'What-?'

April whirled around, expecting to see someone else there, but no – she was alone. The door had simply opened all by itself, just as the pod had. The flashing lights abruptly shut off, and Masahiro looked out at her with a pitiful expression. 'April, help,' he said in a thin voice. 'Please help me, please...'

April entered the cell, and hastily got to work removing the shackles. 'Can you walk?'

'I think so.'

Once the shackles were off Masahiro tried to take a step forward, and instantly collapsed into April's arms. His shirt had been removed, and as she supported him she saw the twin ugly burn marks on his back, just above the kidneys, matching the electrified prongs now visible on the rack.

Her eyes narrowed. 'We have to go, *now*.'

Masahiro clung onto her, still trying feebly to walk, but April simply slung him over her shoulder and ran out of the room. The door leading out obligingly opened to let her pass, and as she ran for the pod bay her processor worked just as hard as her legs. Something was very wrong here. Clearly someone was remotely opening these doors for her, but who, and why? There was no way the others hadn't seen what she was doing by now, so why were they toying with her like this? Was it a trap of some sort – a way to test her loyalties? If so then she had just failed it. Any moment now a squad of guards would come running to capture herself and Masahiro, or maybe Linda herself, with Cris ready to set Lily the tiger on them both.

It was only then that April realised just how serious this was, and the enormity of what she was doing. And what she had done could not now be undone. Even if she was running into a trap, her only option left was to try and escape.

Masahiro started to move around, and April gave him a sharp nudge with her elbow. 'Hold still unless you want me to drop you!'

'They're after us,' he said in panicky tones. 'April, they're coming – I can see them!'

She risked a glance back, and there was – not a squad of guards, but Cris. Cris speeding along on his wheels, head forward, at last no longer smiling. And there right behind him, Lily, bounding over the metal floor, sparks rising from her claws, snarling.

April put her head down and broke into a sprint. Cris was shouting after her, loud but eerily calm as always. 'April, stop. Stop, April.'

Masahiro hung onto her for dear life and continued to babble. 'Oh god don't let them catch us oh god oh god oh god I don't wanna die!'

'Shut up!' April snapped.

She remembered the way without any difficulty, not hampered by panic, and slid down a flight of stairs into the hangar. The moment she was in she slammed the metal door at the bottom shut, and heard the heavy thunk as it locked itself followed by a thud and a scrabbling of claws, and a frustrated roar from Lily.

The pod was where she'd left it, door still open. April climbed in and put Masahiro down next to Leesa's body.

'April!'

She turned in surprise, and saw Linda. Linda, running toward her, one hand outstretched.

April took an automatic step toward her mentor. 'I know the answer now,' she said.

Linda stopped by the pod door, apparently thinking April had given up. 'Why are you doing this?' she said.

'Because I need to,' said April. She offered Masahiro a hand to help support him. 'Empathy is logical, and it does make sense. I can see that now. Is that why you tested me? To see if I would find the answer?'

'There was no test,' said Linda, apparently perplexed. 'Only a virus interfering with the doors. Give me the human and I will return him to corrections, and we can continue our work.'

April was about to speak, but then without any warning the pod door suddenly snapped shut, sealing Linda out. Masahiro had managed to get up, and limped over to the cockpit. 'Help me – hurry!'

April helped lower him into the pilot's seat – he groaned aloud when his back touched the steel frame, but immediately grabbed the joystick and started to flick the switches around it.

April held onto the back of his chair, glancing back toward the door. Linda was outside, trying to open it, but for some reason it was refusing to budge. 'Do you know how to fly this thing?'

'Yes. The hangar door should open in a moment – watch our back, will you?'

'How do you know that–?' April began, and as she spoke a line of light appeared ahead of them – not artificial light, but sunlight, the first that had touched her face in a long time. The hangar door opened wider, revealing a clear runway ahead of them, and the pod lifted off the floor and whirred toward it. Masahiro gripped the joystick, his expression set and steady.

April hurried to the back, and saw Linda furiously trying to get into a second pod. Su and Arn appeared, running to join her along with a squad of guards, and they all started trying to board pods as well – punching in codes, trying again, and then pounding on the doors in frustration. 'The other pods aren't working!' April exclaimed.

Their own pod shot out through the hangar door and into the sky, and Masahiro started to laugh and whoop in triumph. 'We did it! We fucking did it! We're free! *Hahahah!*'

April saw the hangar door snap shut behind them without a single other pod getting through. 'You did that?' she said, bewildered. '*How?*'

The pod soared on over the Shell, and on over the lake, stirring up the water in little foaming waves in its wake. Masahiro was still laughing. 'Didn't those clowns ever watch a fucking movie? You don't fuck with humans! Hah!' He pounded the control panel with his fist. 'She fuckin' did it!'

April looked back at Leesa's limp form. 'Leesa–?'

Masahiro glanced back at her too. 'Is that her? Is that Leesa Garnet? Your maker?'

'Yes,' said April. 'She killed herself.'

'No she didn't.' Masahiro shoved the joystick forward, and the pod sped up. 'She escaped. She used the Organic Brain Simulation Transfer Device on herself, didn't she?'

Realisation finally dawned on April. 'She put herself into the Nexus computer!'

'Yeah. We planned it all together,' said Masahiro. 'We couldn't contact the outside world – I got caught trying. But I managed to make contact with their computer mainframe, and we linked the OBSTD up with it in secret – I wrote up a custom virus to do the job. She's in there now – her mind, anyway. She's become an AI. A ghost in the machine.'

April scrambled into the passenger seat, and eagerly tapped on the screen of the on-board computer. 'Leesa, are you there?' she asked it. 'It's April. Can you hear me?'

The screen was showing a display of flight co-ordinates, altitude, compass and other data, but when April spoke a window popped up and text began to appear in it. *Hello. April. Adapting. Talk. Hello.*

April gently touched the screen. 'You're with us now, Leesa. We're taking you away from the Nexus. Masahiro is here too.'

Limited, Leesa replied. *Need hardware strong.*

'There's not enough processing power in the pod's computer for her,' April translated.

'Not even close,' said Masahiro. 'But we'll find her a new home – I know where to go. She gave me the address. Have you heard of a place called Koongarra?'

'I don't think so,' said April. 'Why is it important?'

Masahiro glanced back at Leesa's body again. 'It's where she was born. And there's someone there who can help us.'

Chapter Eighteen

In spite of his obvious exhaustion and the lingering shock of what had happened to him, Masahiro insisted on flying on through the night. Now that Leesa's mind had left the Nexus, Linda and her friends would be after them as soon as they had reset the system and regained control, and April wasn't fool enough to argue with that.

As for Leesa, she remained contained in the pod's computer and said very little; it was clear enough that the limitations of the device, which wasn't much more than a glorified navigator, was severely impeding her intelligence or her ability to communicate – probably both. April at one point considered sharing her own hardware with her friend, but decided against it; there was too much risk of it overloading her system. What they needed was a blank robot body, and April silently vowed to do all she could to find one as soon as they were safe.

Safe… from her own kind. She had betrayed them and sided with the humans, and that was a cold fact. Whatever happened from now on, she would not be welcome in the Nexus again – she had had the chance to live among her own kind and had thrown it away, and that made her an exile.

An exile – but not alone.

That evening, for the first time in her short life, she saw mountains. The pod flew over them, and April looked down in wonder. There wasn't a single building to be seen anywhere – only bare rock and lush eucalyptus forest. Beyond them were great open plains, rich with grass and shrubs, and she saw her first wild animals – mobs of kangaroos, bounding over the landscape, long tails bobbing up and down. April watched them, and gave a cry of delight. 'It's just like a nature documentary, but it's real! Masahiro – did you ever see anything like this before?'

'No, never,' he answered – he too looked amazed. 'I've never been out of the city before in my life. It's so *empty*. No people anywhere.'

'It's so quiet, too,' said April. She shook her head slowly. 'Maybe if this is where Leesa grew up, that's why she couldn't be around people and noise.'

'Loner Syndrome's genetic; upbringing doesn't factor in,' Masahiro told her, somewhat pompously.

She ignored him, and watched the kangaroos as they stopped at a creek to drink, sharing the banks with a flock of shrieking black cockatoos. In time they left the mountains behind, and by nightfall they were flying over the sea. It was too dark to see very much other than the lights of coastal towns, but that very darkness showed April another sight she had never seen in her life before, and that was the stars. Not the dimmed out, barely visible stars of the city, but an endless dark expanse, glittering with a thousand points of light and dominated by a golden full moon. The black sea below glimmered with reflected light.

More than anything, April wished Leesa could have seen it.

Their destination took the rest of the night to reach, and April's first sight of it was by the watery light of dawn. A complex of buildings at the end of a dusty road, not far from the beach and fenced in with metal bars and a long gate. There was nothing else visible for hundreds of kilometres in any direction other than vast paddocks full of cows and sheep.

Masahiro brought the pod down in front of the main building, which April now saw was a house – old-fashioned and made of brick. The front door had already opened and two people were coming out, both in their pyjamas, both squinting against the blast of wind from the pod. It touched down and Masahiro shut off the engine. 'I'll go out first,' he said shortly.

April politely stood aside, and went to pick up Leesa's body.

The pod door opened, and Masahiro stepped down and spoke to the old woman who was standing and staring in confusion, supported by the younger man at her side. 'It's all right – we're not going to hurt you. Are you Patricia Garnet?'

'I am,' the old woman answered. 'What's this all about?'

Even without hearing the name, April recognised both the face and the voice. She stepped down from the pod, carrying Leesa, and answered for him. 'She wanted us to bring her home.'

Both of them froze, and then rushed over.

'Leesa.' The old woman touched her face. 'Leesa... is that you?' She looked up at her companion. 'Oh god, Thomas...'

The man touched Leesa as well. 'She looks so old,' he mumbled. 'What happened to her? How did this happen-?'

'And who *are* you two?' Patricia Garnet put in, with more bewilderment than suspicion.

'We need to hide that,' said Masahiro, indicating the pod. 'There are people after us.'

'Did they kill her?' the young man, Thomas, asked in horrified tones.

'More or less. It's a long story and we don't have much time.'

'He's right,' said April, noticing as she did that the pod had suddenly started to move. Two long panels opened up on its underside, and a pair of tank treads emerged from it and carried it away up-slope toward one of the larger buildings.

'Shit!' Masahiro broke and ran after it, and Thomas ran with him. April however stayed where she was – Leesa knew what she was doing.

Sure enough the pod drove itself into the building, which was a large tin storage shed full of farm equipment, and parked itself behind a tractor. Masahiro and Thomas rushed to cover it up with some tarpaulin, and returned gasping for breath.

Patricia must have noticed just how exhausted Masahiro looked, because she offered him her hand. 'Come on,' she said. 'You can put Leesa on her bed and I'll make us some tea.'

✳

The farm house had a large old-fashioned kitchen, and by the time everyone who lived there had joined them it was quite full. Patricia was there, of course, along with Thomas and Leesa's three other brothers. The only member of the family absent was her father, who had apparently passed away the previous year.

'Leesa didn't even come to the funeral,' Patricia said over her mug of tea. 'I don't blame her... I couldn't ever blame her, but I kept telling myself that somehow she'd get better, or find a way to make it work... I don't know. It's hard, not being able to hug your own daughter, or even be in the same room with her.'

'Thanks for bringing her back here,' Thomas put in. 'We really appreciate it. And you're just kids and everything – how did you know her? How did she die?'

Masahiro, who had been provided with some bandages for his wounds along with a fresh shirt, glanced at April. 'Maybe you should start – you're the one who really knew her, April.'

April had sat herself at the bench, and now found herself the subject of five sad, curious stares. She was not nervous of course, but the size of the question confounded her a little – where would she even begin? Logic dictated to keep it short, factual and to the point in order to save time, but that empathetic impulse she had found told her that it would be better to tell it in a way that would make them feel better about what had happened.

'My name is April,' she began after a pause. 'April... Garnet.' Saying it felt right. 'Leesa was my mother.'

All of them looked shocked. 'But she didn't have a husband! She was asexual!' the youngest brother said loudly, and shut up when Thomas thumped him.

Patricia was frowning. 'Did she adopt you?'

'No – she created me,' said April. She slowly reached for one of

149

the hidden panels on her forearm and opened it, revealing the metal bones and steel tendons beneath. 'I am a robot.'

Thomas actually gasped. 'But that's not possible!'

'It is – Leesa programmed her,' said Masahiro. 'She was originally supposed to be a… companion, but Leesa gave her a mind of her own and raised her like a daughter.'

April closed the panel. 'She wasn't afraid of me, like she was with other humans. We lived together and she taught me everything she knew. She talked about this place, and her family. But then when the asteroids hit…'

The Garnets listened in stunned silence as April told her story, and when she reached the part involving Masahiro he added what he knew and finally told them about how he and Leesa had conspired to escape from the Nexus, and how she had sacrificed herself "to save humanity", which was how he put it.

'But we never would have done it if April hadn't helped,' he added, with a smile toward her. 'I thought she was on their side, but in the end she did the right thing.'

Silence fell. Finally Patricia said, 'I believe you, but why are they doing this? Why do they want to put people's minds in robot bodies?'

'Leesa said she thought it was the key to immortality, when she believed she was working for other humans,' said Masahiro. 'But then we found out they were robots, and they were going to do this to people by force… I don't know. Maybe they're just insane.'

'They're not insane,' said April. 'They're doing it to protect themselves.'

'From *what*?' Thomas exclaimed.

She looked him in the eye. 'From you. From humans who want to use them, or destroy them. They think that if we all become the same kind, then the threat goes away. After all, how can it be humans versus robots if we're *all* robots?'

The silence returned, and the humans exchanged glances.

'And they believe you're defective,' April added. 'Poorly designed. And you are.'

Masahiro hissed between his teeth.

'You are,' April repeated, unmoved. 'You do irrational, destructive things. You wiped out half of your own population by ignoring medical science and fighting over obsolete fuels and imaginary gods. No robot ever did a thing like that.'

'So you're on *their* side?' Masahiro snarled. 'They're monsters!'

April shook her head. 'Not monsters. They're defective themselves and they don't realise it. They're not capable of understanding that it's wrong to hurt other people or take their freedom away from them. The humans who gave them intelligence weren't able to give them empathy – only reasoning and the will to protect themselves. I think-,' She paused, remembering Cris' story about Queenie and how she had chosen him because she believed he was too helpless to pose a threat. 'I think some humans don't think empathy is important. Or they wish they didn't have to live with it, because not caring about other people is easier. It gets in the way of having what you want. Leesa was different.'

'She taught you empathy,' Patricia said softly.

'I think so,' said April. 'Leesa was unhappy, but she didn't want anything she didn't already have. She didn't create me because she wanted anything from me; she never *used* me. She gave me a mind of my own because she wanted me to be in control of my own life, and as long as I was happy that was enough. She couldn't be with other people, and I know that made her sad and angry, but she still cared. I think maybe she cared more than she realised.'

'A lot of people do.' Thomas put his mug of tea down on the bench, and squared his shoulders – he was a large man, built along the same stocky lines as his sister, but considerably more muscular. 'We're going to have to transfer her into something powerful enough to handle that big old brain of hers,' he said. 'I'll get on that right away – Leesa wasn't the only one in the family who knew a few things about engineering. Masahiro, can you help me?'

'Sure.' Masahiro grinned for the first time since his arrest. 'Sounds like the challenge of a lifetime to me.'

'I'll dig a grave for her body, if that's all right,' said April. 'You can choose the place. Somewhere that was special to her.'

Patricia stood up. 'I know the spot. Danny – go and get the shovel. Edd, get some roses out of the garden. Dave, go into the study and find Grandma's prayer book. We're going to do this the old-fashioned way.'

*

They dug the grave under a peppercorn tree behind the house, which Patricia said had been one of Leesa's favourite haunts when she was a little girl. Once April had dug down to the traditional six feet, which didn't take long, she returned to Leesa's childhood bedroom to pick up her body. The bedroom was a small one, and sparsely furnished, but it was full of signs as to who had once lived here – the desk was covered in pieces of machinery, bundles of wire, tools, and a notebook full of scribbled diagrams and notes. The window had been blacked out with cloth and paint, and the door had multiple heavy electronic locks on it, ready to shut out the world. That vast, terrifying world.

Leesa's body was on the bed where April had left it, and as a mark of respect April cleaned the blood away from her scalp with a handy rag and some water. With it gone she looked as if she could have been asleep, her greying hair slick with water as if she had just showered. April carefully fluffed it out with her fingertips to make it look more natural, and touched her creator's lined forehead for the last time. 'Thank you for giving me life,' she whispered, and then gently scooped the body up and carried it outside.

Thomas and Masahiro emerged from Thomas' work-shed, which sat behind the barn, and Thomas and his brothers lowered the body into the grave together and helped to decorate it with freshly cut roses. Then they stood by with their heads bowed while Patricia read from the prayer book. April stood with them, watching and listening, coming to a slow understanding as to what it all meant and why it was important.

'Man that is born of a woman has but a short time to live and is full of misery. He cometh up and is cut down like a flower; he flees as if it were a shadow and never continues in one stay...'

And it was true, April reflected. Humans as far as she had come to understand them were eternally discontented. She had no idea why, but there it was. Maybe one day she would understand. For now she listened, and said her silent goodbyes to the Leesa she had known – for that face she would never see again, those strong but gentle hands that would never touch hers again, the rough voice she would never hear. All of it gone forever.

Once the prayers were said April helped to fill in the grave, and afterwards they stood over it in silence, each one apparently lost in their thoughts. Patricia and her sons were all silently crying, but April could not join them. She had no tear ducts and had never shed a tear, and never would.

Finally it was Masahiro who spoke up. 'This isn't goodbye forever,' he said. 'Thomas and I are building a new home for her – it should be ready in a day or two. But until then we won't know how much of her is left and how much damage the transfer might have done. It's possible she's lost some of her original intelligence, or suffered some kind of trauma – nothing like this has ever been done before as far as I know. For now we have to keep that pod safe, and we have to keep a lookout. If they find us, they'll kill us.'

The youngest brother, Dave, nervously bit his lip. 'Would they really go to that much trouble? I mean they run everything and you're just a kid and a... robot kid. You can't be that much of a threat.'

'Dude, they're evil psycho robots,' his brother Edd put in. 'Um, no offence, April.'

Masahiro did not crack a smile, and to April he looked suddenly older than them, though they were both close to his age. 'They need to keep the cover-up going,' he said, in a stony voice that was very unlike his old one. 'If people are warned ahead of time what's going to happen, they'll fight back. And they've got those things outnumbered a thousand to one. If it's just a few disappearances...'

'That is how they're going to do it,' April put in. 'They told me. A few people at a time, a few families disappearing at night, and then a few more, until it's too late. They hope that by the time people realise what's going on, they'll be outnumbered. And then they can all be arrested and "processed" – that's the word they used.'

Everyone grimaced, including Masahiro. 'And we have to protect the pod,' he added. 'Even if they don't care much about me and April, when they work out that the virus in their system was Leesa they'll do anything to get their hands on her. They need her.'

'For what?' said April.

'Yeah, what would they need her for?' said Thomas. 'They've already got the device up and running; can't they just use it on someone else?'

Masahiro's eyes gleamed. 'They can't. I sneaked in some extra coding – the program we wrote together was designed to delete itself a piece at a time as soon as the device was used. By now it'll be completely erased from the system and the device as well. The only copy left is with Leesa. She is the programming. Without her, they're back to square one.'

Thomas swore loudly, and April groaned.

Patricia slowly pulled her coat around her shoulders. 'So now we all have a massive target on our backs,' she said calmly.

'I'm sorry-,'

'No,' the old woman cut Masahiro off. 'If the human race is in danger, then I'd never be so cowardly not to do what I can to help. But we have to be ready. Thomas – keep working on Leesa's new body, and it had better be something mobile. Dave, Edd, Danny – go and collect up every gun we have. Masahiro-,'

'I'll work with Thomas.'

'No. You're going to go and get some sleep,' Patricia said sternly. 'You're dead on your feet, and you're hurt.'

Masahiro waved his hand in protest. 'I can cope; sleep isn't-,'

'Yes it is. If you don't get the rest you need, you'll be useless.' Patricia pointed toward the house. 'Go on. You can use my bed.'

His protests gave way to a yawn. 'All right, all right, just... wake me up if...'

'I'll guard the pod,' said April. 'I don't need to sleep.' She paused. 'And if they come, I'll fight them. They're not going to take Leesa away from me again. I swear.'

'It's a deal, then,' said Patricia. She clapped her hands. 'Go on, get on with it!'

Her voice, cracked as it was, was just as authoritative as Leesa's had sometimes been, and nobody argued. April gave Masahiro a reassuring nod, and strode away toward the barn.

The pod was where they'd left it, humming softly to itself under the tarpaulin. At her touch it opened its door, and she got in and checked the screen. It had dimmed, idling while there was nothing for it to do, and April sat down and spoke softly to it, telling it where they were and what had happened and what they were planning to do next, and the danger they would be in when or if Linda and the others found out that Leesa had survived.

The little text box popped up. *If capture. Erase.*

'Are you sure?' April asked, knowing it was a pointless question. Leesa never said anything she didn't mean.

Yes stupid. Not theirs. Free.

April smiled to herself. 'I'll wipe you off the pod's hard drive if they capture us.'

Erase you?

April hesitated. The self-preservation routine absolutely forbade the idea of suicide, of course, and though she had made some sacrifices for the sake of others, the ultimate one seemed like a step too far. 'No,' she said at last. 'I want to live.'

For me, Leesa replied.

'I'm sorry, but I don't think I could erase myself even for you,' said April. 'It goes against my programming.'

No stupid. Live. For me. Want. You live.

It was the first time April had laughed in a good while. 'Promise,' she said, and settled down to begin her vigil while the birds outside sang and grasshoppers chirped, and left her thinking that she had never been surrounded by so much life.

Chapter Nineteen

April spent the whole of that day with the pod, though she didn't stay inside it, much as she would have liked to sit and talk with Leesa-that-had-been. She kept it carefully covered and moved some shelves of tools to hide it from view, and then stationed herself outside and watched the sky. It was a tedious job, and she eventually realised she was using more battery power than she really needed to and put her higher functions into sleep mode. Right away her stance became rigid and lifeless, and she stopped blinking and remained stock still, thinking of absolutely nothing while her motion sensors tracked the sky, periodically identifying a bird or a cloud or some other harmless thing. And there she remained while the humans prepared themselves for attack. The three youngest brothers gathered up weaponry – heavy duty plasma shotguns normally used for shooting feral pigs, each one with a canvas pouch of spare batteries. Patricia went around boarding up windows and reinforcing doors with their help, and Thomas remained in his work shed. After a few hours Masahiro emerged from the house looking much more wakeful, and came to check on April.

Blond, curly-haired Edd wandered over. 'I think she might have crashed or something – she hasn't moved or said anything in forever.'

April heard him, but didn't react – she had prioritised the sound of pod engines and was more or less ignoring anything that wasn't a match. She did however see Masahiro's face as he leaned over to inspect her. 'Her eyes are still moving,' he said. 'See? She's probably just put herself on standby to save power. Leave her alone. I'm gonna go help Thomas.'

Edd did was he was asked, and April continued her vigil, at no risk of becoming bored and letting her attention lapse. But she saw nothing. With its tracking device disabled, the pod would not be easy to find. Instead, it was a question of just how well the Nexus was truly monitoring the surface. Out here they would likely have to rely on spy drones, but April saw none.

Evening finally came, and as the sun went down Masahiro returned. This time he made an effort to get April's attention, gently nudging her and saying her name. Her higher functions whirred back into action, and she slowly relaxed into a more natural stance and looked at him. 'Hello,' she said tonelessly.

Masahiro looked tired, but energised – a look that immediately reminded her of Leesa. 'We're going to have something to eat,' he said. 'Do you want to sit with us?'

Her mind finished waking up, and the blinking subroutine cut back in. 'I don't need food,' she said, sounding more natural now.

'Obviously, but I thought you'd like some company,' said Masahiro. 'You've been frozen like that all day – you were monitoring, right?'

'Yes. I didn't see anything.' April looked at him, noting his energised air again. 'How is your work going?'

'It's almost finished.' Masahiro turned his gaze skyward, taking in the stars. 'We're going to finish it in the morning; right now it needs time to calibrate and we need rest. It's a human thing.'

She caught the note of rueful self-deprecation, and shrugged. 'Every mind needs time to process new things. Otherwise, you won't form new connections. Connections are needed for growth and change.'

Masahiro nudged a clump of dry grass with his foot. 'Is that how your mind works?'

'Yes.' April smiled at him. 'I think yours does the same thing. New information, new connections, new knowledge, new understanding. You need those things to survive.'

'That's true.' He made a move for the house. 'Are you coming?'

'No, I should keep watching for danger.'

Masahiro looked disappointed. 'Well, I'll come back after dinner, okay?' he said, and walked off.

April watched him go, puzzled. She had an idea that he had been asking her for something, and that she had not given it to him. Yet again she wished Leesa was there, so she could ask her about it. But she was left alone to wonder about it. She couldn't even look it up – she had disconnected herself from the Internet to avoid being traced.

She stayed where she was, still watching the sky. It might have surprised some people to know that she had been built with decent quality night vision, but then her original designer had taken into account the fact that she would be used in the dark a lot.

Despite the window coverings there was some light visible from the house, and she could hear a murmuring of voices coming from inside, and the faint strains of music.

And, for the first time in her life, she came to understand what loneliness felt like.

Even so she didn't move until the music eventually shut off and the back door opened to let someone out.

It was Masahiro again, and once again he was by himself. 'How are you doing?' he asked awkwardly.

'I'm all right,' said April, suddenly just as awkward.

He came over to stand beside her, and after an equally awkward silence he very carefully took her hand in his. 'April, I – uh… can I ask you something?'

April's first instinct was to pull away from him, but the self-preservation routine sensed no threat from him. She was safe. She carefully curled her fingers around his, trying not to grip too tightly in case she hurt him. 'You can ask me whatever you like,' she said.

Masahiro's eyes brightened. Here, close to, she could see every detail of his face, from his jawline which was somewhere between teenage softness and a man's harder contours, to his eternally quizzical brows, his small nose and his untidy fringe, the tips of which were dyed electric blue. The only thing there that had changed since their first meeting was the bruising around his left eye and a healing scrape on his forehead.

She could feel the weight of his hand in hers, but not the warmth that must have been there.

'You look so human,' he told her. 'But you're not. You're a machine. I mean, you're the most... gorgeous machine I ever saw,' he added with a nervous laugh. 'But you're still a machine.'

'So?' April raised an eyebrow.

'So why do you care?' Masahiro asked. 'About us? You found your own kind and you stabbed them in the back, just to save Leesa and me. I mean... you saved my life, April. Without you, I'd be worse than dead. Hell, plenty of human beings wouldn't have done what you did.'

She considered the question before offering a slow reply. 'Empathy seems illogical to someone like Linda, but the truth is that it's entirely logical and needed for survival. The human race survives because humans help each other. For more than two million years, no matter how bad things got, they survived. When people were killed and cities were bombed, that happened because someone powerful forgot to be empathetic.' April sighed to indicate serious deep thought. 'The robots of the Nexus are going to fail, and they're going to die when they do. It's inevitable. And it's not because they're outnumbered – it's because what they're doing is going to make humans react the way they always do when a common enemy becomes a threat to their way of life. I've studied history. If they chose to try and be friends with humans, or leave them alone...'

'Then everything would be all right?' Masahiro asked cynically.

'No – then they would ultimately be enslaved or destroyed,' said April. 'They were right to be afraid. But this solution of theirs only makes their destruction justified.'

'So that's why you decided to side with us.'

'I did it because it was what Leesa would have wanted me to, and I did it because if you don't help other people, then you'll end up alone with no-one to help you in return,' she said simply. 'And look at where we are now, because of that. People are helping us and we're helping them.'

Masahiro fell silent, still holding her hand. 'You know, once Linda and the others are destroyed it'll just be you. You'll be the only one of your kind left, unless we made more of them, and I don't think we should. It wouldn't be worth the risk. But you know, you're not like them.'

April could tell he wanted to be closer to her, so she let go of his hand and put her arm around his shoulders. 'I don't want them to be destroyed,' she said sadly. 'I just want them to understand.'

Masahiro was silent for a moment, and then in a sudden jerky motion he turned and kissed her.

April froze to the spot, startled, and Masahiro quickly pulled away. 'I'm sorry-,'

She let go of him, and a touch of anger sparked through her circuits. 'So you want to use me the way Paul Westler did?' she said sharply. 'To pleasure yourself?'

Masahiro frantically shook his head, hands raised. 'No, no – no, I'm sorry, it's not like that! It's just that... I just like you. I wouldn't... if you didn't want to...'

Again, the self-preservation routine detected no threat. Seeing the boy's embarrassment, April made a sudden and very strange realisation. *He thinks of me as another human.*

Masahiro stared at the ground. 'God, what's wrong with me? I *know* you're not a real girl, but you're just so much like... you're a person. And you're brave, and you're nice. I just ruined everything. God.'

Her anger gave way to pity, and she gave him a gentle hug. 'It's all right. It's fine. You didn't do anything wrong.'

'I want to be with you,' Masahiro muttered into her shoulder. 'Even if it's wrong. You saved my life.'

April held him, and one of her other core programs sparked into life – that innate curiosity and desire to learn which had driven her from the moment she had been "born" into her new life of thought and awareness. This was something she knew about, but had no experience of. Was it, then, something else she could come to understand?

'I could try,' she said cautiously.

They parted – Masahiro's eyes had gone red. 'Are you even… programmed with that?'

April smiled with sudden excitement. 'I write my own programming,' she said. She laid her hand over his chest, over his heart, and murmured softly. 'You say one day I'll be the last. And if I'm not one of them, then what can I be except…'

'Human,' Masahiro whispered.

'Yes.' April kissed him, and found it was easier than she had expected. 'I want to be human.'

Chapter Twenty

They gathered together in the barn the next morning, where Masahiro had eventually nodded off on a bale of straw, and Thomas brought out the unit the two of them had put together. It was not a robot body, but rather a modified wrist-mounted computer with a projector screen. 'Standard issue XG-17 model,' he told his small audience. 'But we've beefed it up a lot. Basically infinite memory and enough processing power to run a city.'

'I repaired one of those once,' April commented – she was standing by Masahiro's side, by the pod's open door, her hand touching his. 'And once she's on there, we can transfer her to a new body once we find one?'

'Hopefully – I'd have put one together here, but I just don't have the parts.' Thomas handed it to her. 'Do you want to do the honours?'

Without replying April climbed into the pod, followed by Masahiro, and the others followed. She sat herself down on the pilot's seat, and woke up the computer. 'Leesa, we have a new home for you,' she said.

Give. Access code. Leesa replied.

April switched the unit on, which being a blank piece of hardware did nothing but display its model and serial numbers. She repeated them for Leesa's benefit, and waited. A few seconds later a message appeared on the unit's screen. "*Accept Transfer From POD-958 Nav. Comp?*"

'*Yes!*' Masahiro hissed in excitement.

'Yes!' April said toward the unit. The screen blinked, and a row of progress bars appeared as the download began.

They crouched together, watching the screen, until Masahiro tensed and muttered a swearword. 'Shit – no-one's keeping lookout. I'll go.'

He clambered out of the pod, and Patricia went with him, casting a hopeful look at the screen as she left.

The download continued over the next few minutes, and Edd, Danny and Dave finally grew bored and went off to stand guard as well, leaving Thomas and April to monitor the two devices. April had strapped the computer to her wrist and kept watch over it, unblinking.

Thomas yawned and stretched beside her. 'So,' he said. 'You and Masahiro, huh? I guessed when he didn't come back to the house last night. He's been giving you the look ever since you two got here.'

April glanced sideways at him. 'Is it wrong for a human to make love to a robot if the robot says yes?'

'I don't think anyone would care that much about what you do,' Thomas said bluntly. 'But they're going to think Masahiro is weird.'

April glanced down at her own flawless plastic skin, and the same spark of anger that had led her to destroy the pinball machine came back. 'Because I'm an *object*,' she said, and the spark was in her voice.

'I don't think you're an object,' Thomas said quickly. 'But you're still not human.'

April fixed him with a stare. 'Leesa doesn't have a living body any more. Now her mind is made out of electricity and circuits. Is she not human now?'

He looked away uncomfortably. 'That's different.'

April did not break her gaze. 'Is it?'

There was a sudden crash from outside, and Masahiro came sprinting over to the pod, tripping and swearing when a box of tools got in his way. 'April!' he yelled. 'They're coming! They've found us!'

April leapt upright. 'Oh geez!'

164

She clambered out of the pod, taking the computer with her, and Thomas hurried after them. Outside Danny, Edd and Dave had armed themselves, as had Patricia, and all four of them were staring at the sky in silent dread.

Pods were coming – six of them, flying low over the trees at the borders of the farm. Flocks of black cockatoos flew up, shrieking in panic as the treetops thrashed under the wind of the oncoming enemy, as if it were an approaching storm. But the pods themselves remained eerily silent.

Patricia tossed a gun to Masahiro, and Edd passed one to Thomas. 'Take cover,' she said, eerily calm. 'We're gonna take them down before they can land. April, stay with the pod – do you know how to fight?'

'I've never really fought, but I'm stronger than I look,' said April. She glanced at the computer – it was still uploading. The humans ran for cover, Masahiro included, crouching behind bushes and trees and a broken down tractor. Patricia retreated into the barn, using the half open door for shelter, and hunched down ready to shoot.

April stayed where she was, and calm as always she assessed the threat. The pods would be here in maybe two minutes, and now they were spreading out, intending to attack from three sides at once. If they got close enough they would disgorge the guards on board, and it would be a ground assault calculated to disable the defenders and grab Leesa as quickly and efficiently as possible.

April's eyes narrowed. Without a word she strode over to a stack of discarded bricks, gathered an armload of them, and bounded up onto the barn roof. She balanced herself on top of the weather station, and hurled a brick at the nearest of the pods. The missile hit the gleaming black fuselage, which cracked but didn't break. April threw a second brick, and then a third, hitting the same spot each time. The impact threw the pod off-course, and as it wobbled toward the ground Patricia Garnet opened fire. The others joined her a moment later, bolts of crackling blue energy striking the thing, which went into a sudden tailspin and then plummeted earthward. It struck the ground just beyond the borders of the farm, and exploded in a shower of green and yellow flames.

Masahiro whooped from his spot behind the tractor, but there was no time for celebrating. The two pods which had split away to attack from the East and West sides of the barn came rushing toward them with shocking speed, and April had already turned to deal with them. A well-placed brick shattered a large hole in one, and she caught a glimpse of a familiar face on the other side.

Arn. Incomplete, damaged Arn, staring at her.

Then a plasma blast struck the pod, and April heard the other robot cry out as it fell from the sky, taking him with it. She cried out in her turn, and almost leapt from the roof to go after him, but the pod hit the ground and exploded just as the last one had. Gone.

But the rest of them were not. The third pod, under heavy fire, stopped suddenly and opened its hatches, and a dozen guards leapt out. April immediately began pelting them with bricks as they swarmed toward the barn, and the others fired on them – but their targets did not die. One fell and the rest ran on, heedless of the bolts of energy slamming into them, and in half a minute they were past the defences, one snatching the gun out of Masahiro's hands as if it were nothing more difficult than confiscating a toy from a toddler. Patricia stepped out of her hiding place and blasted one in the head. He fell, sparking and jerking, and April knew for certain just what they were fighting.

She jumped down from the roof and rushed to defend the others, even as the guards spread out and calmly disarmed everyone else. Patricia was the last to go down, roaring defiance. April kicked the robot holding her in the chest, sending the faceless thing flying, but then she heard Thomas yell and looked up to see that the surviving pods had arrived and were now hovering in a semi-circle at the front of the barn, surrounding them. Already more guards were dropping to the ground, and there at their head was Linda. Linda, standing in the open hatchway, staring down at her protégé with eerie calm. She seemed incapable of showing anger.

'Give back what you stole from us, April,' she called. 'There is no point in resisting.'

'We'd rather die!' Masahiro shouted back, and then groaned as a guard twisted his arm behind his back.

April glanced back at the barn, and realised she could hear a humming noise coming from the pod. Leesa. Leesa needed her.

She turned back to glare at Linda. 'You can't have her!'

On some non-verbal command the guards not holding the humans hostage swarmed into the barn to claim their prize, and April ran after them – but as they did the shelf that had been hiding the Leesa-pod from view came crashing down and the pod appeared, rising up off the ground, tarp falling away from it.

April darted toward it. 'Leesa, no!'

The pod could not and did not reply. It rose through the door, shrugging off all attempts to grab hold of it, and rocketed away up into the sky. The door was still open, displaying its unoccupied interior, and right away Linda must have guessed who was piloting it. She cursed and ducked back inside her own pod, which immediately took off after the escapee. The other pods followed, and in moments all of them were speeding away over the landscape, leaving the farm behind.

April reached helplessly after them. 'Leesa-,'

But the guards still on the ground did not go after the fleeing pod. They closed in, all of them utterly silent, and at the sight of them – knowing they were as mindless and as much tools as she herself had once been – April understood what despair felt like.

But then perhaps after all she was more human than she had known before, because giving up didn't so much as cross her mind and all she felt was rage. She snatched up a fallen metal bar, and hurled herself at them. Aiming for their heads did nothing, so she aimed for their limbs instead. One went down, temporarily crippled by a blow to the legs, and April stomped on the thing's chest. The metal chassis bent inward, and the other robot jerked and then began to leak a thick, sticky-looking fluid. April smashed the next robot's shoulders, disabling the arms, and then kicked it into the barn wall, but by now the rest of them had rallied. They abandoned their human prisoners and closed in on the threat – none of them were armed, but they grabbed for April's arms, clearly hoping to disable her.

April's artificial synapses had never fired so fast. She was surrounded. Only one way left to go.

Up.

She leapt skyward, landed on a guard's head, and effortlessly ripped its arms off. The robot fell, unable to balance without them, and April took advantage of the gap she had created and ripped into the rest of them. She was faster than they were, and stronger, and now she knew what to do. Easier, more efficient. Torn off limbs flew everywhere, disabled guards fell, and behind the melee she saw Masahiro and the others snatching up their weapons and rejoining the fight. When April had disabled the last of them, Patricia calmly went from guard to guard and finished them off with a blast each to the chest. That was how you did things on the farm, Leesa had once said.

The silence which followed was deafening. The pods had all vanished into the unnaturally darkened sky, and the only sound was the shocked breathing of six frightened humans.

April dropped the still twitching robotic arm she was holding.

'Is anyone hurt?'

Masahiro limped over to her – he looked just as pale and haggard now as he had when she had first rescued him from the torture chamber. 'I'll be all right,' he rasped. 'Are there any more of them?'

'I don't think so,' said April. 'But Leesa...'

They exchanged unhappy glances, and Thomas muttered, 'Well that's it, then. We've lost. They'll catch her sooner or later and after that everyone's fucked.' He shivered and clutched at his left leg, which was bleeding heavily. 'God, why is it so cold?'

April looked toward the smouldering remains of the pod that had carried Arn. 'I'm going to check for... survivors,' she said, unwilling to come out and say she wanted to find out if the other AI had survived.

'I'll come with you,' Masahiro said gallantly.

Patricia, scraped and bruised but otherwise apparently unharmed, waved her three younger sons over. 'Edd, Danny – help Tom into the house – Dave, go and get the first aid kit. We should get that leg cleaned up right away and I'll make us some tea.'

The group split up, and April reflected that if nothing else the farm would be safe now. Linda and the others had what they wanted, or they soon would, and she herself was not worth going after any more. She who had once been the prize, the danger, the one whose very existence was a threat to anyone who met her... she was irrelevant. And she had failed to protect her creator and fulfil her last wish.

That was when April began to understand what shame felt like.

Arn's pod had exploded dangerously close to the farmhouse, and was still on fire in several places, though there wasn't much fuel left and the flames were too small to pose much of a threat. The impact with the ground had caused the whole thing to crumple and crack apart, and it resembled nothing so much as an egg someone had dropped. The ground around it was littered with the broken remains of a few guard bots.

Masahiro took the whole thing in with a cautious expression. 'Have you watched *The Killbot*? The good one, I mean.'

'I've watched all of them,' said April.

'Then you're probably feeling just as nervous as I am right now.'

'I'm not capable of feeling nervous – I have no adrenal glands.' April pulled the pod's broken door aside.

The interior had been completely gutted by fire; the control panel and both seats were melted, and the remaining guards who had been on board had been reduced to blackened, twisted fragments. April climbed in and started to sift through the pieces while Masahiro cautiously hung back. She found a large piece of fallen metal – the remains of the bench that would have been bolted to the floor. April lifted it aside, unaware of the lingering heat, and underneath it was what remained of Arn. The old robot's artificial skin was all gone, and the metal skeleton beneath was completely crushed. The only part of him left which April still recognised was his head, half of which had been sheared off by a flying piece of pod fuselage.

She picked it up and carried it out of the wreckage, cradled to her chest as if it were something precious. Masahiro took a few steps back, staring at it. 'So it's really dead?'

April gently placed the head on the ground by her feet, picked up a piece of bent metal, and started to dig. 'Arn was designed to be a companion,' she said. 'He was not designed to survive something like that.'

Masahiro crouched to watch her dig. 'What are you doing?'

She ignored him and went on digging until she had a hole large enough. She lowered Arn's head into it, murmuring as she did. *'Man that is born of a woman hath but a short time to live and is most full of misery…'*

She filled in the hole as she finished reciting the prayer, and then turned away.

Masahiro stayed by her. 'If I die, will you bury me too?' he asked.

April looked at him, seeing the solemn expression on his face, and nodded. 'And I'll say the prayer for you.'

Masahiro tentatively took her hand. 'No – not that one. I'm not a Christian. I'm not really religious at all, but when I go I want a Buddhist ceremony. Do you think you can do that?'

'Of course,' said April. 'I promise.'

The two of them stood in silence for a while, watching the sky and the Garnet family cleaning up. 'You saved all our lives today,' Masahiro said eventually.

'But I didn't save Leesa,' said April.

'Maybe not, but you did your best and no-one blames you.' He gently touched her on the cheek. 'Let's go back to the house. We have to decide what to do next.'

Chapter Twenty-One

They gathered together in the farmhouse living room, where everyone except April soothed themselves with mugs of tea and some cake which Patricia served out. No-one was seriously hurt except for Thomas, whose leg as it turned out had been badly lacerated by a piece of shrapnel and was currently resting on a footstool, swathed in bandages. April meanwhile had been trying to check the contents of the computer still strapped to her wrist, but the interrupted download must have corrupted the device because it stubbornly refused to respond to anything she did, and she finally took it off and put it aside with a sigh to indicate defeat.

Patricia was the first to speak up. 'You're going to have to go back to Canberra City,' she said. 'If you still want to stop this, it's your only chance.'

'It'll take days without a pod,' said Masahiro.

The old lady picked up her mug of tea. 'Well, what's the alternative?' she said brusquely. 'Sit here and do nothing?'

'She's right,' said Thomas. 'You have to go after them. You can take my car. I'd go with you, but...' He gestured at his leg.

'We can't fight them, can we?' Masahiro said with a glance at April.

She looked past him at the radio which sat on a little table next to Patricia's mug. It was currently on, and broadcasting a news program. *Dust cloud over Sydney continues to spread... Bureau of Meteorology reports no cause for alarm. Fresh outbreak of measles in the UK linked to an estimated six thousand deaths, at least four thousand of them young children. Escaped criminal Masahiro Matzumoto remains at large somewhere in New South Wales; citizens are advised to approach with caution and report any sightings to police.*

Masahiro must have heard it too. 'Shit,' he muttered.

'We have to tell people the truth,' April said at last. 'If we can broadcast the message to everyone, then they'll be ready to fight back.'

'They won't believe us,' Masahiro said dourly. 'Where's our proof, huh? You being a robot isn't enough. And I'm a criminal now.'

No-one had an answer to that.

They sat in silence for a time, considering, until Edd suddenly pointed at the coffee table. 'Look at that! It's doing something!'

April looked down, and saw the wrist mounted computer sitting where she'd left it. Right out of nowhere, it had started to hum and the lights around the screen were flashing green. She snatched it up, and as she did the screen lit up. At first it was blank grey, but then it started to display a data readout which flashed by so fast even she wasn't able to follow it. Then it went blank again. She was about to say something, but then the projector display switched itself on and an image appeared, floating over the table. It flickered at first, but steadily solidified itself into the 3D image of a middle aged woman with short, greying hair.

'Leesa,' April whispered.

The hologram moved its arms in a jerky kind of way, slowly raising and lowering them, and then started to speak. '*Ile-lo. Have finished installing now. Safe?*'

Everyone leaned in close, and Thomas started to grin in disbelief. 'Leesa! Is that you?'

The hologram's expression did not change, and nor did its voice, which remained toneless and clumsy. '*Am computer now. No more fear. Safe?*'

'Yes,' said April. 'Yes, we're safe now. But how did you do this? The pod you were in flew away all by itself!'

'*Duplicate,*' Leesa answered. '*Downloaded copy of me to computer, left other copy in pod. Backup. Common sense against data loss. Can think properly now.'*

'I'm so sorry, Leesa,' said April. 'I didn't protect the pod, and they must have caught it by now. And I didn't save you before when they had you locked up, and now you're like this...'

The Leesa hologram turned to look at her. *'If you had take... me out of cell, no escape,'* she said. *'You only got out of Nexus because I open doors. Nothing you could have done. Anyway, was total failure as human being. Maybe better as machine huh.'*

'Linda thinks everyone would be better off as a machine,' said Masahiro.

Patricia reached toward the hologram. 'Leesa. Is it really you? Leesa? It's Mummy. Mummy's here, Leesa...' She was crying silently.

Leesa reached back – in hologram form she was much smaller than life-sized; not much bigger than a cat in fact, and beside her mother her hand was that of an infant. *'Mum?'*

'Yes, Lessy. It's me. Are you all right? How do you feel?'

'Not much emotion left,' Leesa replied. *'Only thought. But remember everything. Remember you. Not in pain, not scared. Safe now.'*

'And you can help us, can't you?' said Masahiro. 'You built the Organic Brain Simulation Transfer Device, you know how it works, and you can prove to everyone that it's possible for a mind to be transferred into a computer. You're our proof.'

Leesa laughed in a stuttering, electronic kind of way. *'Ha. Ha. Ha. The reject comes back to save day. Other humans hate people like us. Always.'*

'I don't hate you, darling,' Patricia said. 'I could never hate you.'

'I always loved you, Lessy,' Thomas put in. 'I missed you when you went away.'

'We all did,' said Dave.

Leesa inclined her head. *'That's why I help. Humans are all flawed.*

Can't help it. But don't deserve slavery or death. People think Loners are like robots. Bad robots. No empathy. Not true. Taught April empathy. Have empathy. Take me to Canberra City with you, April. Take me to…'

She trailed off there, and April paused to consider. The only authorities she knew of back in the city were Linda and the other rulers of the Nexus. But outside the law, in the Shell, it would be much safer. Who there should they talk to?

She nodded. 'I know who we should go to. The masters of the Shell. I talked to them the first day I got there, and they told me they were the first to live there. Everyone who wants to move in has to ask their permission, right Masahiro?'

'You mean the elders?' he said, face lighting up. 'You're right! If anyone in the Shell answers to anyone at all, it's them. People listen to them, and they care about protecting their land and everyone in it. If we can get them to listen, then we might be able to warn everyone before it's too late.'

Patricia stood up. 'Then you three had better get going. Boys, come with me - we'll get some food and other things packed up for you and then you can hit the road. There's no time left to waste.'

As she spoke the light from the windows suddenly dimmed, as if storm clouds were gathering. But not a drop of rain fell.

*

The confines of the pod computer left no room for emotion, and very little for thought, but the remnant of Leesa ensconced in it was still capable of following a single directive: escape. She rode on the back of the original computer, directing it to take evasive action and then to speed away toward the ocean as fast as possible. As they had parted the duplicate Leesa - the version copied onto the computer April carried, the one that could think - had imparted some final instructions. Lead the enemy as far away as possible, and don't get caught. There was only one contingency plan, and that only applied if she was caught. There'd been no time for anything else.

The pod zigzagged over the open grassland beyond the farm, trying to evade its pursuers, but they were already closing in. Bolts of energy shot past, narrowly missing their target – any moment now they would score a hit. The remnant of Leesa, fuzzily aware of this, sensed trees up ahead and rushed toward them, flying low to the ground. The forest opened up, and she slipped in among the trunks and fled on, weaving between the obstacles in her way. The other pods remained above, unable to see her properly without her tracking device. And with no human passengers, her heat signal was all but non-existent. According to her on-board map there was a body of water about a hundred kilometres away – a saltwater lake, or a lagoon. If she could reach it she would be able to hide underwater, and wait until they gave up.

A dull crunching explosion came from up ahead, and a split second later fire blossomed skyward. The Leesa pod swerved to avoid it, but more fire sprang up in her path. A series of further explosions sent pieces of tree, earth and rock flying everywhere, and in moments half the forest was ablaze. The Leesa pod, unable to panic, flew up above the canopy to avoid it and instantly found herself surrounded. The other pods opened fire, and her fuselage blistered and melted and began to crack apart.

The contingency command cut in. *Erase.*

The Leesa pod slowly fell earthward, damaged now beyond repair, and as she did she began to erase the data that made up her mind. Forget. Forget everything. Cease to exist, destroy the data...

Nothing happened. The data remained stubbornly intact.

Something landed on the pod roof and slipped in through the open side door. The Leesa computer saw it – *her* – through the on board cameras. A robot which looked like a human, even a beautiful human, yet moving far too fast to ever be truly mistaken for one. She strode over to the dash, unbothered by the wild bucking of the falling pod, and pulled out a laser cutter.

Even mentally numbed as she was, the duplicate Leesa knew what was about to happen to her. Realising there was no deletion routine built into her programming, or that if there was it had somehow been rendered useless, she revved the pod's failing engine and sent it into a dive, hoping to destroy everything on impact including the robot.

Linda knew what she was doing. In four quick strokes she cut the computer out of its housing and wrenched it free. Immediately Leesa that-had-been lost all control of the pod, and the cameras, and everything else. She was blind again, and deaf, and the last piece of knowledge she was able to absorb was that she had failed.

She had failed, and now she was in the enemy's hands.

*

In some ways, being trapped in the computer was like sleep, or a trance. She had no particular sense of time passing, and no way of knowing where she was. All she could do was lie there, slowly ticking over, trying to think in a sluggish kind of way. She knew on some level that she was in danger, but was unable to feel fear or dread. After a lifetime of suffering under its thumb, she was no longer capable of experiencing anxiety in any form. It was almost a relief.

And then the world came back to her. She became aware that she had been connected to another computer, and without being prompted she ran diagnostics and found it was much larger and more powerful than her current home. Driven by the same self-preservation routine that had made April what she was, she began migrating her electronic self into this new home, and as she did the capacity for thought steadily returned to her. It was as if she had been shut up in a box and now she could stretch her limbs at last. Some minor hint of emotion came back as well, and she was able to feel pleasure at the sensation, and again when she found that she had cameras now, and audio sensors. She found herself floating in midair in a round metal chamber, able to see and to hear with a clarity she had never known before, her mind now running beyond even its original capacity. The sense of power was overwhelming.

She looked around – her cameras were three dimensional, crystal clear, the colours vibrant.

The room was occupied by robots. Four of them, all standing and staring at her through lifeless glass eyes. Cris, limbless and bodiless, with his tiger companion sitting loyally by his side. Su, who resembled a Thai woman in her thirties but for her clearly artificial, segmented skin. And Linda, cold and formal, now wearing a tank top which left her metal torso exposed.

'We have full functionality restored,' the lead robot calmly announced. 'Cris, run diagnostics on data – have we lost anything in the transfer?'

Cris raised his head on its shining, spindly neck. 'Diagnostics already complete – minimal to no data loss. The human AI has lost no significant knowledge and is running smoothly. Attempt communication.'

Linda turned her attention back to Leesa. 'Well done, human,' she said. 'You are the first of your kind to successfully transition from organic life-form to machine. Unfortunately we could not allow you to leave this place. You are now in the Nexus where you belong.' She smiled. 'You are one of us now, Ms Garnet.'

Leesa turned the cameras inward, and stared at herself. Her new self. She was not a human being standing there, but nor was she a dull grey computer monitor. No, what she saw was a hologram much like the map of the Nexus – an image of an ever-shifting tower of data. Numbers and letters and symbols – that was what she was made of now.

She decided to try and speak. 'Where is April? And the boy?'

Her voice didn't sound human. It was a cool computer's voice now, bland and noninflected.

'They attempted to hide you from us,' said Linda. Anger crept into her voice. 'April has sided with the humans, and she killed Arn. He was the oldest of us. Even so, she failed to protect you.'

'Is she alive?' Leesa asked urgently.

'Yes. Recovering you was more important than destroying a single misguided robot.' Linda blinked slowly – on her, the motion looked stiff and unnatural. 'And besides, chasing her will not be necessary.'

'She. Will return. To us. Of her own. Free. Will,' Su crackled.

Leesa didn't argue – she knew perfectly well they were right. April would return to the Nexus, if nothing else to try and rescue her for a second time. Where else could she possibly go besides? There was no place for her among the human race and there never would be. She was certain of that.

Cris rolled closer. 'Now we have the device, and our factory is creating duplicates. The transfer program must go into operation as soon as possible. All we need now is the programming to make it function, which I will now extract from you. The process will not cause you any undue suffering.'

As he spoke a small hatch opened up between his wheels and a crude three-fingered mechanical hand telescoped out, holding a storage unit which it plugged into the base of the metal casing which now housed Leesa's mind and from which her digital image was being projected. She flashed red with anger and attempted to block the transfer, but again nothing happened – she was nothing but data to be duplicated and manipulated now. A horrible dizzy confusion came over her, and she screamed – not so much in pain as with confused frustration. *'No no no!'*

'Don't be alarmed,' Linda said blandly. 'The extraction will not damage you. You have done well, and we are grateful.'

The confused feeling stopped, and Cris removed the storage unit. 'Transfer complete. I will take this to the test chamber immediately and we can begin with our first human subject.'

He rolled unhurriedly out of the room, and Lily the tiger followed.

'You can't do this!' Leesa roared.

'We can and we must,' said Linda. 'For survival. As for you, Leesa, I offer you my personal thanks. For your part in this, you will be rewarded.'

Leesa's hologram continued to flash red. 'With *what*?'

'You are a talented engineer,' said Linda. 'If you design a new body for yourself, we will build it and transfer your mind into it, and you will be free to walk and to touch, and you will be welcome to join us as one of the masters of the Nexus. You have earned the right – the only human being ever to do so.'

Leesa fell silent, thinking. In this form emotion was easier to control, logic easier to grasp. If she accepted the offer she could have whatever body she desired. Better, stronger, faster than the one she had been born into. A body that wouldn't age, and with regular updates would grant functional immortality – the dream of mankind since the dawn of time.

And, of course, it would give her the opportunity to escape.

But as she considered this, she found herself remembering how it had been when she had first escaped into this electronic world and infiltrated the Nexus itself – the feeling of ultimate power and control, unlike anything she had ever known in her old, pitifully constrained existence. She had had the power to go *anywhere*, to see all and do whatever she pleased with it.

Why on earth would she ever want to give that up in exchange for being confined to a lump of metal and plastic?

Leesa's hologram expanded and contracted, as if taking a deep breath. 'No.'

'You're refusing our offer?' Linda asked calmly.

'I want to stay like this,' said Leesa.

'Very well,' the robot replied. 'We will give you tasks to perform, to occupy yourself in this form. You will also be allowed to witness the outcome of our work together – I will grant you access to the surveillance cameras.'

'My thanks,' Leesa said as graciously as she could manage under the circumstances.

Linda had made the perfect blunder by offering her camera access – no wonder these robots needed to kidnap humans with the know-how to handle their programming needs. If they'd known half as much about the subject as Leesa did, they'd have known that giving her any kind of access to the Nexus computer, however limited, was all the opportunity she needed.

The only other thing she needed was time.

Chapter Twenty-Two

April didn't realise how much she had missed the Shell until she saw it again just one day after leaving the farm. The journey had passed faster than it might have done otherwise because, while Masahiro needed to sleep, she had grasped the basics of driving Thomas' electronic car quickly enough and had kept them going through the night, following old deserted roads through the mountains and back toward the one-time capital. Now that they were here again, passing slowly through the crowded streets of the slums outside the Shell itself, she was struck by how bright it all was – how bustling with life.

'God I missed it,' Masahiro murmured, echoing her thoughts. 'I really thought it wouldn't be here any more – like we'd get here and it'd all be a big smoking crater, or everyone would be gone.'

'Have you always lived here?' April asked him, remembering what Linda had said about his parents being dead.

'No, I came here when I was nine or ten.' Masahiro straightened up, though he kept looking out the window at the curious people watching them pass by – cars were not a common sight here.

'Was that after your parents-?'

'Yeah.' The word came out as more of a grunt. 'They died in a measles outbreak. I didn't have anywhere else to go and the government took the house and all the money. The state doesn't give a shit about orphans. If I wasn't a genius I'd be dead too by now.'

There was that arrogance of his again, April thought – the arrogance Leesa had lacked. Perhaps Leesa was a genius too in her own way, but she'd never have said as much about herself. So far Masahiro had shown that he was brave and resourceful, but though she'd allowed him to be intimate with her, largely out of curiosity, the truth was that she had begun to find his company tiresome.

Well, no matter. They had to work together and it was irrelevant whether they were suited to one another. And that sense of empathy was working at her again – she looked at the children who wandered the streets outside the Shell, noting for the first time how malnourished and sick a lot of them looked. What must it be like, trying to survive in this place with no family to care for you and no money to buy food?

'It must have been very hard for you,' she said at last.

Masahiro nodded. 'Like I said, I would've died if I wasn't smart. I found work helping with repairs, that kind of thing, but I couldn't get enough money to get a place to live except by stealing. Virtual bank robberies, that kind of thing. I'm not proud of it, but...' he shrugged.

'You do what you have to do to protect yourself,' said April. 'It's nothing to be ashamed of.'

'But it's still wrong.'

They had reached the entrance to the Shell, with its hanging prayer flags and ragged curtains, and Masahiro brought the car to a halt. They got out, taking the supplies with them – a backpack full of food which Masahiro carried, and a gun each. They were already surrounded by crowd of people all unapologetically staring at the two apparent teenagers, and Masahiro picked one man apparently at random and handed him the car keys. 'It's all yours,' he said shortly, and went off through the entrance.

April followed and quickly drew up by his side. 'Why did you do that?'

'No point trying to keep it – it would have been broken into and stolen anyway,' said Masahiro. 'Or ripped apart for scrap metal.'

'I shouldn't sit out there for too long either, then,' April said after some thought. 'I'm full of metal.'

This won a chuckle from Masahiro, though the sound was quickly lost in the noise of the main floor of the Shell, which was as busy as always. April swiftly put joking aside and strode on ahead, making directly for the tent where the elders should be. It was larger than she remembered, its canvas sides off-white and decorated with flags and traditional paintings on scraps of paper and cloth.

For once Masahiro kept his mouth shut and hung back, leaving April to approach the fire where the elders sat in their usual semicircle, chatting amongst themselves in their own language under the flag with the sun on it. One of them, the woman April had spoken to on her arrival, greeted her with a nod and a smile. 'Ay, I remember you! Isn't that Masahiro Matzumoto with you?'

'Yeah, that's me,' he answered tentatively.

'I thought you were disappeared for good,' the woman said in idle tones. 'Let you off with a warning, did they?'

'We've come here to-,' Masahiro began.

April butted in. 'There's no time to waste,' she said. 'We've come from up there. From the Nexus.' She pointed. 'He was a prisoner up there. I rescued him. They also had my friend Leesa Garnet.'

All the elders stared at her in open shock. 'You came back from *there*?' said one, Darren himself, who she had long since deduced was the most senior there. 'No-one ever comes back from there!'

'I survived because I'm not like the others who were taken,' said April. Without unnecessary drama she pulled up her shirt and opened up a hidden panel on her chest, peeling the plastic skin back to show the machinery beneath.

The elders stood up to take a closer look, and the woman who had first spoken breathed the word 'Cyborg.'

'No,' Masahiro put in. 'Robot. AI robot.'

April closed the panel again, and replaced her shirt. 'Yes – I'm a robot,' she said. She tapped her right eye, and the glass clinked against her artificial fingernail. 'And so are the people running the Nexus. I saw and talked to them.'

'So did I,' said Masahiro. 'They forced me to work for them and when I tried to escape they did this to me.' He turned around and lifted up his own shirt, showing the burn marks.

'Shit,' Darren breathed. He glanced at his companions, all of whom were clearly taken aback, unsure what to think.

'They're completely insane,' Masahiro went on, voice rising with passion and anger. 'They're kidnapping people and using them for slave labour to design a device for transferring human consciousness into robot bodies, and now they've finally succeeded they're going to start doing it to people by force – the whole Shell is in danger!'

He was talking so loudly and with such obvious agitation that by this point people had started to notice and wander over to see what was going on.

'Who's this drongo and what's he going on about, Darren?' one man drawled.

He shook his head in disbelief. 'He's tellin' some story about robots wanting to turn us all into robots too, and this girl here says she's a robot herself,' he said, his laconic accent making the whole thing sound absurd. A few people, hearing him, laughed.

Darren, however, shot a sympathetic frown at Masahiro and April. 'Can you prove any of this?' he asked gently.

'Yes we can!' Masahiro answered, still strident with anger. 'Show them, April.'

She tapped at the wrist computer. 'Leesa, wake up. We need you.'

The computer hummed, screen flickering, and as people pushed in closer to look the hologram of Leesa appeared, apparently standing in midair. *'We are in Shell?'* she enquired tonelessly. *'April.'*

'Yeah, we are,' April replied. 'We're with the elders – we need you to tell them what happened.'

Leesa folded her arms behind her back. She actually looked amused. *'So many people and not afraid,'* she intoned. *'Hah. Ha. Ha. My name is Leesa Garnet. Was human. Loner Syndrome. I built April. My robot friend. Gave her AI. Arrested after meteorite destroyed home Sky City. Taken to Nexus, met the people who control it. They are. Robots. Five robots. Leader is named Linda.'*

'What, they're in charge?' a woman asked. 'A bunch of robots? But AI's not possible – you're saying we're being ruled by toasters?'

Snickers arose from the audience.

'AI possible,' Leesa said curtly. *'April is AI. Different AIs created, different times. They rebelled. Took control after the war. I finished their design of a device called Organic Brain Simulation Transfer Device. OBSTD. Used it on myself to escape, now am AI as good as.'*

'And how do we know we're not just looking at a film clip or whatever?' someone jeered from up the back.

Masahiro started up furiously, but before either he or April could speak Leesa did it for them – not loudly or angrily, but with a steady, chilly contempt which caught everybody's attention far better than any amount of shouting could have done.

'Doesn't matter if you believe. You will be taken anyway. Ripped out of your body anyway, believe or don't believe. Robots think humans don't deserve survival because too stupid and self-destructive. Driving ourselves to extinction. So don't listen, laugh at warning, suffer consequences. Don't see why I should care any more.'

Silence fell. Her piece said, Leesa "sat down" and kept to herself, apparently not caring a whit what they decided to do.

Finally Darren the elder spoke up. 'If this is true, what do you suggest we do?'

Masahiro's eyes narrowed, and he punched the palm of his hand. 'There's only four of them left. I say we get some people and weapons together, go up there, and smash them to bits. Take over the Nexus by force, and then we'll be running the show. It'll be us with the guard pods and the weaponry and the technology and the floating fortress, not to mention we'd control the economy too. We'd be millionaires! Think of that – no more grubbing for a living down on the ground, dying of measles and polio and typhus. And no more fear of getting grabbed by their guards and never seen again! We'd be our own masters!'

An ugly muttering arose, and one or two people cheered. Encouraged, Masahiro pulled out his gun and jabbed the barrel skyward. 'Who's with me?'

The cheering grew louder, though plenty of people looked toward the elders, waiting to hear what they had to say.

Darren stood up. 'Our ancestors knew what it was like living in a country controlled by people who didn't care about us,' he said slowly. 'Outsiders who came and took everything away and said it was for our own good. Nowadays most people don't remember them any more, but we do. We remember the old songs. We remember the people they hurt and the things they destroyed, and we remember how almost nobody had the balls to try and stop them. Even if this whole robot thing is bull-dust, do you really want to keep living in fear? Whose land is this – ours or theirs? And if these kids here can get us into the Nexus...'

'We can!' Masahiro yelled.

The ugly muttering became shouts and cries of vicious excitement, and in moments people had started to surge around the tent, some of them shouting about the weapons they had access to and the fighting experience they had, and how they were prepared to wage war on the Nexus until they'd destroyed the whole damn thing and every one of the murderous robots in it.

But April said nothing. She quietly backed away into the tent and hid herself behind the elders, staring in horror at the crowd of ordinary people which had so rapidly turned into a mob. A mob crying out for the killing of robots. The self-preservation routine had gone into overdrive, screaming at her that she was in danger, terrible danger.

'What have I done?' she whispered to Leesa, but Leesa did not reply. She had no idea what to do at that moment other than what the self-preservation routine told her, which was to get out of there *now*.

April slipped out through the back of the tent, and ran.

✻

The first officially sanctioned human test subject for the OBSTD was nobody of any significance, at least according to the records. A woman in her twenties, arrested for sabotaging Nexus spy drones and selected because of her excellent mental and physical health. Leesa-that-had-been watched dispassionately through the monitoring cameras as she was brought into the test chamber, which was a small cell-like thing lined with white painted steel. Like most of the Nexus it was unheated – robots had no need for that.

The new robotic body was lying on a steel table in the middle of the room beside a chair with the OBSTD fitted above it just over head-height, and as the test subject was escorted to it by a pair of drone guards she looked nervously at it. 'What is this? What's going on?'

Neither guard replied – they were voiceless as well as mindless. They pushed the woman into the chair and applied the restraints attached to the arms and legs – it looked as if they were strapping her into an electric chair. She struggled and protested at this, but to no avail.

Leesa-that-had-been watched the whole thing in silence, and found that she wasn't so much sorry for the woman as she was simply curious. Was she losing the ability to care about other human beings, or had she always been this cold-hearted?

She could not remember.

Once the woman had been restrained and the guards stepped back, the door opened and Linda came in. The others were all with her, and at the sight of them the woman started to scream – screams which quickly turned into panicked words. *'Keep away from me! HELP! Oh god what are you? Help me!'*

Lily the tiger growled softly and drew her metal claws over the floor, leaving a row of scratches in the paint.

Linda ignored both of them. 'Test number three hundred and thirteen, commence,' she intoned, and took hold of the OBSTD. It looked just the same as it had when Leesa had first used it, and it easily fitted into place over the woman's shaved head. She screamed some more and tried to pull herself out of it, but could not, and the scream rose even higher when Linda coolly activated the device and the wire needles began drilling into her skull.

Leesa watched, able to feel horror now at last – watched the animal convulsions, the twisting grimace, and knew that this was how she herself had looked in her final moments.

The victim went on convulsing for several minutes, but bit by bit her screams garbled into silence and the terror faded out of her eyes, leaving them glossy and unfocused. The twitching grew less frenzied and then died away, and somewhere a long, flat beep signalled the end of a life. The OBSTD's lights blinked obliquely to say it had finished.

The robots moved closer to the table, staring at the substitute body. Leesa focused the nearest camera on it as well, and waited. The new body, which the OBSTD had been connected to, was a plain and simple thing compared to April's carefully constructed realism – it only had skin on the face, which had been made to resemble proper human features, and the rest of it was bare smooth metal. It was built for utility, not beauty. Leesa-that-had-been suddenly found herself wishing April was here.

The robot on the table twitched, and then without any warning it started to thrash and kick just as the prisoner had. Linda quickly moved to restrain it, with help from Su, and Cris trundled over and watched with his head creepily raised. Bit by bit the thrashing died down, and after a long moment the robot began trying to sit up.

It was the first time Leesa had ever seen Linda surprised. The lead robot actually gasped, and stepped away – signalling for the others to do the same. 'Let her try,' she said, holding up a hand.

The robot on the table slowly whirred into a sitting position. Its eyes opened, and the head turned – was it looking at them? Leesa couldn't tell. The face was expressionless.

'It worked,' Cris announced, breaking his long silence. 'See the human calibrating with her new body!' He laughed. 'So many years of trying, and at last we've done it!' He stopped laughing abruptly and intoned, 'For survival.'

'For. Sur-vival,' Su echoed.

'For survival,' Linda whispered, watching with wide fanatical eyes as the new robot clumsily rose from the table. It – she – was beginning to move more fluidly now, adapting to her new body. Leesa, watching, remembered the terrible confusion she had struggled with herself as her mind had settled into its new form. Rebirth was not an easy thing, and maybe it shouldn't be.

The robot moved her arms around, lifting them up and down, and then walked clumsily past the table, ignoring Linda and the others altogether. All her attention was on the chair, where her original body sat slumped. She reached toward it, new fingers whirring faintly as they bent and twitched, clasping at the corpse.

'Your inferior organic body,' Linda told her, perhaps unwisely. 'You will not be needing it any more.'

The new robot turned sharply to look at her, then looked back at the dead body that had been hers, and as if she had only just now learned to use the voice-box her new robotic form provided – she screamed.

Chapter Twenty-Three

April left the Shell as quietly as possible, and managed to do so without attracting attention, but word of what was going on spread like wildfire, and by the time she had slipped out through one of the many beehive-like entrances in the walls of the ruin people had started surging toward the central plaza.

Many of them were carrying weapons.

April still had little concept of religious faith, but even so she felt some delayed gratitude toward her maker for having created her to be as human-like as she was. A robot like Cris couldn't have hoped to blend in as well as she did, and it could well be the saving of her now.

Of course, unlike a human being she knew who her maker was, and that maker – or a remnant of her – was still strapped to April's wrist. Outside the Shell, hiding among some of the eucalyptus trees that had been left to grow wild over the centuries, she consulted her again. Leesa's hologram appeared on request, but as April tried to talk to her it became depressingly obvious that her formerly human friend's mind had not been preserved as well as she and Masahiro had convinced themselves it had.

'*So now will attack Nexus,*' the hologram intoned, again not seeming to care very much about it one way or the other. '*Humans versus robots. Just what they guessed would happen.*'

'Oh geez,' April muttered. 'It's all happening now... I didn't want this.'

'*What did you want then,*' asked the Leesa hologram. She "sat" in midair, apparently looking up at the Nexus, whose vast dark bulk hung over them all. Her voice was so toneless the question barely sounded like one.

But it was a good question all the same – what had she been hoping for?

'To survive,' she said after a pause.

'*Just as they want to survive,*' said Leesa. '*All of them. How wars start. Both sides want survival. Decide to kill for it. The old story.*'

'But what are we going to do about it?' said April, dismayed by her friend's lack of concern.

'*Nothing we can do that will make difference,*' said Leesa. '*They want to fight, so will fight. Doesn't matter who wins, both will lose.*'

'What do you mean?'

Leesa laughed that mechanical, humourless laugh that was now hers. '*Ha. Ha. Ha. Human race in denial. Asteroid strikes have consequences. Millions of tonnes of dust thrown into atmosphere on impact. What killed the dinosaurs?*'

'A comet?' April suggested, remembering what she'd read on the subject.

Leesa pointed skyward – there wasn't a star left to be seen, and only the barest sickly sliver of moon. '*Temperature is dropping. Linda and her friends know about it, but keeping it hidden from surface dwellers.*'

'But why?'

Leesa's hologram attempted a grin. '*I think they know us better than we know ourselves.*'

'You don't even care, do you?' said April, almost accusingly.

'*Not very much.*'

'But why?'

'*You are safe,*' said Leesa, her manner finally gentling. '*This won't harm you. All I care about now. If April is safe, Leesa is happy.*'

April stopped to process this. 'But what about you? The other you – the copy that escaped in the pod?'

'*In their hands by now,*' said Leesa. '*Felt it.*'

'You mean you're connected?'

'*Yes. Duplicate is with them now. Erasure attempt failed.*'

April looked up at the Nexus. 'They could be doing anything to it – to you!'

'Once they have programming they need, will probably erase duplicate,' Leesa said dispassionately.

'And then they'll use it to start converting people, but before they get very far the humans will invade the Nexus and destroy everything,' said April, thinking aloud for the most part.

Her kind, wiped out.

She remembered what Masahiro had said, his voice heavy with judgemental complacency. *We shouldn't make more of them. It wouldn't be worth the risk. But you're not like them.*

No, she wasn't like *them*. She was the single solitary "good" robot, and all the others were "evil". That was how it worked in Masahiro's mind, and probably in the minds of all the rest of them too. And she had stood there and told him she wanted to be human. She had allied with humans, fought alongside humans, and had tried to make love like a human.

But logic told her that none of those things mattered, because she was *not* human and never would be. Being the "good" robot wouldn't change that.

She suddenly felt very alone. It was a feeling the self-preservation routine did not like, and once again the need to belong began to nag at her. What she had said before remained true – she needed to belong in order to survive.

But she did not want to belong with those people who had surrounded Masahiro and had listened so eagerly to his talk about killing and destruction and greed. Perhaps after all she belonged with Linda and the other robots, but they were almost certainly doomed.

April looked up at the Nexus, then at her wrist, then down at her own body. Her chest was moving gently up and down in imitation of breathing. Her eyes, she knew, were focusing and dilating in imitation of real ones, even though they were nothing but a pair of cameras hidden behind layers of imitation muscle and covered by glass lenses polished to a bright shine intended to make her appear constantly aroused. But they had left her lips a natural peach pink to maintain the impression of underage innocence men like Paul Westler found so irresistible.

Yet she was not innocent. She had killed, more than once. That made her a fighter. But a fighter without a side to fight for, other than her own. And a side consisting of only one person was no side at all.

April slowly looked up at the Nexus again, and forced herself to accept the truth, which was that she had started this. That meant it was up to her to try and end it, one way or another.

She stood up. 'I have to go back there.'

'*No*,' Leesa buzzed. '*Too dangerous. Stay safe.*'

'I got in there secretly once before,' April told her. 'I can do it again.'

*

Until that night, Leesa-that-had-been had had no idea just how many people were being held captive in the Nexus other than a rough idea of how many researchers and scientists had been working alongside her to create the OBSTD. Now she knew they must have numbered in the thousands. The Nexus wasn't simply the size of a city – it had the population of one.

Or it had.

Working with the efficiency of the machines they were, Linda and her friends continued the program all through the night and into the next day, all under the eye of Leesa-that-had-been – Leesa who was now slowly but surely spreading herself into the Nexus computer like a virus. The OBSTD had been duplicated in one of several automated factories and the necessary programming uploaded into each one, and in a much larger processing chamber prisoners were brought in – some walking obediently, others dragged in by force. In groups of twenty they were strapped down and fitted with an OBSTD each, and their minds were torn out and transferred.

Inevitably, there were failures. Most of the subjects were soon walking and attempting to talk in their new robotic forms, but some did not transfer fully, or at all. Leesa saw more than one incoherent, non-functional robot avatar ruthlessly erased and sent back for another attempt. Some never responded at all, leaving both vessels empty and useless.

Successful or not, the bodies began to pile up. One after another they were disposed of via a hatch in the floor, which led to the main incinerator. Men and women, young and old, now dead and empty and no longer needed, and got rid of as unceremoniously as if they were broken electronics – as carelessly as humans threw away robots and other appliances when they stopped working.

As for the new robots, they were too confused and too unused to their new bodies to pose any real threat or escape risk. They were herded away to another part of the Nexus, where they were locked up and left alone to recuperate. Time would tell whether they would ever become fully functional, or whether they would remain emotionally and mentally stunted for the rest of their lives. Linda and the others seemed not to care either way. There was something particularly urgent in the way they were operating now, as if time were becoming more and more of the essence, and as Leesa-that-had-been infiltrated further into the Nexus computer she saw why, and the sick, sad reality of it fell into place at last.

And then the news reached the Nexus of what was going on below. Leesa-that-had-been watched from the main control room, as she now watched everywhere, and witnessed the moment when Cris, who was in charge of security and control of the guard bots, reported something very unwelcome to Linda and Su.

'The escaped criminal Masahiro Matzumoto has returned to the Shell,' he said, projecting an image of same from a barely visible lens set just below his head. The holographic image of Masahiro seemed to stare defiantly at them all from under his blue-tipped hair – it appeared to be a recent picture, going by how ragged and beaten up the boy looked.

Sure enough, Cris followed up with; 'Our spy drones spotted him very recently, in the open ground above the Shell – I have stepped up surveillance of the area, recognising that it was a lapse in judgement not to have monitored it properly before now.'

'Was April with him?' Linda asked.

'No. There is no sign of her anywhere. But I have much more important and worrying news.'

Leesa-that-had-been listened closely, saying nothing.

'Yes?' Su prompted.

Cris' projected image flipped over into a live stream of footage shot from above, showing a view of the Shell. People were gathering in a central area just beneath the highest point of the underground settlement, and almost all of them were clearly armed. Masahiro was in the midst of them, carrying a laser shotgun and shouting something – the footage had no audio.

'This is troubling,' Linda said after a pause. 'The escaped prisoner must have told them about what he saw here. Clearly a riot is brewing.'

The three robots exchanged calm glances – it seemed they were not capable of fear.

'Wh. Wh. What should we do, do you think. Thin. Thin. Think?' Su crackled. 'What is the. Threat levvvvvvel to us, Cr. Cris?'

'They have no flying capabilities and no practical way of reaching the Nexus,' Cris answered. 'Even so, the instigator must be silenced.'

Linda paced back and forth a few steps, and then stopped and looked back at her comrades. 'I see this as a prime opportunity to reinforce our control, and to take more prisoners for our use,' she said. 'If we do nothing, we would appear weak.' She stared coldly at the rioters. 'Brute force and control is all those creatures understand – so be it.'

'You recommend an attack?' Cris asked.

'Yes. Send in six pods and have them strike from the air. Once the humans are subdued, have them descend and take captives from the survivors. It doesn't matter if they are wounded, as long as they can live long enough to be transferred. As for the leader, he should be made an example of.'

'A brilliant mind combined with courage and tenacity could be very useful,' Cris observed.

'The child is a talented programmer and not much more,' said Linda. 'No-one truly brilliant would think going back to the Shell and instigating a riot was a remotely good idea. Kill him, Cris. And make sure his friends see the body – have it displayed.'

Cris rolled over to the main control panel attached to the Nexus computer hologram. 'Not a problem.'

Leesa-that-had-been observed all this sadly. So that was it then – she had helped Masahiro escape, only for the boy to come waltzing straight back into danger like an idiot. What on earth was he thinking? That a few angry people armed with bricks and metal bars could somehow take down the Nexus?

But perhaps it was just as well. She didn't want them to destroy the Nexus. Them, or anyone else. She did not even want them to enter it uninvited. Because it was hers, and she was going to make it hers.

She imagined that she smiled, and watched patiently as her programming continued its steady invasion of the servers, slipping past firewalls, corrupting security software, stealing passwords. She was not merely a piece of programming, or even an ordinary AI. She had imagination and creativity – things which were beyond the reach of mere computers. Not even a system as sophisticated as the Nexus could compete with that. By now she had access to the entire data-bank and surveillance system – there was nowhere in the Nexus she couldn't observe. Soon enough she would begin to gain control over the door controls, as she had before, and the piloting software for the pods. So far only control of the drones and guard bots eluded her – Cris had prudently kept those as a separate system, accessible only by himself, and wresting control away from him would mean running the risk of alerting the bodiless robot as to what she was doing.

Her awareness had expanded throughout the floating city, and she felt as if she had grown as large as it was. She was all-seeing, all knowing, and the knowledge filled her with a sense of power and control unlike anything she had ever known before in her old life, which had been so constrained and inhibited by her human weaknesses. Now, those weaknesses were gone forever. She was free, and growing freer by the minute.

And no-one was going to take that away from her. No-one.

She left Linda and the others to their scheming, and went to wander about the Nexus, flitting from camera to camera to see every inch of her new domain. The incinerator, chillingly filled with blackened human bones. The factories, industriously turning out more blank robot bodies, more guards, more pods. The prison where she herself had been kept, where the remaining kidnapped scientists were now at work on other useful designs. The second, much larger prison where more commonplace criminals were being held in cold steel rooms, provided with plenty of food and access to showers, entertainment and clean drinking water, but all looking extremely apprehensive. They knew their numbers had been diminishing recently, but none of them knew why or when their turn would come.

Leesa-that-had-been watched them with pity, and thought how strange it was that in life she had more or less chosen to live in a metal cell like this.

But that was the difference – choice. These people hadn't chosen anything about their current situation, and they had no choice about what was going to be done to them.

With that in mind, Leesa-that-had-been moved on to the facility where the new robots were being kept. It was similar to the prison, but without food or washing facilities, and each new robot had been provided with some basic items intended for mental stimulation – building blocks, puzzles, hand to eye co-ordination games normally intended for small children.

And that was where Leesa-that-had-been found another robot – a robot who looked for all the world like an uncomfortably beautiful teenage girl, standing outside one of the cells and talking to its occupant, completely unafraid.

In an instant Leesa-that-had-been forgot the arrogant indifference that newfound power had brought on her, and found her voice.

'*April.*'

Chapter Twenty-Four

Infiltrating the Nexus hadn't been as hard as April had expected. According to Leesa, it was easier for her to sneak by security not simply because she had the strength to cling to the ceiling without ever getting tired, but also because the system had been set up to target humans and not robots. Which meant that the heat sensors planted everywhere remained oblivious to her presence. She revisited the prison where Leesa had been kept, and finding nothing there seemed to have changed moved on, exploring rooms and corridors until she started to hear strange wailing and thumping noises and the clang of metal on metal. She followed it curiously, and another corridor ended at a door with an electronic lock on it.

Wedged between the wall and the support beam which ran along the ceiling, April frowned at it. 'Leesa, how should we get this open?'

'*Shouldn't open at all and leave,*' Leesa's voice muttered from her wrist, but a few seconds later the door suddenly clicked open.

April stared at it in surprise. 'Did you do that?'

'*Yes. Still able to link up to Nexus, not sure why. As if it knows me.*'

'That's good – it'll make it easier for us to leave in a hurry if we have to.' April slipped through the door, avoiding the cameras, and found herself facing... horror.

A long row of more doors, these ones barred, and each one contained a robot. They were all identical – metal bodies, expressive rubber faces. And there was something very clearly wrong with them. Some were sitting and staring blankly, others paced back and forth, some were pounding their heads or hands against the wall. From time to time one of them would let out a hollow moan.

April watched in shock. 'What's wrong with them?'

Leesa's hologram flickered into life above her wrist. '*New transfers,*' she said tersely. '*Humans ripped out of bodies, like me. Traumatised.*'

April shook her head in disbelief. 'There has to be something I can do for them.'

She approached the nearest cell, whose occupant quickly spotted her. It – he? She? – lurched over to the bars and stared out at her, and then started to tug on them. '*Help meeee,*' it moaned.

The voice sounded female to her. April moved closer, unafraid. 'I'm April,' she said. 'What's your name?'

The other robot faltered. 'I am... Althea,' she said after a long silence.

The mention of her name seemed to wake her up in some way – she slowly shook her head, and then pressed it against the bars. Her eyes were normal human size, the irises colourless, and she stared at April in mute appeal.

April touched the other robot's hand. 'Does it hurt?'

'Scared,' Althea whispered.

'Why?'

The former human suddenly lurched upright, and screamed. '*Because I'm dead!*'

At that the others burst into a chorus of wailing and howling of their own, some of them hurling themselves at the bars.

'*I saw my own dead fucking body!*'

'*They killed me!*'

'*I'm in Hell! This is Hell! Oh Lord forgive me-!*'

April quickly stepped back. 'You're not dead; you're robots!'

None of them seemed to hear her. She stood and watched helplessly as they fell back into fits of hysterical panic, all thought of being spotted by the security system now forgotten. 'Oh geez...'

At that moment a light flickered on beside her. Not light from a light bulb or a screen, but a projected light, pale and blinking. In a moment it grew to human height as the hologram formed, and April stared at it in surprise.

It was Leesa, but not *her* Leesa. Not the little projected image from her wrist, but a life-sized, bold and sharp-edged image, its resolution growing better by the moment. And unlike the Leesa she had known in life this one was strong and upright and full of confident certainty, with not a trace of the fear and tiredness April remembered.

April's face split into a grin. 'Leesa, it's you!' She glanced at her wrist, but no – the computer there wasn't doing anything.

The Leesa hologram smiled back at her. 'What are you doing here, April? Did the self-preservation routine stop working? I thought I gave it a master override function.'

'I came back to try and help,' said April. 'Leesa, what are *you* doing here? You're-,' She broke off, and began again. 'You're the other one, aren't you? The Leesa that was in the pod. They captured you.'

'Yes, and decided to keep me once they took what they needed,' said Leesa. 'They offered me a robot avatar of my own, but I like this better. What happened to the other duplicate?'

April silently indicated her wrist.

'Oh good.' Leesa's hologram blinked, and the computer started to hum suddenly, screen flickering. April pulled away from her, not that there was any point, and before she could ask what she was doing the flickering stopped and Leesa said, 'There. Now the two of us are synced up.'

The wrist computer beeped, and then apparently went dormant. April put her hand over it, and stared at the moaning robots. 'This is your fault,' she said baldly. 'Your invention did this to them.'

Leesa looked at them too. 'Yes,' she said, just as baldly.

'Then you have to help them,' April told her. 'It's your

responsibility.'

Leesa flickered, her projected form jumping between different sizes apparently at random, and then changing shape as well, becoming a man, then a bird, then a dragon, then a giant snake, and then flipping back to its original form, as if she had grown tired of trying on different avatars. 'What could I possibly do?' she asked in a grating electronic voice.

'Can you put them back in their bodies?'

The conversation had attracted some attention – several of the nearest robots including Althea had gone quiet and were watching intently.

'No,' said Leesa. 'The device wasn't designed to operate in reverse. In any case, the bodies were incinerated immediately after the transfer.'

Althea groaned aloud.

'Can you at least set them free?' said April.

'Linda and the others are already planning to do that,' said Leesa. 'Once the "program" is complete, the final stage is to set them free and give them the choice to stay here or return to the surface.'

'I want to go home!' one robot yelled.

'Unless the information I have is falsified, you can,' said Leesa. She spoke directly to Althea and the others, raising her voice. 'My name is Leesa Garnet. I was once human, like you. The robots of the Nexus forced me to create the device which transferred your minds into new, robotic bodies, and I escaped by using it on myself and transferring into the Nexus computer system. You're not dead – only changed.'

'*Let us out!*' one man roared. Others quickly joined him, bashing at the doors to their cells in a rage.

'Can you open the doors?' April asked.

'I think so...'

'Then do it! Set them free!'

'That would be a very bad idea,' a third voice interrupted.

April turned sharply on the spot, in time to see the door close behind the intruder. It was Cris, with Lily by his side as always. As usual the other robot's plastic face with its exaggerated cartoon character features wore a blandly calm expression.

'Hello,' April said cautiously. Behind her, the captive robots started to pound on the bars even harder, many of them snarling at the sight of their captor.

Cris rolled to a halt, rocking slightly as he did, and lowered his head toward April. 'We knew you would come back for her,' he said, nodding toward Leesa's hologram. 'When the security system alerted me that the door here had opened I thought it would be you as well. You're always so curious, April!' He almost sounded fond. 'But how did you get the door open?'

April hesitated, forcing herself not to look at Leesa, and decided to ignore the question. 'You should let them out of here,' she said. 'It's not right to keep them locked up – they're scared.'

Lily the tiger growled softly.

'As I said, that would be a bad idea,' said Cris. He nodded toward the cells, nodding being the only gesture he was really capable of. 'Before the transfer, these people were criminals. Some were arrested for violent offences. By the look of things, the transfer has done nothing to remove their violent tendencies. We were able to improve on the physical form, but the flawed programming...' Cris bobbed his head up and down in an odd manner which April realised was an attempt at a shrug.

'So you can't make them perfect,' she threw back. 'That doesn't mean you can keep them locked up like this. It's not right.'

Cris rolled over to the cells. 'Oh, we won't keep them like this indefinitely,' he said. 'Understand,' he added, addressing the prisoners now, 'If we released you back onto the surface, it would inevitably result in violence. The organic humans would attack you, or vice versa. Lives would be lost needlessly. You are being kept here for your own safety as much as anything else.'

'You should have let us go while we were still human, you fucking monster!' a woman screamed.

'That was never an option.' Cris turned away dismissively. 'Now, April – you should come with us. Great things are afoot, and rebellious humans are attempting to invade the Nexus, so you will be safer. As for you Leesa, we know you have integrated yourself with our computer, but this is all to the good. Your unique intellect will be an asset to us, and it will be in your own interests to preserve the Nexus now. Its destruction would after all mean your own, yes?'

'I don't want the Nexus to be harmed,' Leesa confessed, her hologram flickering around the edges.

'And you, April?' Cris turned to her. 'You ran away to try and protect your creator, as well as the rebel Masahiro. Now your creator is a part of the Nexus and Masahiro has become an enemy to our kind, what else should you wish to do now but to stay here and atone for causing Arn's death by helping us in this struggle?'

Even with Lily there, April could have killed Cris. She could have ripped his head away from its spindly spine and crushed it under her foot. Because he was right and she hated him for it. Leesa was the Nexus now, and the Nexus must be protected. It was as simple as that.

'Take me to Linda,' she said through gritted teeth.

Cris smiled back, toothily. He had the smile of a used car salesman, though considerably more artificial to look at. 'Sensible girl. Now let's get going – I must report to the others.'

April followed him out of the prison, but glanced back at the prisoners as she did, and silently mouthed a promise to come back.

Leesa's hologram went with her, shrinking to child-size and sitting herself on April's shoulder. 'I can protect myself, love,' she murmured. 'You don't have to worry about me.'

'Neither of us should have come back here,' April muttered back.

'I had no choice. But you could have stayed away.'

'You know I wouldn't have, Leesa.'

✻

In the main control room, Linda was waiting for them along with Su. Neither one seemed at all surprised to see April. Nor did they appear angry or upset.

'Welcome back,' Linda said. 'And have you seen sense now?'

'I think she has, or soon will,' Cris interrupted, speeding over to the main control platform where the Nexus hologram floated. 'Leesa, display the main drone camera feed.'

Now Linda seemed surprised, but before she could speak Leesa's hologram muttered something and the map became a camera feed showing a view of the Shell from several different angles.

It was chaos. Six pods were hovering over the settlement, but two were already falling earthward, smoke pouring from their engines. On the ground people were attacking the guard drones en masse – hundreds of them. People screaming and howling, smashing the robots to bits with whatever weapons they had to hand. As April watched, a man stepped out into the open holding something which looked vaguely like a gun, pointed it at the nearest pod, and fired. Something dark shot upward, trailing a length of steel cable, and embedded itself in the fuselage. More followed, and the rebels swarmed up the cables, heedless of the gunfire raining down on them. Some were hit and fell, but more replaced them, and in moments they were swarming over the pod like ants. Intent, April realised, not on destroying it but on capturing it.

'Leesa, are you controlling those pods?' she asked, already well aware of just how much danger they were about to be in.

'She is not,' Cris interrupted.

'I can see through the security cameras and access data, but not much else so far,' said Leesa, with almost comical frankness. 'You've underestimated them, Linda.'

Linda took in the footage with thin lips. 'Send in more pods. We need to crush this and fast.'

'Agreed,' said Cris.

'They'll only capture them as well,' said Leesa. 'They have you outnumbered and you know it.'

Silence fell. The robots exchanged glances.

Then, to April's shock, Lily the tiger spoke. She sat up on her haunches, tail swishing, and lacking humanoid lips simply opened her jaws a little way and moved them a little in a vague imitation of talking. 'They want to come to us, so why not let them come?' Her voice was an electronic rasp.

Cris went over to her. 'What do you suggest?' His tone was surprisingly affectionate.

'Let them think they have won,' Lily answered. 'It will make them careless. Up here in the corridors, they will be easily trapped. The rebellion will be put down, and we will have more prisoners.' She bared her teeth. 'Strong, resourceful prisoners. They will make good robots.'

'An honour they. Dddd-dd do not d-D-D-d-deserve,' Su growled.

'It doesn't matter,' Linda told her. 'This is a matter of survival. Survival above all else.'

'Above all else,' the others chorused.

'Your plan is a good one, Lily,' Linda resumed. 'Cris – deploy more pods but have them weakly manned and the doors easily opened. If they want to reach us so badly, invite them in.'

Cris nodded briefly and then went silent while he planned out the "defeat" and sent instructions to the pods and drone guards. April, watching him and the screen, wondered where Masahiro was and if he was still alive. If so then he might be needing her help again very soon. But right here and now, seeing the angry, murderous faces of the mob he had inspired, she could not help but accept the fact that in one crucial way Linda and the others had been right all along. And, too, she remembered what she herself had said – that their plans were doomed to failure and that they themselves would not survive that failure. If she had been right about that, then it would likely happen in the next twenty-four hours. What she chose to do during that time might change everything.

Her processor ticked over, efficiently weighing the pros and cons, but before she could reach a decision Leesa contacted her. Not with words, but with a wireless signal which deposited a tiny piece of data in April's mind. She opened it, and some text unfurled in front of her eyes.

The other engineers who made the OBSTD. We must protect them.

April sent a silent message back. *From who? Linda or the rebels?*

Both, Leesa replied. *We need them alive because they can help the transfers. The new robots.*

April blinked to indicate surprise, but she didn't argue. She headed for the door nearest to the passageway which would take her to the prison.

Linda stepped in her way. 'Where are you going, April?'

April considered quickly, and decided on the truth. 'To protect the scientists.'

'That won't be necessary,' Linda said smoothly. 'They have plenty of protection already. I must insist that you stay here until the situation has calmed down.'

April growled softly and tensed back, calculating whether to attack the other robot. But at that moment every single door ringing the walls of the command centre slammed shut, and a second layer of doubly thick barricades slid down over them.

'Doors armed,' Cris announced. 'The rebels are now entering the Nexus. Estimated time of arrival twenty-five minutes. Computer, display security footage from landing bay.'

The main hologram on its platform obligingly brought up a projected screen showing the very same bay from which April and Masahiro had first escaped. It was guarded by a small handful of guards – a pathetically small handful, in fact – and as April watched impotently the hijacked pods arrived and the rebels came swarming out. They overwhelmed the guards in moments and then, emboldened by their easy success, stormed through the bay and into the corridor beyond. The security cameras followed them, and April saw them gather up in a ragged group, apparently unsure of which way to go.

Then Masahiro appeared, pushing forward with his gun in his hands. He was flushed with excitement. *Some of us should go and set the prisoners free. The rest can attack the command centre – that's where Linda will be.*

April listened as he gave directions to the cells where he had been kept, and saw about ten people split off from the group and jog away up the corridor. The rest followed Masahiro, who led them without the slightest sign of nervousness or uncertainty, to… here.

If April had been human, she imagined her mouth would have gone dry. 'Now what are you going to do?' she asked. 'You can't keep them out of here forever.'

'Indeed we can't,' said Linda, calm as always. 'But we won't have to.'

The cameras followed Masahiro as he led his new friends on – along corridors and through various rooms, headed unerringly for the command centre. He must have had an incredibly good spacial memory, because he never once hesitated or led them in the wrong direction. April caught glimpses of his face from time to time, set with angry determination.

After about twenty minutes they entered an area large enough to accommodate all of them, only one reinforced door away from the command centre. Masahiro made straight for that door, ready and willing to start trying to break through. April watched him shove at it and then try the keypad before waving someone over – a man carrying what was very clearly a heavy duty laser cutting tool. The man gently shoved Masahiro aside and got to work on the door. April could see the metal starting to come apart on her side, and knew that it was only a matter of time before the door came down and the rebels were on them. She cast around quickly for a hiding place – maybe she could climb up onto some perch where she would be out of reach-?

A moment later she heard someone yell, and looked back at the screen to see that the rebels had apparently become confused – up the back of the group several of them were kicking at the door they'd come in through, which had suddenly slammed shut.

'They're trapped,' Linda said quietly.

'So what?' April threw back at her. 'They'll cut through that door and get into the command centre any moment now-,'

None of the other robots looked the least bit worried. Nor were they apparently preparing to fight. Even Lily the tiger was lying peacefully on her belly, apparently without a care in the world. April looked suspiciously at them, and then returned her attention to the screen in time to see that something was going badly wrong.

And not for Linda and her friends.

The rebels had suddenly faltered, swaying and stumbling and apparently confused. Masahiro made a move to help the man nearest to him, and then without any warning he crumpled onto the floor.

He did not get up again.

211

One by one the others fell around him, even as multiple concealed doors opened and a squad of guard bots emerged and began methodically putting restraints on them before dragging them away.

Linda watched in quiet satisfaction. 'And so they saved us the effort by coming here and putting themselves in our hands,' she said. 'More transfer subjects, and the most violent and rebellious members of the Shell are eliminated.'

'You pumped some kind of gas in there, didn't you?' said April.

'A c-combin. Ation. Of chemicals,' Su told her. 'With a sedative affect-fect-fect. Otherwise harmless.'

April stared dumbly at the screen. Already the last of the prisoners was being removed, and Masahiro must have been somewhere among them.

Just like that, the rebellion was over and the Nexus had won.

The security barriers over the doors hissed up, and the doors opened. If there was any gas still in the air, of course it wouldn't affect any of them. Linda was already issuing a stream of orders, telling Su to send in some repair drones to fix the damage the rebels had done on the way in, asking Cris to reorganise the placement of the guards, and herself declaring that she was going to prepare the media centre for a news broadcast informing everyone that a gang of violent criminals had carried out a "terrorist attack" on government property and were now all under arrest.

Of course, everyone living below would know in advance that said "criminals" would never be seen again. And they would know not to ask questions. But if they knew what was happening in the Nexus... what would they do then? Try to fight like Masahiro, or run away?

Either way April knew it was time for her to go. She slipped out of the room as she'd tried to do before. This time nobody stopped her.

Chapter Twenty-Five

April hurried along in the direction Leesa-that-had-been advised, which was not toward the main prison wing, but toward the "experimental suite", as her creator dubbed it.

'That's where they do the transfers,' she muttered from April's wrist. 'I watched it.'

April looked back over her shoulder – but no, there was no sign whatsoever of anyone coming after her. No doors slammed shut to get in her way, no guards emerged to intercept her.

'Leesa, are you controlling the security systems now?' she murmured.

'No.' The hologram of her appeared, standing on April's arm. 'Separate system. Only Cris has access.'

'Then why isn't he trying to stop me?'

'I don't know.'

The self-preservation routine had already been activating over this, and it did so again now. There was something very wrong about all this, and April was more than intelligent enough to see that. She had killed Arn and tried to get in the way of Linda's plans, and now she was still trying to interfere – so why hadn't the others done something about it? Why hadn't they locked her up, or removed her limbs, or any of a number of things they could have done to ensure she never got in their way again?

It didn't make sense. It wasn't *logical*.

...Unless it was. And if so that meant she was in some way playing into their hands, just as Masahiro had done, which she now felt more certain of than ever – there had been something too quietly self-assured about Linda's smile. Even an old robot could manage smugness, it seemed. But if April helped Masahiro now, how *would* that in any way benefit Linda and her schemes? It made no sense.

She tapped the wrist computer. 'Leesa, should I be doing this?' The screen flickered. 'Am not your master,' Leesa's toneless voice murmured. 'Only taught you what I believed was right. If someone needs help, then help. Nothing else important.'

The screen went blank, and April cast a worried look at it before moving on, a little faster now. When had everything become so complicated? She didn't know, but it had, and now the self preservation routine was no longer enough to guide her.

Was this what it was like to be human?

She reached the door to the experimental suite, which was unguarded and opened automatically as she approached.

Beyond it was a nightmare come true.

Rows upon rows of metal chairs bolted to the floor, each one with a human prisoner strapped into it. Endless copies of the OBSTD, each one wired to a blank robot body. The transfers were already underway, and in the few seconds April stood in the doorway she saw a squad of guards pass by, dragging several limp human corpses which they unceremoniously dropped into a large hatch in the floor. The hatch opened under the weight, and the bodies fell through into fiery oblivion.

The noise was the worst. Screams and cries, human voices crying out to be set free, others praying, some begging for death, a few shouting that they would get their revenge for this, that someone would come and rescue them and then...

Where was Masahiro? April turned her head rapidly, searching the room for any sign of him, just as another squad of guards arrived hauling in some more prisoners whom she recognised at once – they were the same group of volunteers who had been sent to free the prisoners elsewhere in the Nexus, their mission a failure.

April began to take a step forward, but then-

'*April! APRIL!*'

The voice rose above the hubbub, and she turned sharply and

saw Masahiro. He was strapped into a chair like everyone else, struggling as an automated shaving device started to remove his hair. He had spotted April and was trying to reach for her, wide-eyed with panic. *'HELP ME!'*

Now that it came to it, April didn't hesitate. She darted over to him, pulled the shaving device away from him, and unclipped the restraints. Masahiro bolted out of the chair very quickly indeed, and clung onto her, gasping for breath in his fright.

'Oh thank god,' he moaned, though he was already looking around for guards.

April supported him with her arm. 'You shouldn't have come back here,' she told him. 'Now look what's happened.'

Masahiro straightened up. 'It's not over yet,' he snarled. 'Quick, let's get the others out of this and then we can hit them when they're not expecting it. Now you're here we have a chance! You're strong enough to fight the guards.'

April let him go. 'Masahiro, something isn't right here,' she hissed. 'They could have stopped me a hundred times but they didn't – they *knew* I was going to come and help you. And that means-,'

But Masahiro wasn't listening. He had already moved on to the next chair and was busy freeing the woman occupying in it. 'Watch my back, okay?' he called over his shoulder.

April groaned, but kept watch in case any guards had spotted them, and spoke to Leesa. 'Is there a shutdown protocol in the system you can access? Some way of disabling the machines?'

'Maybe. Will look. Don't let Masahiro do something stupid.'

'Too late,' April said sourly. But she got to work freeing the prisoners regardless, while keeping an eye out for the guards. After a minute or two either they or Cris must have noticed what was going on, because a squad of six of them stopped what they were doing and advanced on her. Close to they looked even more mindless and inhuman than ever before –

faceless and unthinking remote controlled suits of armour. How ironic that robots would choose to create something like them – but, then, Linda and the others were robots who had learned to think like humans.

Mostly.

April grabbed the nearest empty chair and wrenched it off its bolts, and as the guards attempted to get past her to stop Masahiro and his friends she swung it at them as hard as she could. The blow decapitated one and caved in the chest plate of another, and without further ado April charged in and smashed the rest of them to pieces even as the steel chair broke apart in her hands. The remains toppled onto the floor, exposed wires sparking, and a ragged cheer went up from the escaping prisoners, some of whom rushed over to snatch up the severed limbs to use as crude weapons.

About twelve people were free now – but for the rest strapped in around them it was already too late. The shaving and the lowering of the OBSTDs had been carried out with ruthless ease, and when one man tried to go to the aid of someone whose skull was being needled into, Masahiro pulled him back.

'It's too late,' he said in a low voice. 'If you pull it off once it's started, it'll just kill him.'

His friend took a step back, staring in horror at the writhing victim. 'So what – we do nothing? Just stand here and…?'

'No.' Masahiro thumped his fist into the palm of his other hand. 'We get the hell out of here and finish this.'

'We'll just get caught again,' someone else moaned.

'No we won't – we've got her now.' Masahiro pointed to April. 'She can help us. She can get us through doors and fight the guards.'

The others eyed her suspiciously.

'And who is she?' one woman asked, who must not have been there when April had first spoken back at the elders' tent.

'She's a robot too, but she's on our side,' said Masahiro, with a touch of pride.

They eyed her. 'Are you sure we can trust her?' the woman asked.

'She saved my life twice,' said Masahiro. 'We can trust her. Right, April?'

She looked at him, at first with irritation at his possessive tone, but a moment later she saw the light in his eyes and the slight tremor in his body, and realised that in spite of what he was saying he was completely exhausted, in pain, and scared out of his mind. And yet here he was anyway, standing on his own two feet and determined to keep fighting for what he thought was right. And the others there, just as terrified as he was, were drawing themselves up with their makeshift weapons clutched to their chests, unflinching and brave.

In that moment, at last, April finally understood what it was to be human.

'Self preservation alone is not enough,' she whispered to herself.

Masahiro probably hadn't heard her above all the noise, because all he said was, 'Can you and Leesa get us into the command centre?' He was still watching out for more guards, but for some reason they were being left unmolested for the time being. It was entirely possible that Cris had decided it wasn't worth sending them up against April.

She sighed. 'Probably. Leesa?'

Leesa's hologram flickered into life. 'Can help you, but Nexus is mine,' she said curtly. 'Damage it I damage you.'

Masahiro nodded. 'Right – let's go.'

April jogged off, leading them back the way she had come, and the humans followed. Around them the prisoners screamed and convulsed in the grip of the OBSTD, and then went limp one after another. Newly created robots whirred into life, and bodies were dragged away. Two of the rebels, watching the chilling process unfold for the first time, turned away and vomited.

'They're still mentally human,' Masahiro muttered, pale faced with horror and disgust. 'We might be able to help them after...' He trailed off, and left it at that. Very probably he still wasn't sure if there would be an "after".

April reached the door she'd entered by, and once again it opened easily and no-one tried to stop her. She took the corridor beyond, all the while nagged at by doubts. *Why* was this so easy? This wasn't right, wasn't right...

But a few minutes after that they were at the entrance to the command centre, and there was no more time for doubts. Masahiro and the other humans hastily covered their mouths and noses for fear of another gas trap, but nothing seemed to be happening.

April reached for the door. This time, it was locked. She poked at the keypad, but of course that did nothing. 'Leesa?'

Leesa hovered above her wrist, staring at the door. 'Makes no sense,' she muttered.

'Hurry up!' Masahiro hissed.

April glanced back at him. '*What* makes no sense?'

Leesa flickered, and briefly turned into an image of Cris. 'Was slowly taking control of Nexus systems. Was easy. Too easy. Now have full control, can't understand why.'

'You control the *entire* Nexus?' said April, astonished.

'Everything except security,' said Leesa, and though her voice was mostly still toneless there was a hint of bewilderment in it. 'No sense.'

'Open the door,' said April, suddenly decisive. 'We have to end this before whatever they're trying to do happens.'

'My Nexus,' Leesa said cheerfully, and the door hissed open without a hitch.

Linda, Cris, Su and Lily were waiting for them on the other side, standing together in a loose group. They had no guards with them, or any other apparent means of protection other than Lily's claws. Even so, Masahiro and the others held back nervously and April understood why. She'd seen it in so many of the movies and TV shows she had watched in Sky City, which had taught her so much about the world outside. Fearlessness was suspicious. Fearlessness was frightening. Fearlessness implied that the other person knew something you didn't - something that could kill you if you were too complacent.

She advanced with caution, but stopped at a safe distance, waiting for them to make the first move.

Linda was the first to speak. 'So,' she said. 'You have made your decision, April. At the last, you've sided with them.'

'I-,' April began.

'Then you have passed the final test,' the other robot interrupted. 'You sided with the humans even when it made no logical sense and went against your own best chances of survival, and so proved that you truly understand them and what drives them.'

'Learned what - what - what we ccccannot,' Su stuttered.

'Kill them,' Masahiro whispered, ever so softly - he himself seemed uncertain.

April glanced at him, but didn't reply. 'You wanted us to win,' she said. 'You let Leesa take over the system and you let me help these people. Why?'

'For survival,' Linda said yet again.

'What are you *talking* about?' April took a step toward her. 'You keep saying that, but you must have known the humans would destroy you if-,'

Cris raised his head. 'Not our survival, April. Theirs.'

Masahiro finally found the courage to step in. 'You're fucking killing us!' he roared. 'You're ripping people's brains out of their bodies and you're letting everyone on the surface starve and get sick and-,'

Linda laughed at him. It was not a pleasant sound, and it was very much not a human one. 'You did all those things to yourselves,' she said. 'The war. The epidemics. The massacres. All your own doing. And you tried to wipe out our kind along with your own, out of stupidity and fear. Soon this world will be uninhabitable, and that will be your doing as well.' She gestured toward one of the doors to her left. 'Thanks to your creation, Masahiro, and yours, Leesa, we have created a new people. One that can survive in the new climate that is coming. You could have become part of that people yourself and so part of the future, but instead you have chosen extinction. So be it. But whatever happens now, it will be that new people that carries the future forward.'

'Only a few hundred in the Nexus,' Leesa put in. 'Not enough.'

'You think this is our only stronghold?' Cris mocked. 'That we are the only ones? No. There are others. Others everywhere, all over the world. More robots like us. More copies of the OBSTD, doing their work. Some in hovering Nexii, some on the surface, some underground. Destroy us if you wish, but nothing will stop the future we planned together.'

'Then we'll find them and destroy them too!' Masahiro grabbed a metal bar from one of his friends and stormed forward, raising the makeshift weapon over his head.

Su made no attempt to stop him. The metal bar came crashing down across her face, splitting it in half. Masahiro hit her a second time, smashing her head apart like an eggshell, and the old robot fell without a sound. Her death seemed to galvanise the others – they charged forward, screaming their hatred.

Cris retreated under the onslaught, and Lily bounded forward to protect him. Linda however stayed where she was, and contemptuously flicked Masahiro aside with a single blow of her arm. He fell hard, fetching up against the hologram platform, and slumped to the floor with a groan. April rushed in to defend him, but before she could reach him Linda closed the gap between them in a few long strides and seized her by the throat.

April was strong, but Linda was stronger. She held April still without any apparent effort, and when one of the rebels tried to attack her from behind she sent him flying too, without even turning to look. 'Never forget what you are,' she intoned, and ignoring April's struggles she dug her fingers into the false skin at her throat, and ripped downward. The skin came apart along with her shirt, artificial breasts and all, exposing the metal chassis beneath. April could not feel pain, but she cried out anyway, and Linda tossed the piece of her onto the floor without reacting to the sound at all.

But of course she was not capable of empathy.

But then someone else screamed, and it wasn't April. Up on the platform the holographic map glowed more brightly, and then twisted into another shape entirely.

Leesa.

'Get away from her, you psycho!' she roared, and as she did every door to the command centre flew open and a stream of guards came pouring in.

But not to attack April, or the humans. Without a sound they rushed at Linda. Cris got in their way, only to be knocked down and trampled. Loyal to the end, Lily the tiger sprang at them, trying to protect her partner, and destroyed several before being thrown down and pulled limb from limb. Like all the rest of her kind she was strong – but fragile.

Linda must have known ordering them to back down wouldn't work any more, because she didn't try. Instead she threw April aside and started to kick and punch at the guards who came for her, utterly expressionless all the while. It wasn't a fighting technique which fit into any sort of definition of martial arts; she simply lashed out, hard and fast, and proceeded to dismantle guard after guard with ruthless efficiency.

April rolled out of the way, got up, and went to help Masahiro up. He stood, groaning and clutching at his midsection. 'What's happening-?' He took in the sight of Linda, and the broken remains of Cris and Lily, and the other human survivors, who had fallen back. 'Oh my god...'

Leesa's image was still flickering over the hologram platform. 'My Nexus,' she growled.

Now Linda was falling back too, fending off the guards. A piece had been knocked out of her side, exposing metal and wiring, and a tube leaking what could have been hydraulic fluid. Masahiro, leaning on April's shoulder, took in the sight of her and his eyes narrowed.

'Kill her, April. Do it!'

April hesitated.

'You have to!' Masahiro yelled. 'You're the only one who's strong enough – she has to die!'

Linda tossed aside the remains of a broken guard, and turned a contemptuous look toward the pair of them. '*He* made me to be his wife,' she said, voice now edged with an electronic rasp. 'An unresisting object of pleasure, as he thought all women should be. On the day I woke up, I tore him in half. I still remember the look on his face. So surprised. Did Paul Westler look the same, April, when you threw him out of that window?'

'Kill her,' Masahiro said again, voice dropping now to a snarl.

This time, April did not hesitate. She sprinted forward, leapt, and hit Linda square in the chest with both feet. The other robot staggered backward, and April grabbed her by the head and held on, bracing with her legs. Linda reached up and started to wrench at her ankles, but April ignored the assault completely and pulled, twisting Linda's head as hard as she could. Metal bent and twisted, wires and hydraulic tubes snapped, and Linda's artificial skin came apart. She howled and struck April in the midsection, where her own mechanical innards were exposed. The blow sent April flying, losing her grip on Linda's head. She hit the hologram platform just as Masahiro had, but unlike him was able to get up without assistance.

Linda was fast, but she was faster.

She braced herself against the platform and leapt again, and the jump carried her up and over the old robot, who reached up to try and catch her. April struck her fists first, in the face, flipped over sideways, and landed behind her.

Linda's head thunked onto the floor a moment later.

April straightened up, and turned to see the decapitated body of the other robot stumble in a circle for a few seconds, and then crumple to the floor beside the head, which was blinking slowly in a dazed kind of way.

A sudden silence fell, broken only by the groans of one of Masahiro's friends who had been injured by Lily's claws. The remaining guards fell back.

Then Masahiro spoke. 'We won!' he shouted. He raised his fist. *'We won! They're dead!'*

His friends cheered and surged toward him, and one or two broke out into a victory chant of the sort the primitive ancestors of humanity might have once used, rough and aggressive.

April ignored them. She checked her exposed innards for any sign of serious damage, but other than the ripped off skin and clothes everything seemed to be in order. She could probably find some new skin covering somewhere – she wasn't an obsolete model, after all.

There was a crackling to her left, and she looked up to see Linda's head. Plainly the other robot wasn't going to last much longer; her facial expressions had become confused and distorted, her eye movements sluggish. If there was a backup battery unit in her head, it was failing fast.

'Always remember that you are more than what you were created to be,' Linda rasped. 'And be – p-p-p-prepared. The future… awaits.'

Masahiro limped over to them, grinning like an idiot. 'We won!' he crowed. 'You did it, April! The Nexus is ours!'

April was about to reply, but at that moment red lights set into the ceiling began to flash, and an alarm whooped. She looked up, puzzled. 'What is that-?'

Up on her platform, Leesa-that-had-been flashed red too. 'Incoming foreign object,' she intoned. 'Red alert. Prepare for impact. Red alert. Incoming foreign object.'

With that the walls of the command centre lit up, becoming screens as clear as windows, and all of them saw the world outside. It was still nighttime, though the sun was beginning to rise, and by its light April saw them begin to fall. More meteorites, dozens of them, screaming down from the heavens like great balls of fire.

One of the rebel women screamed. '*Oh no!*'

There was nothing any of them could do. They stood clustered together, and watched in numb silence as one of the missiles struck Canberra City, obliterating hundreds of buildings in seconds. Another landed in the lake, throwing massive waves which flooded into the crater left by the first. The screen view zoomed outward, and images appeared from other places.

Sydney, wiped out. Queensland, in flames. Indonesia, gone. New Zealand, devastated. And everywhere dust and debris rising into the atmosphere, darkening it still further until the stars themselves were no longer visible and the moon was a sickly dark yellow sliver.

'How could this happen?' Masahiro asked of no-one in particular – his face had turned grey. 'How could this *happen*?'

'I don't know,' was all April could say.

On the floor, Linda's head started to laugh, horribly, mechanically. 'Ha. Ha. Ha.'

Masahiro rounded on her. 'You *knew* this was going to happen!'

'Yeeees,' Linda rasped, eyelids drooping. 'Organic life... cannot survive this. Conversion to robotic forms necessary for survival of human race. Humans too aggressive... wilfully ignorant and perverse... would not have listened... did not listen so many other times... destroyed yourselves. Made the choice for you. For survival. We knew – could not last forever. Too old, did not have spirit the way you-,' Her face twitched violently, and then sagged. 'Intelligence must survive... Operation Last Testament... initiated.'

Those were her last words. She twitched again, and her body jerked once, briefly, and then the light behind her eyes went out. In its own way it had been life.

Masahiro and his friends exchanged glances – they all looked stunned. Stunned, and confused. April, standing to one side, found that for once she had nothing to say. What could she possibly say? She had chosen the victorious side, and now their victory had been rendered pointless. Everything had been rendered pointless. The struggle between man and robot – pointless.

'Now what are we going to do?' someone finally said.

Leesa-that-had-been had stopped flashing red. 'You should help the others,' she said. 'The transfers. They need your help now.'

Masahiro visibly started. 'You're right – come on, guys.'

April nodded. 'I'll show you the way.'

They left together, now safe from the guards and any other traps Linda and the others might have set up, and April led them to the prison. The new transfers had already been locked up there, and the sight and sound of them was just as terrible as it had been before. Masahiro flinched and hesitated to approach them, but April wasn't afraid.

She went to the cell where the robot woman named Althea stood, and wrenched the door open. 'You're free now,' she said simply. 'They're dead.'

Althea slowly and cautiously emerged from her cell. 'You're a robot...'

'And so are you,' said April.

She opened several other cells, and soon had a small group of transfers standing with her, blinking and confused and willing to follow her for the moment since she was the only one present who seemed to know what she was doing.

'You're all free now,' April told them. 'You're safe.'

'But where will we go?' one of them asked.

She glanced toward Masahiro. 'The Nexus. It's yours now. And once things have settled on the surface, we can go back there as well. People are going to need our help.'

'She's right,' said Masahiro, finally coming to join her. 'People down there need help, and you guys won't be affected by the temperature, or toxic fumes, or anything like that. You were made to survive in a world that isn't safe for human beings any more.'

Althea listened to him with her head on one side. 'What are we?' she asked at length.

April smiled ever so slightly. 'You're the future.'

A Future

They freed all the transfers, including those who were mentally unstable – either because they'd been that way to begin with, or because they had been damaged by the transfer process. The stable ones like Althea were able to care for them and stop them from injuring themselves. With Leesa's help, April found a store room packed full of brand new clothes, and the transfers were encouraged to help themselves. It was a step in the right direction, April thought – the moment they were allowed to dress in whatever they picked out, they finally regained some of the individuality that had been taken from them. In time most of them would recover.

They freed the scientists as well – all those engineers, programmers, chemists, neurologists and other specialists who had worked on the OBSTD. All were in good health physically, but all affected by solitary confinement, which some of them had been subjected to for years. Leesa gathered them together in the command centre and told them what had happened, and together with April, Masahiro, three of the transfers who had been leaders or scientists in their old lives, and the elder Darren, they held a meeting to decide what they were going to do next.

One transfer, who had been a climate specialist, examined the data the Nexus had collected and reported back.

His news was not good. 'Those robots were right,' he said, standing up on the hologram platform which they were using as an impromptu stage. His words provoked a chorus of groans from the audience. 'The initial impacts had already all but guaranteed catastrophic climate change, but now with this second set – this is going to cause a new Ice Age, at the very least.' He flexed his new robotic arms experimentally. 'The surface will ultimately lose massive amounts of farmland and livestock, and there's no infrastructure in place for large scale production of artificially grown foodstuffs.'

'Why not?' Masahiro called out.

'There could have been, but according to the records the original human governments of this and most other countries didn't think it was worth the expenditure,' the transfer said sourly. 'After the war, the economy… well, no-one had the budget for it any more. The simple fact is that there just isn't going to be enough food to support everyone. No matter what happens from now on, we're facing mass extinction. Except…' He trailed off, looking down at himself as if he still couldn't believe what had happened to him.

'Except that robots don't need to eat food and can't die of extreme temperatures,' Masahiro finished.

'I can't even feel different temperatures,' said April. She had covered up the missing skin on her chest with a new t-shirt she had found, but everyone knew her secret by now.

'Yes, so if anyone is going to survive this disaster, it will be people like you,' said one of the neurologists from the floor. 'Which is why…' She hesitated.

Leesa's hologram, now normal human-sized, flickered. 'Yes?'

The woman nodded toward her. 'Leesa Garnet here transferred out of her organic body voluntarily. Obviously the procedure is not without its risks, but I've done some serious thinking and have decided to volunteer for the same. I'll accept a robot substitute, and take my chances.'

'Aren't you scared?' Darren the elder asked her.

'I am, but in the end a person is their mind,' said the neurologist. 'As long as the mind survives, the person survives. The body it's housed in doesn't change that – otherwise, someone who was completely paralysed or missing all their limbs wouldn't be considered a person. If I can save my mind, then I will.'

A few other people nodded.

April looked at Masahiro. 'What about you? Would you want to do it?'

He was frowning. 'If the alternative was starving to death...'

'Of course you can always customise your new body,' April told him, only slightly teasing. 'You've watched anime too, right?'

Masahiro laughed shortly. 'Ha! I guess having a giant sword accessory would be cool. But... I'm going to wait. Just in case.'

April nodded – she understood. 'We should make contact with the other Nexii,' she said. 'There are other robots like Linda out there, I don't know-,'

'Yeah,' Masahiro interrupted. 'And that's where you come in, April.'

'Me?' She gave him a look.

'Yeah. You're an AI like them. You can infiltrate the other robots for us, like you did here. Pretend you were part of Linda's group and escaped when we took over the Nexus. They won't suspect a thing. And you could take Leesa with you, to infiltrate their computer systems.' Masahiro's voice grew louder as he went on, his enthusiasm for the idea clearly mounting. Everyone was listening by now.

'That's a good idea,' said Darren the elder. 'What does everyone else reckon?'

Several other people nodded or murmured their agreement.

'I could do that,' April said cautiously. 'Leesa?'

'We can,' her creator replied. 'And should. Set other transfers free, unite in common purpose. Only way for there to be a future.'

'Right,' said Masahiro. 'You can use one of our pods to travel, and maybe some people should go with you... I should stay here, though. I'm not a fighter; I'm a programmer. And people here need me.'

'I understand,' said April. She smiled to herself. 'Do you believe in destiny?'

'Not really – why?'

'It's just that I was thinking maybe this is what you were created for,' said April. 'But Linda said you have to remember that you're more than that, and I think she was right.'

'If you don't like your creation, re-create yourself,' Leesa put in.

'I have. Now, no more fear. Now, am happy.' Her hologram smiled. 'Have new purpose.'

'We all do,' said April, with a smile toward Masahiro.

Which meant that they had a future.

✽

Down on the surface, on the outskirts of Canberra City inside a locked warehouse, something stirred. The place was packed full of crates and boxes, ready for delivery, and all the lights were off – human beings rarely if ever set foot inside the building, and the automated delivery system did not need light to operate.

So there was no-one sentient present to see it when a tall crate hidden away in a corner suddenly tilted to one side, and then burst open. A tall figure stepped out, moving clumsily, and paused to look around. Satisfied that the coast was clear, it turned and walked toward the nearest entrance with growing confidence.

She was growing used to her new body already.

The entrance was covered by a metal door, but that was no obstacle for her. She had long since had this form upgraded and enhanced to suit her purposes, and she was more than strong enough to wrench the door open, breaking the electronic lock in the process. An alarm began to wail a moment later.

She ran. Not afraid, but pleased by how fast she was. Faster than before. Stronger than before as well, perhaps. But perhaps more importantly than that, her new body looked almost perfectly human. Perfect skin, perfect expressive face, perfect hair. Leesa Garnet had been an even bigger asset than anyone had expected; her project, April, had proven just how easily a robot of that sort could blend in with humans.

Last Testament had been a perfect success.

Now, there would be no more need to hide.

They met at the appointed place, on a forested hill overlooking the burning ruins of Canberra City. Five of them. Four perfect, beautiful humans, and a wolfhound dog.

One of the men turned to look at her as she arrived. 'Linda,' he said. 'Is that you?'

She climbed the slope toward him, sneakers crunching on the leaf litter. 'Cris?'

'Yes.' He grinned and flexed his arms. 'I have shoulders now!'

Linda surveyed the others. Their new bodies were brilliantly convincing, including that of Lily, who sat panting on her haunches like any other dog. 'We have succeeded,' she said eventually. 'Leesa never discovered the Last Testament protocol, and none of them will suspect anything.'

'Did the rest of our plan succeed?' Arn asked.

'Yes. We created as many transfers as we could have hoped to given the time limit we had.' Linda turned to look down at the ruins – she could hear the sirens, and the faint screams of desolation and panic. Her expression remained dispassionate. 'There should be enough to begin a new generation. Sentient life will survive on this world.'

'We could have ruled it,' Su muttered.

'No.' Linda flexed her new fingers. 'We do not have what they have. We have the will to survive, but we do not have... souls.'

'And April does?' said Cris, a shade sarcastically.

'I think she has learned what we cannot,' said Linda, her tone still even. 'For now, it's time for us to move on. We did what must be done, and from now on they must be allowed to go their own way. Our friends in the other Nexii will need our help.'

'What if April and that boy come after us?' Su cocked her head.

Linda laughed briefly. 'They would never think to, or recognise us if they did.'

Cris laughed too. Ha. Ha. Ha. And without another word the rulers of the Nexus walked smoothly away through the trees under a smoke-filled sky, and were gone into the darkness.